6

FLY ME to the MOON

Also by Alyson Noël

Laguna Cove

Art Geeks and Prom Queens

Faking 19

FLY ME

to the

MOON

Alyson Noël

St. Martin's Griffin

New York

This is a work of fiction. All of the characters, organizations, and events portrayed in this novel are either products of the author's imagination or are used fictitiously.

www.stmartins.com

Design by Maggie Goodman

Library of Congress Cataloging-in-Publication Data

Noël, Alyson.
    Fly me to the moon / Alyson Noël.—1st ed.
        p. cm.
    ISBN-13: 978-0-312-35508-1
    ISBN-10: 0-312-35508-4
        1. Flight attendants—Fiction. I. Title.

PS3614.O385F56 2007
813'.6—dc22

                                    2006051192

First Edition: January 2007

10 9 8 7 6 5 4 3 2 1

For my mother, who never tried to clip my wings

And for flight attendants everywhere—past, present, and future

ACKNOWLEDGMENTS

Many thanks, *merci beaucoups,* and hearty *efharistos* are owed to:

My mom, who encouraged me to soar, who never held me back, and who struggled to keep the nest so that I'd always have a safe place to land.

My husband, Sandy, who reads everything first, who will go any-where once, who can find the best restaurant in the most desolate town, and whose enthusiasm, optimism, curiosity, resilience, and never-ending quest for fun are truly inspiring.

Jolynn "Snarky" Benn, who can make me laugh like no one else, who personifies the definition of "fun," whose trips to New York became legendary, and who knows how to pronounce "Jan."

All of the amazing, hardworking New York flight attendants who can take the most dreadful hell trip and make it, well, a lot less hellish. Including but certainly not limited to: Kenny Blake, who knows what really happened to Bud and Sophie; Justine Tumolo, who has the craziest stories of anyone I know; Nancy Lane, who packs the best candy and who makes recurrent a lot less miserable; and Cissy Shores, who has the amazing, almost magical ability to turn Podunk into paradise.

My uncle, Captain Dick Jarrell, who's nothing like the guys in this book, and who's the only person I'd trust to pack my parachute. His son Brad, the professional hero, his former flight attendant wife, Pat, and current flight attendant daughter, Kristy, who I wish I could've flown with.

Jackie Nunes, who joined me on my first three-month odyssey through Europe that left me wanting more, and who told me about the job opening that changed everything.

Michelle Lane, who keeps me amused and entertained from thousands of miles away, who happens to be a former f/a, and whose last name I borrowed.

My old friends from my Mykonos days, who so generously shared their island and their lives, and who taught me how to catch, prepare, and actually enjoy eating octopus.

My agent, Kate Schafer, who keeps me right on course with her uncanny wit, wisdom, and guidance.

All the good people at St. Martin's, especially Sally Richardson, Matthew Shear, Jennifer Weis, and Stefanie Lindskog, to whom I'm completely indebted.

And, last but not least, in memory of Gary Edwards, who loved a good adventure.

FLY ME to the MOON

PREPARE FOR DITCHING

When an airplane makes an
unscheduled landing into the
ocean, it is important to don
a life vest.

1

So there I was, awkwardly reaching for the *USA Today* left outside my hotel room, determined to ignore the fact that my black, opaque, control-top pantyhose were seriously impairing my ability to breathe, when I heard the muffled sound of the phone ringing from the other side of the door.

Now, on any other day, I would have just grabbed the newspaper and made a mad dash for the elevator, since a ringing phone at 3:55 A.M. can only mean one thing: that some overbearing, micromanaging, type-A Flight Attendant in Charge is trying to track me even though I still have thirty-two perfectly good seconds before I actually *have* to be in the hotel lobby.

But today was different. Not only was I a full five minutes ahead of schedule, not only was it my twenty-eighth birthday, but I also knew that by the end of the day I would be engaged to Michael, my boyfriend-slash-roommate of the last four years.

It had all started the day before I left on this trip. I was cleaning the bedroom and singing along to the latest U2 CD, and just as Bono and I shouted *"Uno, dos, tres . . . Catorce!"* my right hip slammed into Michael's flight bag, sending it soaring off the dresser and crashing to the ground.

Now I admit, up until that very moment his bag had never held much interest. I'd always thought of it as a briefcase, or a man purse—something completely benign but totally off limits. But as I stared at the wreckage spilled all around me, I instinctively dropped to my knees and examined each artifact as though it were the gateway to a secret world I never knew existed.

Oh sure, there were all the predictable items, like well-used navigational maps, half-eaten protein bars, his company photo ID, and a big yellow flashlight to be used in case of emergency. But there were also a few surprises, like the brand-new tube of Rogaine that landed next to the half-empty bottle of Levitra that was covering the red plastic card from a video store that obviously didn't cater to families.

And just as I lifted his bulky, FAA-mandated flight manual I discovered a small, robin's-egg blue box with a crisp white ribbon tied snugly around it.

My breath grew shallow, my heart beat faster, and my hands were actually trembling as I lifted that tiny box to my ear, shaking it ever so slightly as I imagined Michael kneeling before me, eyes misty with emotion, asking me to be his wife. . . .

And I was almost positive I would say yes.

So, anticipating an early-morning birthday greeting from my almost fiancé, I frantically slid the key card back into the lock, hurdled over the mound of soggy white towels I'd left piled on the bathroom floor, and grabbed the receiver conveniently located next to the toilet. Before I could even get to hello, a disembodied, Southern-accented male voice said, "Hailey Lane? This is Bob in scheduling." And the fourteen words that followed were the ones that flight attendants around the globe live to hear: "The rest of your trip has been canceled. You are scheduled to deadhead home."

Wow.

But even though I was expecting something great doesn't mean

I wasn't skeptical. "Come on, Clay, quit fucking around. I'm on my way down," I said, peering in the mirror and smoothing my out-of-control auburn curls while checking my teeth for lipstick tracks.

"Ms. Lane, let me remind you that all scheduling calls are recorded," said the unamused voice on the other end.

"This isn't Clay?" I whispered, my breath caught in my throat.

"You are scheduled to deadhead on flight 001, nonstop from San Diego to Newark," he continued, in a crisp, no-nonsense tone. "You will arrive at fifteen hundred."

"Are you serious? You mean I don't have to fly to Salt Lake, Atlanta, *and* Cincinnati before I get there?" I asked, still not totally convinced I wasn't dreaming.

"I still need to contact the rest of your crew," he said, beginning to sound annoyed.

"Okay, okay. Just one more question: Can I deviate?" I asked, fingers frantically reaching for my flight schedule book, trying to spin this into an even better deal for me. "Let's see, there's a nonstop landing in La Guardia an hour earlier. Can you put me on that instead?"

He sighed. "Your employment date?"

"Three, twenty-five, ninety-nine," I told him, listening to the distant sound of his fingers tapping on the keyboard.

"Done."

"Really? Oh my God, thanks Bob! I mean *really*, thanks. You have no idea how much this means to me! It's my birthday, you know, and, *hello*?" I said, staring at the receiver, listening to the steady hum of the dial tone.

Tucking the newspaper under my arm, I dragged my roll-aboard all the way down the hall to Clay's room, where I knocked twice, paused, and then knocked twice more, which had been our secret code for the last six years, even though it was kind of lame and all too easy to crack.

Clay and I had met the very first day of flight attendant training, and I give him full credit for getting me through it, because without him, I would have bolted two minutes into the creepy, overly peppy orientation. But every time I mentioned escape, he'd remind me of all the guaranteed fun and adventure that awaited us once we earned our wings: The long layovers in chic foreign cities; unlimited duty-free shopping; and the hordes of handsome, successful, single men all jockeying for a shot at the free first-class standby travel enjoyed by airline employees and their significant others.

All we had to do in return was get through six weeks of unmitigated, soul-destroying, personality-quashing hell that only someone who's survived a brutal military boot camp can relate to.

The flight attendant training regime is something rarely discussed outside the industry. Too many soft-core stewardess movies have dwelled in the public's consciousness for too long, making it impossible for us to get the respect we deserve. But truth be told, there is nothing sexy about a system of such carefully calculated, institutionalized paranoia, where forgetting to smile can result in an immediate charge of insubordination and a one-way ticket home.

Over a span of six long weeks, two trainers eerily resembling Stepford Wives taught us the art of surviving days adrift at sea with nothing more than a couple of flares, a bailing bucket, and a lone box of ancient, fruit-flavored candy bearing a label never seen in stores. We learned how to deal with an in-flight death (never use the word "death"); how to handle an alleged in-flight sex act (offer a blanket, look the other way); how to secure an unruly, irate passenger to his seat using company logo plastic tie-wraps; how to deal with head injuries, burns, profuse bleeding, childbirth, vomiting, urination, defecation; and how to clean it all up afterward by donning a "one size fits most" plastic biohazard suit and using club soda for stains and coffee bags for foul odors.

We fought fires; crawled through dark, smoke-filled cabins; and even evacuated a mock airplane by sliding down an authentic, double-lane inflatable slide, resulting in three pairs of torn pants, numerous rub burns, and one broken arm whose owner was "dismissed" for having weak bones.

They restyled our hair, reapplied our makeup, vetoed our jewelry, fed us propaganda, and actively discouraged questions, jokes, comments, and any other signs of freethinking individuality.

And once our spirits were deemed suitably broken and our formerly vibrant selves sufficiently rehabbed into paranoid automatons, they pushed us out into the world, onto an airplane, and reminded us to smile.

"Happy Birthday, doll," which came out "duaawl" in Clay's lazy, Southern-accented impersonation of an old lady from Staten Island, which isn't very good but always makes me laugh. "You look great," he added, opening the door and slipping into his navy blue blazer.

"Four A.M. and no undereye puffiness," I said, pointing proudly at my face. "See, being a slam-clicker and not going out with you guys last night paid off."

"Yeah, but you missed out." He shook his perfectly tousled, blond-highlighted head and closed the door behind him. "We met downstairs in the bar, and when the check arrived the first officer divided the number of chicken wings each of us ate and split the bill accordingly."

"You're making that up." I walked alongside him and laughed.

"True story. He wears this calculator watch that does fractions. My share, including the glass of wine, was eight dollars and eighteen cents."

"Did that include tip?"

"You think he tips?" Clay looked at me, one eyebrow raised. "I waited until he left; then I paid the tip. So, are we deviating?" he asked, following me into the elevator.

"I am," I said, pushing the L button and watching the doors close.

"Good, because I told scheduling I was just gonna do whatever you do."

"That sounds pretty codependent." I raised an eyebrow at him.

"It's way too early to make an important decision when I know you can do it for both of us. And this way we can share a cab to the city." He smiled.

"Fine, but no detours this time." I gave him a stern look. Clay was well known for running all of his errands on the way from La Guardia Airport to whichever apartment he was staying in that week. "No ATMs, no Starbucks, no wine stores, no video rental drop-offs, and no gay bars," I said, dropping my key card at the front desk. "I have a big night ahead, and now that I'm gonna get home even earlier I want to take a bubble bath, and maybe even get a pedicure."

"So is tonight the night?" he asked, handing our bags to the van driver.

"Definitely," I said, smiling brightly in spite of the nervous ping I felt in my stomach.

"Are you gonna say yes?" he asked, eyeing me carefully.

"Probably." I nodded, avoiding his eyes and biting down on my lower lip.

"Probably?" He raised his recently waxed brows at me.

"Well, yeah, I mean. It makes sense, right?" I said, suddenly wondering which one of us I was trying to convince. "I mean, we live together, he's good to me, he's normal. . . ." I shrugged, unable to come up with more good reasons, though I was sure they existed—*didn't they?*

"Perfect. So, what's the problem?" he asked, peering at me closely.

"I guess . . . I don't know. I guess I just thought it would be more exciting." I shrugged.

"Hailey, he's a *pilot.* How much excitement do you think you're gonna get?"

"But he's not like the others!" I insisted. "He lives in Manhattan, not some tax-free zone in Florida! He doesn't starch his jeans, doesn't wear white tennis shoes with dress pants. *And* he's taking me to Babbo tonight for my birthday, where I know he'll leave a very generous tip, thank you very much." I climbed into the van.

"Okay, so he's a *metrosexual* pilot." Clay shrugged. "But let me just say, you'd be a lot more sure of your answer if you'd just looked inside that Tiffany's box."

2

I had just spent the entire flight making a mental list—I couldn't make an actual *written* list, as I'd been feigning sleep for the past five and a half hours in order to avoid conversation with the two smelly size-XXL men I was wedged between—of all the reasons why I *should* marry Michael.

The *"Just Say Yes!"* side consisted of pretty much all the same, solid, concrete reasons I had given Clay, while the *"Run Away!"* side was mostly a list of adjectives with not one single noun. And as I performed a mental review, poring over it again and again in my head, it became painfully clear there was no way I could base a decision that was supposed to last *forever* on a list of flimsy *modifiers*.

Having spent the first part of my adult life running around and traveling the world while leaving a trail of unfinished projects in my wake—e.g., college, boyfriends, the novel I started writing seven years ago, hell, I couldn't even keep the same hair color for more than six months before I longed for something new—it was no wonder I was having doubts. I mean, the only thing I'd ever really *completed* was flight attendant training, and that was due more to Clay's determination than mine.

So clearly my nervous stomach had nothing to do with Michael and everything to do with, well, *me*.

But things really were different now. So far I'd been working for Atlas Airlines for six straight years (a record), not to mention that I'd been with Michael for four (a major breakthrough!). True, we both traveled so much that if you counted the actual number of days we'd spent together it'd probably add up to no more than six months max. But even that measly amount of time still qualified as a personal best.

Not to mention how I'd exhausted the last few years moonlighting as a bridesmaid, standing on the sidelines in one demeaning pastel frock after another while the last of my single female friends walked down the aisle (with no discernible hint of panic), where they received *a ring from a guy* that somehow qualified them to start tossing all kinds of unsolicited advice my way. Because clearly, having allowed myself to creep dangerously close to thirty with my left hand completely barren meant I was in desperate need of their newly acquired matrimonial wisdom.

And now it was my turn.

Besides, during my six years of flying, hadn't I been told over and over again that *the plane won't wait*? That if I'm late to the gate, I'll be *immediately replaced*? Well, I was beginning to think maybe the same rules applied to life. I mean, maybe Michael wasn't the most exciting person, or the most creative person, or even the person who made me laugh the most, but he was presentable, dependable, made a good living, and treated me well. And I was beginning to realize that hanging back and waiting for someone more exciting would only result in me, stranded on the middle of the runway, way past departure.

So by the time we were on final approach, I'd decided I would look surprised and excited when he presented me with the small blue box and say *"Yes!"* with as much enthusiasm as a not-at-all-surprised person could muster.

The second the wheels hit the runway I tore into my carry-on bag, turned on my phone, and listened to the sound of Michael's cell go straight into voice mail. "Um, hi Michael," I whispered, never one to partake in *yellular.* "Good news! My flights were canceled and I deviated, so I'll be getting home way earlier. I know you're probably at the gym or something, but I just wanted to say hi, and I can't wait for tonight!"

I tossed the phone in my bag and was concentrating on breathing through my mouth, trying to avoid the awful onion breath emanating from the guy on my left, when the captain came on the PA and said, "Uh, ladies and gentlemen, we seem to be having some difficulty attaching the jetway to the aircraft door. It should be taken care of momentarily. We appreciate your patience."

That's all it took.

The guy on my right poked me hard in the arm and asked, "What'd he just say?"

Now, I know that we both heard the *exact same* announcement at the *exact same* volume. So why was it that just because I was in uniform he thought I'd heard something *more*? "Well, uh, I think he said there was a problem with the jetway," I told him, smiling politely while watching his face turn from a sallow beige to bright red, like he was seconds away from a heart attack.

"Goddamn airline!" he screamed, glaring at me as though I was personally responsible for everything from the stingy seat pitch to the stale pretzels. *"Goddamn-piece-of-shit-airline! That's the last time I'll ever fly this piece of crap!"* he yelled, scowling, demanding a response.

I glanced furtively around the cabin in an effort to see if my supervisor or anyone from management was on board, in which case my immediate response would be to calmly defuse the situation while instilling the merits of our exemplary service.

But not recognizing anyone, I just shrugged and turned on my iPod.

Hurrying outside, I found Clay already in the line for yellow cabs, as I figured he would be. "Hey," I said, squeezing through a crowd of people all toting identical black bags with identical red ribbons tied around the handle for easy spotting on the baggage claim carousel.

"What took?" he asked, squinting at his watch.

"I was in coach, remember?" I rolled my eyes. "So how was first class?"

Clay was three months older than me, which in this case had been all the seniority required to get him comfortably seated up front while I was crammed in the back between the two surly "squishers" (flight attendant speak for people who'd clearly be more comfortable using a seat belt extension).

"The service is really going downhill." He shook his head. "Did you know we won't serve pretzels with the preflight cocktail anymore? I swear, it's like the end of the world," he said, opening the cab door.

"Two stops, please," I told the driver. "The first is Seventy-second and Third, and the second . . ." I glanced at Clay, waiting. He'd never been one for a permanent address.

"Twenty-third and Seventh," he said, sliding in next to me.

"Chelsea this week?" I teased.

"It's been a month." He rolled his eyes and popped a breath mint.

"Mr. Right?"

Clay looked at me and shrugged. "Mr. Right This Second. So are you nervous?" he asked as the cab hurtled over the Triborough Bridge, straight into the city.

"A little," I said, gazing out at the Manhattan skyline, wondering how, out of the millions of people living there, I could be so sure I'd found the right one.

"Just don't forget about the little people," he said, tapping me on the shoulder. "You know, the ones who bar crawled with you, sample sale–shopped with you, held your hair back when you got sick from that bad coach-class lasagna, and basically stood by you long before you had that M-R-S in front of your name." He frowned at me.

"Clay, I could never forget you," I said, grabbing his hand and squeezing.

"Please, that's what they all say. But it's an age-old story. Every fag loses his hag eventually." He shook his head and turned toward the window, pressing his forehead against the smudgy glass.

"First of all, you're my best friend."

He turned and smiled.

"And second, don't call me a fag hag; it creeps me out. Besides, Michael *loves* you," I insisted.

Clay just looked at me, brown eyes wary.

"Okay, so he tolerates you. But I promise, *nothing will change!* You'll see." I nodded my head and smiled brightly. But all the while I hoped I wasn't just saying that.

When we arrived at my building, I leaned over and gave Clay a quick kiss on the cheek. "I'll call you tomorrow. We'll meet for coffee, and I'll give you all the dirty details and show you the ring. I promise," I said. Then I grabbed my bags and ran inside, anxious to get upstairs and out of my ugly polyester uniform that smelled faintly of everything I'd come in contact with the last two days.

Riding the elevator to the fourteenth floor, I performed my usual striptease, so by the time I walked through the front door I was shoeless, jacketless, and just about to step out of my skirt when I noticed a navy blue blazer lying on the Turkish rug we'd gotten at the Grand Bazaar last spring. Vowing to be a better housekeeper once we were actually married, I flung the jacket lightly over my arm and pushed through the partially closed bedroom door and straight into a scene I'd heard about many times before, but never expected to see in real life.

There, sitting on the edge of our queen-sized bed, was my future husband, Michael. Dressed in the gray cashmere sweater I'd bought for his birthday, with his dark denim jeans pushed all the way down to the top of his brown suede driving mocs. His head was thrown back, his eyes were shut tight, and his lips were moist and parted, while a petite, dark-haired flight attendant in a crisp white shirt and navy blue uniform pants knelt between his legs, head bobbing up and down *rhythmically.*

I stood there in shock, watching *someone else* do what I had done just two days earlier, right before running out the door to catch the bus to Newark International Airport. Then suddenly, there was a horrible, loud scream.

It came from me.

"Hailey! It's not what you think!" Michael yelled, his face frantic and panicked, waving one hand in the air to distract me while using the other to cover the evidence.

"Oh my God!" I screamed. *"What is going on, Michael?"*

"Hailey, relax. Everything's fine," he said, tugging on his black bikini briefs that were all knotted and twisted around the leg of his pants.

"What the hell is going on?" I repeated, unable to move or close my eyes to the sight of his little friend cowering at the foot of our bed.

"Hailey, please just—*shit!*" he yelled, hopping one-legged around the room, teetering dangerously, while his underwear squeezed around his thigh like a boa constrictor. "I can explain. Just . . . *fuck!*"

"WHO THE HELL IS SHE?" I demanded, my eyes darting between Michael and the tiny dark-haired girl whose face was pressed tightly into the folds of the bed skirt.

And then they both looked at me.

And then I saw.

It wasn't at all what I thought. It was much worse than that.
She was a *he*.

"Oh my God!" I whispered, clutching my stomach.

"Hailey!"

"Oh, I feel sick," I said, backing out of the room.

"Hailey! *Dammit!*" Michael cursed, kicking off both his shoes and pants, and having to start all over again.

I stumbled blindly into the living room, zipping my skirt and searching frantically for my shoes. I had to get out of there, *immediately!*

I spotted my navy pumps right where I'd thrown them, under the glass-topped coffee table, and was crouched on all fours, butt stuck in the air like a bull's-eye, when I heard a tentative voice say, "Hailey? Can I please have my jacket? I'm going to be late for sign-in."

And I looked up to see the guy who just moments ago had a mouthful of my boyfriend's dick. Then I gazed down at the jacket I'd been clutching all this time, thinking it was mine.

And then I threw it at him, grabbed my bags, and ran.

And as the door closed behind me, I heard Michael scream, "Hailey, wait! I can explain! *Don't tell anyone!*"

3

From the moment I gained consciousness I went directly into the stream of questions that mark the start of every flight attendant's day: *Where am I? What hotel is this? Did I miss my flight? How come I didn't get my wake up call? Where's the bathroom?* And in my particular case, *Who's this hairy person lying next to me?*

Slowly opening one eye, I tried to muster the courage to turn over and see just who was spooning my left shoulder. And as I rotated my head to the side, I was greeted by the steely-eyed stare of Conrad, the snub-nosed Persian named after Kat's third husband. And then all of yesterday's events came rushing back.

All of it.

Crap.

After fleeing the scene, I'd flagged down a taxi and without even thinking I gave the driver Kat's address. But it made sense. I mean, Clay was honeymooning in Chelsea, and all the girlfriends I'd hung with when I first got to New York were now either married, had just given birth, had transferred to another base, were no longer working for Atlas, were commuting to another state, or all of the above. Besides, ever since Kat and I worked a trip to Madrid five years ago, she'd become like a mom to me (although a lot less judgmental than my real mom). And since she was the only one I knew who was senior enough to fly to Istanbul and Athens during the middle of the week, I figured she'd probably be home.

The second she'd opened the door she'd taken one look at me and said, "I'm pouring you a drink."

I'd stumbled into her expansive marble foyer, trying to contain the nausea building inside me. "I think I'm going to be sick," I'd warned.

"Nonsense. Just leave your bag and follow me. I want to hear all about it," she'd said, draping her arm firmly around my shoulders and leading me down the long hall and into the library where she keeps her stash.

She steered me to a red velvet sofa, and I burrowed deep into the cushions, watching as she busied herself behind the broad mahogany bar. As always her clothing was immaculate, her makeup professionally drawn, and her golden blond bob blown into perfect, shiny submission. And as she reached her long, heavily ringed fingers toward her collection of cut crystal glasses she squinted at me with her piercing blue eyes. "No, this is definitely not a champagne moment," she said, reaching for a highball and adding several fingers of vodka.

I was in no mood for alcohol, but I took the glass anyway, sipping the clear, cool liquid and feeling a trail of burn as it made its way down my throat. Then I looked at her and took another, because Kat is not a woman you want to argue with.

Katina Wilkes-Noble-Whitmore is a Fifth Avenue penthouse–dwelling flight attendant with over thirty years of seniority. A woman who in her amazing life had both served and dined with heads of state. She was thrice married, now widowed; and with no children of her own, she'd taken on Clay and me as sort of unofficial adoptees.

When husband number three, Conrad, dropped dead of a heart

attack four years ago, she'd become wealthier than she'd ever imagined. And after taking a six-month leave of absence spent in serious mourning, she'd returned to flying. Instantly becoming the enemy of every single junior flight attendant who, stuck in a system ruled entirely by seniority, spends their entire career waiting for women like Kat to either quit or *drop off*.

But Kat couldn't *not* fly, since she was a complete sucker for other people's drama. And other than an emergency room doctor, or a family court judge, no other occupation can compete with the drama that unfolds at thirty thousand feet.

"Kat, I—" I began.

"Don't talk, just sip," she said, motioning toward my drink, which I had to admit was beginning to taste quite good.

So I took another sip, carefully placed my glass on the table before me, and completely lost it in a spasm of uncontrollable tears. And when I finally looked up, Kat was standing by with a fistful of tissues. "Thanks," I said, blowing my nose so loudly I should've been embarrassed. But embarrassment was all relative, and at this point honking with my nose was nothing compared to what I was facing. "I'm sorry." I shook my head and dabbed gently at my face. "I'm a wreck."

"Nonsense," she said, settling onto the chaise across from me. "Just tell me what happened, and we'll get it all sorted out."

So I took a deep breath and told her.

She just stared at me, eyes growing wider than I'd ever seen them. "Are you sure?" she asked. "About what you saw?"

I reached for the bottle of vodka she'd left on the table, topped off my glass, and closed my eyes, consulting the movie screen in my head that was featuring the *Michael Gets a Blowjob* clip over and over again. "Yeah, I'm sure." I sighed.

"Well, who was it? Anyone I know?" she asked, her eyes narrowing as though already plotting revenge.

"I doubt it." I shrugged. "He flies for Lyric."

"The discount carrier?" She was completely aghast. Kat consid-

ered the tracksuit-clad, white tennis shoe–wearing discount travelers to be the very end of a civilized society.

I just nodded and reached for the box of tissues. Another breakdown was the only thing I could count on.

"Well, I'm not surprised," she said, shaking her head and shuddering. "They're complete animals over there, with their all-coach cabins, and their food for sale."

"But I'm such an idiot! I actually thought he was going to propose!" I said, shaking my head and burying my face in a wad of tissues.

"Well, you weren't going to say *yes* were you?"

Excuse me?

I looked up to see Kat peering at me with such obvious disapproval that I immediately regretted coming over. I mean, I was looking for sympathy, pure and simple, and there was nothing sympathetic about what she'd just said.

I watched as she uncurled her feet from under her and leaned toward me, resting her hand on the table between us. "Hailey, I know you don't want to hear this, but I really think it's all worked out for the best."

I leaned against the cushions and closed my eyes, determined to block out the sound of her voice. *I should have gone to Clay's*, I thought. *I should have gone to a hotel. I should have set up camp deep in the bowels of the subway with all the other lonely people. BUT I NEVER SHOULD HAVE COME HERE!*

"You're too young to get tied down!" she continued.

And this *coming from a woman with three marriages under her belt!* I folded my arms across my chest, refusing all eye contact.

"Besides," she said, oblivious to my inattention. "Aren't you glad you found out *now*, rather than five years from now? When you're stranded in some tax-free suburb with your four little brats, while Michael jets around the world, stopping by just long enough to drop off his dirty underwear and the occasional box of duty-free chocolates?"

Okay, even I had to admit that was way bleaker than my current predicament. "But how could this even *happen?*" I begged, desperate for answers. "I mean, how could I not have *known?* Clay always tells me I've got amazing gaydar, yet when it comes to my own boyfriend, I'm totally clueless!"

But she just sipped her drink and shrugged. "So what are you going to do?"

I headed to the bar for more ice, listening to the cubes clink and crackle as they merged with the vodka; then I looked at her and shrugged. "All I know is that I'm now officially single and homeless. Do you think I could maybe stay here a few days? Just until I get my stuff and figure something out?"

"Of course you can stay!" she'd said, her face warming into a smile. "Harold, Conrad, William, and I would love the company!"

I'd glanced at the three Persians who bore the names of her three former husbands (even the girl cat Conrad), as they eyed me from their perch on the velvet settee. Oh, God, I'd forgotten all about the cats, and I was deathly allergic to them. But my immediate prospects were pretty dismal, and I could do a lot worse than hanging out at Kat's kitty-filled penthouse for a few days.

"Thanks," I'd said, tearing up again.

"Don't mention it," she'd said.

And now, grasping my pounding head with both hands, I climbed out of bed and wandered into the kitchen, determined to find Kat and apologize for all the nonstop crying, binge drinking, and going on and on about Michael I'd subjected her to until I finally, mercifully, passed out.

But instead, I found a note, anchored by a pyramid of cat food tins, giving detailed instructions on the care and feeding of "the kids," with a PS at the bottom that she'd gone to visit a friend in Athens for a few days.

Wondering whom she knew in Greece, I was spooning three

different types of kitty chow into three different crystal bowls when Clay walked into the kitchen with a fistful of tulips and a loud, "Mornin', doll," that nearly gave me a heart attack.

"How'd you get in here?" I shrieked, clutching the edge of the counter and fighting to restore my breath.

"Kat gave me an alert call this morning—said I needed to check on you. So we met at Grand Central and she slipped me the keys. Are you okay?" he asked, dropping the tulips and giving me a hug that got me crying all over again. "I'm so sorry," he whispered.

I wiped my swollen eyes and picked up the tulips, bringing them to my nose even though they had no discernible scent. "Did she tell you *everything*?" I asked, peering at him from over the soft red petals.

"Yeah." Clay shrugged, looking down at the travertine floor, clearly feeling uncomfortable.

"Oh, God," I said, collapsing onto a chair. "I'm such a loser."

"Don't say that."

"But I am." I shook my head. "It never occurred to me that he was getting . . ." I stopped and bit down on my lower lip, still uncomfortable saying the words out loud.

"On-the-ground service?"

I buried my face in my hands.

"Sorry, stupid joke," he said, grabbing a vase for the flowers. "Here's the deal. I know you're devastated, and understandably so. And we are going to mourn properly, because trust me, I have a no-fail plan. But before we can even attempt to get started I have to insist you get out of that uniform and take a shower, because, honey, you smell like the middle seat on a 757."

I looked down, startled to see that I was still wearing my navy blue uniform. "Oh, God, I slept in this. I'm a total wreck," I said, eyes welling up with tears again.

"Listen, just get in the shower, then go put on one of those silky robes Kat collects, and I'll dig up something dapper from one of the exes. Then meet me in the den and I'll unveil the rest of the plan."

Wrapped in a cozy red cashmere robe and matching slippers, with my long, curly wet hair smoothed back into a ponytail, I walked into the den to find Clay lounging on the couch, with an unlit cigar dangling from his lips and an oversized smoking jacket cinched tight around his waist.

"Where'd you find that?" I laughed.

"One of the guest room closets. What do you think? Do I look butch?" He leaned against the cushions in his idea of a manly pose.

"You look like the MC in *Cabaret*," I said, plopping down next to him. "What's with the cigar?"

"Have you ever tried one?" he asked.

I shook my head and curled my feet up under me.

"Man, they're so phallic." He held it in front of him. "I say any straight guy that's into these is just fooling himself."

"Oh my God! Michael *loved* cigars," I said, eyes going wide with the memory. "Especially Cubans."

"I rest my case." Clay nodded.

"You know, I probably shouldn't drink this," I said, reaching for one of the two Bloody Marys he'd made and stirring it with the celery stalk. "I should have coffee instead."

But Clay just rolled his eyes. "Please. Do you wanna be alert? Or do you wanna feel better?" he asked.

And knowing I definitely didn't want to be alert, I took a tentative sip, quickly followed by another. "So what's the plan?" I asked, crunching on celery.

"Well, did you open my gift?"

Okay, if I'd needed any further evidence to prove I was losing it, I needed look no further. Not only had I lost his gift, but I'd completely forgotten about it. Giving him a guilty look I said, "Um, I'm not really sure where it is."

"Well, you're lucky I found it, because oddly enough it fits perfectly with the plan," he said, retrieving a rectangular, gold-wrapped package from under a cushion.

"Where'd you find that?" I asked, taking it from him and rubbing my thumb across the shiny, slick paper.

"In the bottom of your carry-on."

"You went through my bag?"

"You have no secrets from me, doll. So go ahead, open it." He smiled.

I pulled on the shiny gold ribbon and ran my finger gently under the tape, removing the paper until a black-and-white picture of Audrey Hepburn holding a very long cigarette holder emerged. "Oh, I love this movie!" I said, leaning over to hug him.

"Okay, so this is the plan." He set down his drink and gave me a serious look. "We're gonna enjoy a Bloody Mary or two while we watch *Breakfast at Tiffany's.* Then we'll order up some food like Thai or Chinese. And by the time we're finished it'll probably be late afternoon, so we'll celebrate *that* with another cocktail, and if you wanna talk, and unload, and get it all out of your system I'll listen. And I promise I won't interrupt or give advice unless you ask. And when that's done, we'll call the deli and have them deliver some essentials like ice cream and the *New York Post,* and then maybe, if we're not too bloated, we'll try on some of Kat's old stewardess uniforms from the seventies. Then at some point I'm guessing we'll probably sugar crash and pass out. And then on Sunday . . ." He paused, merging his eyebrows together and waving his unlit cigar in the air. "Well, I really haven't worked out all the details yet. But by 11:45, Sunday night, we're gonna clean it all up. And at 12:01, when it's officially Monday, you're going to make a new start."

"I don't know if I can do that," I said, realizing I sounded completely pathetic. But hey, at least I was honest.

"Of course you can." He nodded emphatically. "You've got to fake it till you make it," he said, pointing his cigar at me.

"Oh, now you're quoting Oprah?" I rolled my eyes and bit off another piece of celery stalk.

"Dr. Phil."

"You sure?" I asked, talking with my mouth full.

"Trust me, Hailey, it's the big guy. Look, I'm not asking you to forget, because I know that will take a lot longer than a weekend. What I'm suggesting is forty-eight hours of hard mourning, not counting what you already started last night, and then we're just gonna clean it all up and not look back."

"I don't know," I said, tearing up again.

"I know you think it sounds impossible, but you can do it. Now hand me that DVD," he said, sliding it in and pushing PLAY.

4

After one and a half viewings of *Breakfast at Tiffany's,* two bottles of duty-free vodka, three limes, one bottle of Dom Pérignon (I hoped Kat wouldn't mind), two pints of Ben and Jerry's (Chunky Monkey for Clay, Cherry Garcia for me), five Styrofoam containers of take-out Thai food, one thoroughly chewed on but never lit cigar, one bottle of nearly knocked over but quickly recovered pale pink nail polish, one broken hair clip, and two and a half boxes of super-soft, aloe-infused tissues, I'd finally convinced Clay I was ready to move on.

"I don't know what I'd do without you," I said, hugging him in the doorway.

"You sure you're gonna be okay?" he asked, eyeing me carefully.

"Positive." I nodded. "So, are you flying tomorrow?"

"Yeah, I've got that two-day San Juan layover." He smiled.

"You always get the dream trips." I shook my head. "I don't know how you do it."

"Six solid years of bribing scheduling with duty-free chocolate and wine. You could do it too, you know."

I just looked at him and rolled my eyes. "I will not pander to those people." I laughed.

"You should come with me, to Puerto Rico," he said, eyes lighting up.

"I can't." I shook my head. "Besides, I don't want to cut in on your action. I hear old San Juan is quite the party town."

"Please." He rolled his eyes. "You have to come, and you can't say no. I know you're not working, and I also know you have nothing better to do."

"Thanks for the reminder," I said, slumping against the door frame.

"Besides, it's all free. The flight's free, and since you'll be bunking with me, even the room's free."

"Clay, I can't," I insisted.

"I'll even buy your first four mojitos," he promised.

"I'd love to, but really, I can't. Kat's expecting me to feed the kitties, and I have to start looking for a place to live. I can't stay here forever, you know."

He peered down the hall and shrugged. "I don't know why not. You could go months in this place without bumping into each other."

"True." I smiled.

"Listen, I sign in at seven. That's A.M. Promise me you'll reconsider." He looked at me.

"Just call when you get back," I said, closing the door behind him.

The second he was gone, I realized I really did feel better. I mean, it's not like I was so deluded I thought a couple Bloody Marys and a pint of Ben and Jerry's were the antidote. But still, it was nice to know that if I was involuntarily downgrading back to my former life of being single with an uncertain future, at least I wasn't going it alone. I had great friends to keep me company and the freedom to live my life however I chose.

It was like now that I was released from the weight of Michael's never-ending supply of *opinions,* I could finally concentrate on *my* dreams, which, I hated to admit, had been put on indefinite hiatus so that I could live his. Maybe I could even finish that manuscript I'd started writing all those years ago, now that Michael could no longer peek over my shoulder and say things like, "Fiction is a waste of time."

Obviously, it was all just a simple matter of perspective. I mean, being dumped didn't have to be the end, because if you think about it, it's really more like a new beginning.

I headed back to the den, reached into my bag, and turned on my phone, determined to deal with the onslaught of messages I assumed were already piling up, since in a base with just under fifteen hundred flight attendants sometimes New York City felt like a small town. And I knew it was just a matter of time before word got out that I'd been dumped.

Sure enough, within seconds of finding a signal, my cell started beeping and an envelope appeared on the display.

"Hailey? I heard about your breakup. If you want to talk give me a call."

"Hailey? Oh my God! Did you really break up? I mean, where will you live? Do you have any idea how much your lifestyle is going to change?"

"Hey Hailey, it's me. Give me a call if you wanna have dinner. You bring the wine; I'll supply the Ramen noodles."

And then, right in the middle of message number four, a new call beeped in. And wanting to just get it over with and face it head-on, I didn't bother to check the display.

"Hailey! I've been trying to reach you all weekend."

Oh crap. It was Michael. I mean, even though I was secretly fantasizing about him calling didn't mean I actually wanted it to happen. I focused on the END button and considered pushing it.

"Hailey, are you okay? Where are you?" He sounded nervous.

"What do you want?" I said, trying to keep my voice neutral.

"I just want to know if you're okay."

"Well, I'm just *great*. And *thanks so much* for calling." I rolled my eyes and shook my head even though it was a total waste of energy since it wasn't like he could see me.

"Listen, I know you're upset, and I'm sorry. But you need to know that it's not at all what you think."

Was he serious? Did he really have an excuse? "Oh really? Then tell me, just what exactly was it, Michael?" I said, feeling all the progress I'd made with Clay evaporate as the anger grew and blossomed inside me.

"Well, I'm not *gay*, if that's what you're thinking," he said in a small, tight whisper.

"Oh, well, forgive me for saying so, but you do realize that was a *guy* between your legs?"

"Listen, Hailey," he said, sounding extremely agitated. "I'd really prefer you to keep this between us."

"Why should I?"

"Because I'm *not gay*! I was the one *receiving*, okay?"

I just sat there, not quite believing what I'd just heard. "Is that how you justify it?" I said finally.

"I'm just saying it's not a big deal," he whispered emphatically.

"*Not a big deal?* Do you think it was *not a big deal* for me to come home from a trip on my *birthday*, thinking you were about to propose, but instead finding you getting the hummer of a lifetime on *our bed*? You think that was NOT A BIG DEAL?" I shrieked, on the verge of a complete and total meltdown.

"*Propose?*" He laughed. "Where'd you get that from?"

Oh, great. Why did I say that? WHY? "Um, I saw the Tiffany's box," I mumbled, rolling my eyes at myself now.

"Well, I hate to break it to ya, but I never had plans to propose. And while you were snooping through my stuff you should've just opened the box. You would've found a silver key chain I'd had engraved for your birthday, *not* an engagement ring."

He got me a key chain?
For my birthday?
And I was going to marry this guy?

"I'm not even close to settling down," he continued, in his "talking to the small child visiting the cockpit" voice. "But when I do, I assure you it'll be with someone younger."

"Excuse me?" I gasped, white knuckling the phone as my knees buckled and I collapsed onto the couch. *He did not just say that. Did he?*

"Hailey, get real. By the time I'm ready for marriage, you'll be pushing forty," he scoffed.

"And you'll be pushing *fifty*!" I shouted.

"Look, it's just not gonna happen. I never promised you anything. Let's just remember that, okay?"

I threw the phone onto the Persian rug, listening to the soft thud as it made contact and rolled over. I could not believe what I had just heard. *How could I have been so stupid?*

"Hailey?" he yelled, over and over until I finally retrieved the phone and put it back to my ear.

"Are you finished?" I asked, my voice sounding clipped and tight.

"I'm sorry if you're hurt. I'm just trying to give you the big picture, that's all."

"Oh, I got the picture," I said, hoping I sounded strong, practical, and totally in control, despite all evidence to the contrary. "Listen, Michael, I need to stop by and pack up my things."

"Done. Your stuff is with the front desk. You can get it anytime."

I just sat there with the phone pressed to my ear. After four years he'd already packed me up and reclaimed his space. Just. Like. That.

"And Hailey, I'm serious about keeping this between us. These are private matters that should remain private."

My face grew hot, and my hands began to shake as I gripped

the phone even tighter and used his words against him. "Listen, Michael, I never promised you anything. Let's just remember that, okay?" And then I hit END.

And then I called Clay.

5

"No wonder the passengers are so nasty when they come on board; it's all her fault," Clay said, pointing at the surly gate agent who just moments before had performed an exaggerated eye roll/head shake when he asked if there was an available first-class seat for me.

"Clay, I'll be lucky just to get on. Never mind first class," I said, eyes pinned to the overhead monitor, watching the passenger count rise as the number of empty seats diminished.

"Well, I'd just like to take this opportunity to point out what a good friend I am. Sitting here holding your hand while I should be working," he said, crossing his long legs, and inspecting his cuticles.

"Yeah, and I bet your fellow crew members are just thrilled about it." I shook my head and focused back on the screen. "Oh great! Did you see that? The numbers just canceled out! That's it! It's over! This chair is now my final destination," I said, dropping my head in my hands.

It was like, now that I'd made the decision to go to San Juan, I couldn't stand the idea of *not* going to San Juan. I mean, I was packed and ready for two long, hot, lazy days at the pool with a mojito in one hand and my long-abandoned manuscript in the other. And now all I had to look forward to was a never-ending bus ride back to Manhattan, where I would dish out countless tins of Fancy Feast and pore through real estate ads for apartments I could never afford. "This free standby travel is a total scam," I said, grabbing my bags and preparing to leave.

"Where you going?" Clay asked, pulling at a hangnail and refusing to budge.

"Uh, hello? Have you looked at the screen? Nothing but zeros, and that means no seat, *amigo*." Jeez, his irrational optimism was so annoying.

"It ain't over till the door closes." He smiled lazily. "And it ain't closing till I'm on board," he said, patting the seat next to him.

And wouldn't you know it, no sooner had I sat back down when an unruly passenger was escorted off the plane. And then over the PA we heard, "Hailey Lane and Clay Stevens, please report to the boarding door immediately."

I was lounging in a blue leather first-class seat, footrest extended, pillow placed snugly behind my neck while I sipped champagne and flipped through the manuscript I'd started writing over six years ago but had barely glanced at in the last four. And I was thinking, *This is how it should be. Maybe my karma is starting to turn around. Maybe this moment will signal the start of an exciting, new, first-class life. I really should do this more often. I belong in this cabin. . . .*

And then somebody said, "You need to move."

I looked up to see that same surly gate agent glaring down at me. Well, obviously she was having a rough morning, so the least I could do was try to make it a little better. "Excuse me?" I said, smiling pleasantly.

"Don't argue with me. Just get your belongings and move," she said, her voice revealing years of nicotine abuse, as her square-cut,

French-manicured, acrylic nails clutched at her bony hips. "The passenger that booked this seat has arrived, and he's making his way down the jetway as we speak."

"I wasn't arguing," I said meekly, fully aware that as a nonrevenue standby passenger I was in no position to argue with anyone, especially her. "Um, where should I sit?" I tried to sound as accommodating as possible, while the surrounding passengers eyed me warily, like I was some kind of major security threat.

"Lucky for you there was a miscount. There should be an empty seat somewhere back in coach," she said, just as a tall, dark-haired, slightly disheveled but really cute guy ran up behind her. "Oh, Mr. Richards, here you are. We're so sorry for the mix-up. Your seat will be available as soon as Ms. Lane here gets her belongings and heads back to the coach cabin," the agent said, pointing a thick, white-tipped nail at me while smiling flirtatiously at him.

"No bother. Take your time," he said, smiling as he fought to catch his breath.

"Well, actually, she needs to hurry, since we're not allowed to close the door and push back from the gate until she's seated," she said, in a voice that was loud enough for the entire first-class cabin to bear witness. "But why don't we just put your bag right here on top of hers?"

I watched as my carefully laid out garment bag was smashed and flattened by his heavier, bulkier one. But again, due to company-mandated behavioral codes, there was nothing I could do. So grabbing my small carry-on, I strode through the first-class cabin in what had become my standard flight attendant gait: head up, legs moving swiftly, eyes fixed on a distant point lest I accidentally make eye contact with a passenger who might actually want something. But still, nearly everyone I passed shook their head, rolled their eyes, and "tsked" at me. Well, everyone except Clay, who was too busy reading *People* magazine in the galley to even notice my banishment.

And when I finally made it all the way to the very back, I took the one and only empty seat in the middle of the very last row. Then I turned on my iPod, hunkered down with the latest edition of *Sky Mall* magazine, and waited for it to be over.

It was just as I was finishing my third mojito when it seemed like a really good idea to ask, "But do you think Michael *ever* loved me?" I took one last hearty sip and glanced at Clay, who was sunning on the lounge chair beside me. We were at the InterContinental hotel just outside of old San Juan, and we'd been relaxing by the pool for the last two and a half hours.

He removed his black Dolce & Gabbana sunglasses, sighed deeply, and with great patience said, "Hailey."

"Oh God, never mind." I sat up abruptly and folded my arms around my knees. "Don't even answer that. I can see it in your eyes. I've now become the kind of boring, pathetic person we always try to avoid." I gave him a cautious look, hoping he'd deny it and assure me I was just overreacting and wasn't anywhere near that bad. But he just shrugged.

"Honestly Hailey, I never really liked Michael," he confessed.

Oh great, now he tells me. I felt like I'd just been voted off the island. I mean, first Kat and now Clay. Did all my friends secretly hate the guy I'd almost decided to marry?

"*Et tu,* Clay?" I asked, followed by a small, weird sound that was meant to resemble laughter, but didn't.

He took a sip of his drink and looked at me. "He just never seemed very real, you know? He was always so disingenuous, like he was reciting certain conversational lines just to be polite, when he didn't really mean any of them."

"Do you think that's because he didn't really like you?" I asked, realizing that on the surface it seemed like a really rude thing to say, but the fact was Clay and I both knew how Michael felt about him.

"Well, at first I thought that might be it. But as I spent more time with you guys, I realized it was just how he was. I mean, come on, Hailey, what did you guys even talk about besides Atlas? What did you really have in common?" He looked at me with his eyebrows raised, waiting.

"Oh, well, that's easy." I nodded, knowing I could ace this one. "We both liked the same restaurants," I said, using my fingers to list all of our commonalities. "We liked long European layovers; we both liked shopping at Banana Republic . . ." Okay, I had seven more fingers ready to go to work and I was already done. That was one shallow list.

"All first-date stuff," Clay said. "Only you managed to coast four years on it."

"Um, I think I need another drink," I mumbled, sensing Clay was just getting started.

"And I never understood it," he continued. "You read all the time, go to museums, enjoy theater, but it's not like you could share that stuff with Michael."

Yup, he was on a roll.

"But I have you for all that." I smiled, desperately scraping my straw against the bottom of my plastic cup while my eyes searched for the waiter.

"And you wanna know the truth?"

No way. Uh-uh. I absolutely, positively, do not want to know the truth!

"I think you were totally selling out."

I just stared at him, completely defeated.

"And I'm with Kat: It *was* for the best. You *can* do better," he said, finishing his drink and placing his empty cup on the small plastic table between us. Then, shaking his head, he said, "I'm done discussing this, Hailey. And you need to stop obsessing."

I just gazed at him, nodding obediently, knowing he was right. So from then on, I'd stop obsessing *out loud.*

"Man, it's hot," he said, removing his glasses and heading for the pool. "Wanna go for a swim?"

I shook my head and watched as he waded into the shiny clear water, going all the way under until he was completely submerged. And when he finally resurfaced, his wet blond hair was all separated and glistening yellow, like a little baby duck. And I felt so grateful to have a friend like him, someone who would tell me the truth no matter how brutal. But I also wondered why he hadn't bothered to point any of this out until now.

He swam over to the in-pool bar, where some fellow crew members were talking and laughing. And I considered getting up to join them, except that my drink had just arrived and I was beginning to realize that me + 4 drinks + a pool = a bad idea. So I reapplied my sunscreen, leaned back on my lounge chair, and mulled over what Clay had just said.

It was true that I'd sold out. Or at the very least entered into an extreme, one-sided compromise. And as much as I hated to admit it, I'd definitely forfeited shared interests and true companionship for the illusion of comfort and security. I mean, thinking back on all those expensive dinners, well, they pretty much consisted of Michael recanting yet another boring *Top Gun* wannabe story while I sneaked peeks at all the other tables and wondered if those women were as bored as I was. Then, after he'd exhausted all of his glory stories, there'd be complete and total silence—but not the kind that comes from years of comfortable familiarity.

Heck, most of the time, I couldn't wait for the check to arrive so we could go to some bar, meet up with our respective friends, and ignore each other until it was time to go home.

And even though I had to admit it was *his* salary that enabled me to go to all those good restaurants, live in a nice doorman building, and buy all the Banana Republic I could handle, it still wasn't the main reason I'd stayed with him so long.

It was like, until I'd met Michael, my love life was a pathetic string of first and second dates, with the occasional third agreed to in a weak moment. I guess I'd developed a habit of skipping out the second things got serious. But by the time Michael came along, I'd been starting to panic. Suddenly everyone around me was happily pairing off. And not wanting to be left out, I'd endured the last four years the only way I knew how—by ignoring every single warning, every danger sign and flashing red light, until I'd so bought into the *myth of us* that I actually confused convenience with love.

By the time Clay tapped me on the shoulder and said, "Hailey, wake up. Let's get back to the room and change. We're all heading into old San Juan for dinner," the sun was already starting to set, and except for us, the pool was deserted.

"What?" I asked incoherently, rubbing my eyes under my sunglasses. "I must have taken a little siesta." I raised my arms over my head for a leisurely stretch.

"More like you fell into a coma," he said, collecting my sunscreen and paperback and tossing it into our communal beach bag. "It's after six, time for happy hour."

"I thought we just did happy hour." I slid my feet into my flip-flops and shuffled behind.

"Here in Puerto Rico, they give new meaning to the word."

"Oh yeah, 'Livin' La Vida Loca.' I've seen the video."

"You ain't seen nothing yet," he promised.

When we got back to the room I headed straight for the bathroom and turned on the hot water. It wasn't the first time I'd bunked with Clay, and we had a mutual understanding that I always got to shower first since it took me longer to get ready. Even though he obsessed about his hair almost as much as I did mine, he still qualified as the most low-maintenance gay guy I'd ever met.

Tossing my sunglasses onto the counter, I stepped into the shower and felt my wildly frizzy hair (that thanks to the humidity had swelled to three times its normal diameter) begin to lie submissively against my head as the jet of hot water tamed and softened it. I peeled back the paper wrapper of the tiny hotel-supplied soap, and as I foamed it up in my palms and ran it over my body I marveled at how good it felt to get a little sun on my skin.

Of course I knew all about the hazards of premature aging brought on by wanton exposure, but there was no denying that a tan made everyone (not to mention every *body*) look a little bit healthier, sleeker, and just generally *glowier*. And after that weekend-long food orgy with Clay, the bloat-inducing flight (jet belly, anyone?), immediately followed by three and a half mojitos at the pool, there wasn't an inch of my body that didn't need a little help.

I climbed out of the shower, wound a towel tightly around me, and aimed the wall-mounted blow dryer at the steamed-up mirror, watching as the dewy buildup began to dissipate until I could gradually make out my sun-kissed reflection.

Okay, so my shoulders looked a little more red than tan, no big deal. By tomorrow it would be nicely faded to a rich, golden glow. And the halter tie strap marks? No biggie. I'd just wear a halter-top to dinner, problem solved. But as the mirror continued to clear, exposing first my neck and then my chin, my eyes bulged in horror as the rest of my face was revealed. Because even though I was no longer wearing my sunglasses, I might as well have been. Not only were my nose, cheeks, and forehead a bright, blazing red, but right in the very center, smack dab in the middle of my face, was a perfect, flesh-toned outline of the duty-free Gucci sunglasses I'd worn during my three-and-a-half-hour nap in the sun.

I threw the bathroom door open and ran into the bedroom, where Clay was sprawled out on the bed listening to his iPod and watching TV with the sound off.

"Tell me it's not as bad as I think," I begged.

But when he turned to look at me his expression said everything he was too polite to.

"Oh God." I crumpled onto the twin bed across from his.

"What happened?" he asked, removing his earplugs and staring at the middle of my face. The corner of his mouth twitched with barely suppressed laughter.

"What am I gonna do? I can't go out like this!" I said, turning toward the mirror and laughing in spite of myself.

"Um, maybe you should put your sunglasses back on," he suggested as he doubled over, laughing so hard his face was nearly as
red as mine.

"At night?"

"Yeah, I can lead you around. We'll tell people you're visually
impaired. No one will laugh at you then."

"Or, maybe we can cover it with makeup. Didn't you take theater makeup in college?" I asked, looking at him, my eyes pleading
for help.

"I took a semester of stage makeup, Hailey. I didn't go to magic
school." He shook his head.

"Well we have to do something, because I can't go out looking
like this, and there's no way I'm staying in," I told him.

He stared at me for a moment, then got up from the bed and
sighed. "Time to work a miracle," he said, leading me to the bathroom.

By the time Clay was finished, I looked like the best friend in
Working Girl. I know most people make themselves over after a
breakup, but this was ridiculous.

"Okay," Clay said, squinting at me. "Think of it as a sort of retro
disco look."

I stood before the mirror, gazing at my reflection. Layers of
bronzer and powder had served to even out some of the tonal difference, while generous applications of dark, glittery eye shadow,
black liner, and four coats of mascara took care of the rest. And
since Clay forbade me to use my flat iron (a.k.a. "my magic
wand"), my auburn hair fanned out around me in a riot of curls,
just like Nicole Kidman (before she met Tom Cruise).

"Very Studio Fifty-four," he said, standing back to admire his
handiwork.

"Very Tammy Faye," I said, inspecting my spider-leg eyelashes.
"Okay, so what about you?"

"I'm gonna take a quick shower, and then we'll split," he said, retrieving his shower gel from his Jack Spade dopp kit and pushing me out the door.

"Forget it. If I'm going out in drag, then you are too," I insisted.

"But I'm not the one who suffered a tanning accident," he said, closing the door on me.

"C'mon, Clay. It'll be fun!" I shouted through the locked door. "You can do some kind of glam rock, vintage Bowie look. People will think we planned it."

"Go watch TV," he shouted. "I'll be out in a minute."

By the time we met up with the crew, Clay and I had reached a compromise. His eyes were subtly lined with black pencil, his hair was a little more gelled than usual, and he had the faintest touch of gold gloss in the very center of his bottom lip.

"Here come the twins," said Jack, a captain I'd flown with a few times before.

"I didn't know we were going to a costume party," said Bob, a first officer I'd never really cared for.

"Then why are *you* all dressed up like a pilot on a layover?" asked the head flight attendant, Jennifer, motioning to his pristine white Reeboks and sharply pressed khakis.

"Are we ready?" Clay asked.

"There's another crew joining us," Bob said. "I saw them checking in a little while ago. They were just working a turnaround and were headed back to JFK when they canceled the flight. Apparently there's a hurricane headed this way. Supposed to touch down off the coast of Florida. Guess they'll be stuck here for a couple days."

"Really? Where they based?" Clay asked, plopping down onto an overstuffed chair and making himself comfortable.

And no sooner had Bob opened his mouth to answer, when Michael appeared.

BRACING POSITIONS

In an unexpected emergency,
flight attendants must react to
the first sign of impact by
yelling:
 Grab ankles!
 Heads down!
 Stay low!
 Bend over!

6

I'm not gonna lie. I'd imagined a moment like this many, many times since I'd caught Michael with his pants down. But in every single scenario, not only was I ten pounds thinner, with miraculously straight, humidity-defying hair, but I was also (inexplicably) laying over at the Bali Ritz-Carlton, where I was seated at the bar, clad in a clingy, low-cut Gucci gown, sipping a martini and smiling patiently while Bono and Jon Stewart vied for my attention. . . . And then, of course, Michael would walk in, our eyes would meet, and he'd drop to his knees, begging forgiveness. . . .

(Never mind that I now knew it was much more likely that Michael would drop to his knees for Bono and Jon while completely ignoring *me*. It was my fantasy and I was having it my way.)

And even though I'd gone through plenty of variations—sometimes I was wearing Versace, sometimes the hotel was in Capri—never once did I imagine myself standing in a lobby in old San Juan, looking like 1988, with hair that was channeling Carrot Top, as my former boyfriend/roommate whom I'd briefly consid-

ered marrying strolls in looking tan, fit, and totally together with a
pretty, young, adoring flight attendant (female) hanging on his arm.

"I've booked us at this great little place in town called the Pea-
cock Club. Our table's at eight," he said. His all-too-familiar mouth
rose into an easy smile as I stood there feeling damp, awkward, and
nauseous, wondering if I really was going to vomit all over the
shiny marble floor. And then looking right at me, without even
blinking, he said, "Oh, Hailey, hey. I didn't even recognize you."

I wanted so much to have a snappy retort, something that
would make everyone laugh, at his expense of course. But my
mind just completely froze. And by the time it thawed out again I
was watching him walk out the door to round up some taxis.

"I absolutely cannot have dinner with him," I said, I was sitting on
the hump, wedged between Jennifer and Clay, as our small dirty
cab followed so closely behind Michael's there wasn't a chance of
losing them.

"Please, you've had a million dinners together where you barely
even spoke," Clay reminded me. "So why should this one be any
different?"

He had a point.

"I gotta tell ya, Hailey, I never really understood your whole
thing with Michael," Jennifer said, looking at me and shrugging.

"Yeah, apparently that's the general consensus." I rolled my
eyes and stared at my sunburned knees that because of the hump,
were practically parallel to my chin.

"You just seemed so . . . *mismatched*. It's like he's all mapped
out and programmed, and you're like . . ." Clay and I both turned
to look at her. If nothing else, I'd finally learn what people really
thought of me. "Not." She smiled.

"I'm not mapped out? You mean like, *I'm lost*?" I asked, staring
straight ahead at the rosary dangling from the rearview mirror. *Oh*

my God, maybe my mom isn't the only one who thinks I'm just me-andering through life.

"No, not *lost*. Just like, not so . . . *focused*." she said.

"Not focused?" I repeated. *So it's true. People think I have no direction.*

"You know how pilots are." She was beginning to sound flustered. "They're just so . . . *structured*."

I'm nonstructured, unfocused, and totally without direction. And I have hair that is taking over the entire backseat of this cab, I thought, grabbing a handful and trying to smooth it down.

"Besides, if you don't go, he wins," Clay said, tapping me on the shoulder and nodding.

"It's not about winning," I mumbled, focusing on the silver Jesus swaying back and forth. What would *he* do?

"*Every* breakup is about winning! That's why I insist on having the breakup fantasy immediately after exchanging numbers, so when it does happen, I'm ready."

"Clay, that is seriously disturbed." Jennifer laughed.

"He always mourns the end before it even begins," I told her.

"I'm always looking for my next ex." He smiled. "But seriously, you can't let him win. He can't know that he got to you."

"Uh, have you seen my face lately? 'Cause this is hardly the look of someone at the top of their game," I said, holding onto the back of the driver's seat as he cranked a hard turn to the left.

"I think it looks kind of cool," Jennifer said.

"You live in the East Village. You're used to this stuff," I reminded her.

"Well, at least you don't look like that Barbie wannabe cockpit queen hanging all over his arm." She shook her head.

"Yeah, and who is she?" I asked as the cab came to an abrupt halt.

"Only one way to find out," Clay said, reaching for my hand and dragging me into the restaurant.

When we walked into the room the first thing I noticed was how dim it was. *This lighting will definitely work in my favor,* I thought as the host led us past a succession of large and lively tables before taking us back outside to a beautiful, lush courtyard filled with potted palms and orchids, all of it spotlighted by the full moon shining brightly overhead.

So much for dim lighting, I thought, keeping my eye on Michael at the front of the procession, making sure I lagged far behind, since the less contact I had with him the better.

"Will this be okay?" Our host motioned toward a beautiful table set for twelve.

It is so typical of Michael to home in on another crew's dinner, then just totally take over, I thought, rolling my eyes and scoping out the chairs, determined to sit as far from him as possible.

"*Sí, gracias.*" Michael nodded.

And hearing him say that made my knees go so weak I pulled out the nearest chair and plopped myself down. Not realizing until it was too late that it was directly across from his.

Clay gave me a not-so-subtle disapproving look immediately followed by a firm knee knock as he took the seat next to mine, and Jennifer made sure she exhaled long and loud as she sat on my other side.

I knew they were right. I'd been riding an emotional escalator, going up and down for days now. And I was well aware of how completely ridiculous I was acting. I mean, anyone who's ever dined at Taco Bell can say the word *gracias*. It's just, hearing him say that reminded me of all the dinners we'd shared in foreign countries, and how he always used to thank the waiter in their native tongue. And now he was still doing it, as though nothing had changed. Only everything *had* changed. And I was no longer sitting next to him. I was sitting next to Clay. And he was pinching me under the table. Hard.

"Ow," I whispered, giving his hand a firm swat before he could pull it away. *I mean, excuse me for having a weak moment, sheesh.* I shook my head and looked down at the menu.

"Good, read your menu, but stop looking at Michael," he hissed. "He'll get it all wrong and think you still want him."

I rolled my eyes, flipped my menu over, and read the back.

"You don't still want him, do you?" he asked, eyes widening with alarm.

"Clay, please. I am *so* over him," I said, looking up just as Michael ordered four bottles of wine for the entire table, without consulting anyone. *God, I used to think he was so good at entertaining, but now I can see that he's just another control freak.* "Um, excuse me," I said, catching the waiter just as he was about to leave. "I'm not having any wine. I'd like a mojito, please." I glanced quickly at Michael and narrowed my eyes. *Your days of ordering my drinks are o-v-e-r,* I thought.

"Make it two," Clay said, in a show of solidarity.

I turned to him and smiled. Other than the beagle I'd had as a kid, Clay was definitely my most loyal, successful, long-term male relationship.

"Oh, and can you tell me where the restroom is?" I asked, grabbing my purse and standing.

And just as I was about to leave I heard someone say, "Wait up! I'll go with you."

And I turned to see Michael's date smiling and rising from her seat.

7

"Does it hurt?"

We were leaning against an intricately patterned blue-and-white tiled wall, waiting for a stall to be vacated. *Does it hurt to see her with Michael? Do I have to pee so bad it hurts?* She was looking at me, waiting for an answer, and I had no idea what she was getting at.

"Your face," she said, pointing at my forehead with her two fingers, as though indicating an emergency exit. "It's all red, except in the middle."

Oh God, for a few blissful moments I'd forgotten all about my face. I leaned toward the mirror, checking for confirmation. Sure enough, my forehead, nose, chin, and cheeks were morphing into an even deeper blazing burgundy, while the area surrounding my hazel eyes was my usual pale beige, except for the parts that Clay had colored in with heavy black liner. I leaned in even closer, tracing my finger gently down the side of my cheek. It felt hot. And I looked like a negative of a raccoon.

"Um, you can go first," I said, motioning toward the stall that had just been vacated. I mean, even though I was barely able to hold it, I knew if I let her go first, she'd leave first, and then maybe I could have a quiet moment to myself before I had to head back out to that chaos.

But when I was finished, I found her standing right where we'd left off, waiting for me. And never one to indulge an awkward silence, I asked, "So, how long have you been based in New York?" I pumped the soap dispenser a few times, allowing my palms to fill with the thick pink liquid while consciously avoiding my reflection in the mirror.

"Oh, I'm not. I'm Dallas based. But I was supposed to audition tomorrow in Manhattan, so I picked up this trip. Looks like I'm not gonna make it, though," she said, smiling and shrugging, as though it was no big deal. Like now that she'd met Mr. Wonderful, she no longer needed to worry about little things like paying bills or chasing fame.

"What kind of audition?" I asked, scrutinizing her through the mirror while she picked at her cuticles. She was tall, thin, blond, blue-eyed, dainty-nosed, and had perfect dental work—had to be reality TV. She had that kind of pretty, accommodating, homogeneous look they specialize in. She also seemed vaguely familiar. But that could also be the whole homogeneous thing, or the fact that greeting hundreds of people a day for six years straight had made everyone start to look familiar.

"I was up for this nice part on one of the *Law and Orders*," she said. "It was my second call back."

Law and Order? *I love that show!* "Which one?" I asked, grabbing three crunchy brown paper towels from the dispenser and drying my hands.

"Trial by Jury." She shrugged.

That's the only one I don't like. Figures.

"So you're an actress?" I asked, secretly wondering how old

she was. Secretly wondering how long Michael had been trying to better-deal me. Secretly wondering if Michael had told her about me.

"Yeah, I've done a few commercials, a few print ads, some Off Broadway. But you probably know me from the safety video," she said, twisting the cap off her glittery pink Juicy Tubes and rolling it back and forth across her lips.

I watched as she tucked it back in her purse and ran her hands through her shiny blond hair, the fluorescent bathroom light reflecting and bouncing off it, just like in those Pantene commercials, and I thought, *She's the girl in the safety video? The video I've been ignoring my entire career? The video where I've actually heard passengers say, "Dude, check it out, she is so hot," and then make some rude comment when she shows how to manually inflate the life vest?*

She's that girl?

And now Michael is dating her?

"Um, I hate to tell you this, but it looks like your bottom lip is forming a blister," she said, pointing at my mouth with two fingers and giving me a concerned look.

But no way was I checking the mirror for confirmation. It was bad enough that I was sunburned, bloated, and dateless, with worse than usual hair, while Michael was hooking up with the wet dream of safety demos. I certainly didn't need to add my fat, bubbled lip into the mix.

"Oh, and by the way, I'm Aimee. What did you say your name was?" she asked, exiting ahead of me.

I followed behind her perfect size-two self, checking out her cute, wedge-heeled sandals, Juicy Couture sundress, and glossy mane, and I felt like a dumpy hausfrau in comparison. So excuse me for not wanting to be linked to whatever story Michael might one day tell her about his "psycho" ex girlfriend.

"I'm Monica," I lied, following her back to the table.

The second Michael spied our approach, he immediately jumped up from his seat, pulled Aimee's out, and remained standing until we were both seated again.

Oh, brother. I rolled my eyes. *I remember how he did that for me back in the early days. No way will it last,* I thought watching as he wrapped his arm around Aimee's slim but toned, tanned but not burned shoulders.

"I was about to send out a search party," he said, looking from her to me and smiling anxiously.

Pilot humor. I rolled my eyes again and stifled a yawn.

"Oh, Monica and I were just talking," she purred, leaning into him and rubbing his forearm with the same two fingers she uses to point out sunburns, blisters, oxygen masks, and emergency exits, like they are permanently fused together or something.

"Monica? Who's Monica?" Michael asked, obviously confused and looking from Aimee to me, and back again.

Oh, crap. I guess I hadn't really thought this all the way through, and now Aimee was giving me a strange look. But just as she started to lift her two fingers to point at me, our waiter came back to take our order.

We were just finishing dessert when Bob returned from the restroom and said, "That hurricane finally hit just west of the Keys."

"How bad is it?" asked Jack.

"Last I heard it'd been downgraded to a category one, but that can still do some damage," he said, then reached for his glass and polished off the rest of his wine.

"Oh, great, now I feel guilty. I'd been hoping for a storm since yesterday when I got this trip," Jennifer said, shaking her head. "God, I hope no one gets hurt."

Everyone chimed in, agreeing with Jennifer and expressing sudden goodwill toward the good people of Florida. But Clay and I just looked at each other and shrugged. It wasn't like we were trying to be callous; it's just that flight attendants were always wishing for blizzards, tornadoes, fog, driving rain, or any other kind of natural disaster that could possibly lead to a canceled flight. And in the event of a perfectly sunny day, well then we wished for malfunctions and broken airplane parts (but only on the ground, never in the air). I mean, basically, we were a group of professional travelers who never wanted to fly anywhere unless we were occupying a passenger seat and headed either a) home, or b) on vacation. Then we demanded that everything run on a firm, tight schedule.

"Speaking of hurricanes, what did the hurricane say to the palm tree?" Michael asked, looking around the table, the corners of his mouth curling up in anticipation of a punch line only he knew.

Here we go. I cringed. *A couple glasses of wine and now he's Letterman.* I shook my head and waited for the inevitably juvenile answer that would no doubt straddle the murky lines of Atlas's sexual harassment policy. *God, this was how my friends must have felt all those times they joined us for dinner or drinks. Why couldn't I see then what I can now?*

"I give up! Tell me!" Aimee squealed, grabbing his hand and biting him playfully on the knuckle.

Michael paused, looking around the table, making sure he had everyone's full attention. "Hang on to your nuts; this ain't gonna be no ordinary blowjob!" he finally said, exploding in laughter.

Okay, not only was that not funny, but the Southern accent he'd adopted for the final punch was really pushing it. But do you think that kept anyone from laughing? Not a chance. And that's because:

A. The other pilots truly believed it *was* funny.
B. The check had just been delivered, and all the flight atten-
    dants were hoping he'd pay it.

Well, I had my own Atlas AirMiles Visa card, not to mention
just enough rum in my blood to look him directly in the eye and
say, "I don't get it."

Everyone turned and stared. Some laughed, most were curious,
but Michael and Clay looked alarmed.

"It's just a stupid joke." Michael shrugged, gazing down at the
table and running his fingers along the base of his wineglass. He
was starting to look really uncomfortable.

I'll show you discomfort, I thought, narrowing my eyes, hell-bent
on revenge. I mean, if he felt confident enough to tell a blowjob
joke in my presence, then maybe I'd share a blowjob joke that *happened* in my presence. And I had no doubt everyone would remember this one.

"What I meant was, well, just what is an 'ordinary' blowjob
anyway? Huh, Michael?" I leaned back in my seat and crossed my
arms over my chest. *Hah, let's see how you squirm out of that, Mr.
Jet-Flying, Starlet-Dating, Wine-Ordering, Joke-Telling, Hummer-
Getting Sky God!*

Clay moved his left hand under the table and squeezed my leg
so tight it felt like I had a tourniquet wrapped around it. And even
though I was looking right at Michael, patiently waiting for a response, the heat and discomfort emanating from the rest of the
table was palpable.

I glanced quickly at Aimee, who was giving me a strange, hurt
look; and then over at Clay, who was silently pleading with me to
stop; and then over at Jennifer, who was softly shaking her head.
And by the time I focused back on Michael, I was not only losing
steam, but I was beginning to feel a little clammy, self-conscious,
and sad.

I mean, what the hell was I doing, anyway? Everyone was just trying to enjoy a nice dinner in Puerto Rico, and with one stupid comment I'd turned the whole night into my own personal vendetta.

So Michael had a date with a dude and broke my heart. Had I really wanted to marry him anyway? Because the ever-present stomach pings and nausea that accompanied every matrimonial moment in my head pretty much told me otherwise.

It was like, maybe in some weird way Michael had actually done me a favor, by forcing me out of my lazy, comfortable, complacent world so I could finally confront my life head-on. Because even though I hated to admit it, if he hadn't gone and pushed me into the deep end, I'd still be sitting on the edge of the pool, dipping in just a toe or two and telling myself that the water didn't really look all that refreshing anyway.

Besides, hadn't I been there for Clay when he came out to his family five years ago? Hadn't I supported him when they refused to take his calls for a full year and a half after that? And hadn't I seen, firsthand, the pain it caused him? So how could I act so cavalier now? How could I be so vindictive?

Yes, Michael had hurt me, by cheating on me and calling me too old to marry. But the fact is, I was getting over it, while he was still compelled to prove his shaky manhood by dating a cheerleader, throwing his Visa card around, and behaving like a thirty-eight-year-old frat boy.

It was like I'd dodged a bullet.

But now I had to find a way out. I mean, everyone was staring at me, Clay was slowly cutting off all circulation to my leg, and Michael was obsessively fondling his wineglass. And since it was all my fault to begin with, I knew I had to do something. Quick.

"So, um, do you know why women fake orgasms?" I asked, looking right at Michael, willing him to make eye contact so he could see that I wasn't taking this where he assumed I was. That I wasn't going to spill his secret. That I wasn't as small and spiteful as he thought.

And when he finally lifted his head, his brown eyes looked directly into mine. "Yeah, because men fake foreplay," he said, smiling as he hijacked my punch line.

8

During the beverage service, while I was sitting on the jump seat, I realized I'd lost my manuscript. *Great, as if I don't have enough to be freaked about,* I thought, going through my small carry-on bag for the third time and rechecking every single nook and cranny.

Thanks to that major tropical storm, I'd spent the last five days in rainy Puerto Rico, holed up in the hotel, watching pay-per-view with Clay and Jennifer, winning then losing fifty dollars in blackjack at the hotel casino, acting friendly toward Michael and Aimee when I inadvertently ran into them in the lobby, and watching the red portions of my face peel and fade to a nice, raw pink.

And it wasn't until we got to the airport that I realized I'd only left out enough kitty chow to cover the three days I thought I'd be gone and not the five that I actually was.

"Kat is going to kill me!" I'd told Clay while helping him set up the galley.

Due to the recent spate of weather-related flight cancellations, all the seats were full. So if I wanted to get home I had no choice but to sit on the jump seat. And if I was going to ride in the galley, well then, I felt like I had to help out, if only a little.

"You didn't leave out an extra bowl, just in case?" he asked, slamming a bag of ice onto the galley floor over and over again until it broke into smaller, more serviceable chunks.

"It didn't even occur to me," I admitted. "Believe me, animals and children are not safe with me. I don't even possess the minimum amount of nurturing skills required to take care of others." I opened a bag of napkins that advertised a software company (yet another sign of how Atlas was totally selling out), and shoved them into a caddy.

"What are you talking about? Of course you're nurturing; you're a flight attendant! Which also makes you a nurse, a psychologist, a babysitter, a janitor, a dietician, a bartender, a cocktail waitress, a veterinarian, a life coach, a bomb stopper, a crime fighter, a cockpit protector, a luggage lifter, a hash slinger, a magician, a mind reader, a global positioning system, a weather controller, and a human shield. It's like we have superpowers! Think about it: We transport thousands of people a day, feeding and watering them while we're at it!" he said, getting up from the floor and carefully pouring the newly broken ice chunks into a plastic serving drawer.

"Believe me, the only reason I feed and water anyone is because it's my job, and I'll get fired if I don't. And now Kat's gonna fire me as her friend, when she gets home from Greece and finds three starved kitties in her kitchen. Besides," I whispered, shutting the door of the beverage cart and peeking down the aisle, "after six years of this, I don't even like most people anymore."

"Hailey, please." He'd rolled his eyes. "None of us do." Then, shaking his head, he'd charged down the aisle intent on stopping someone from cracking the overhead bin with their oversized bag.

And now, with the contents of my carry-on spilled across the galley floor, the fact of my missing manuscript was something I could no longer deny. And it wasn't just that it was my only copy that had me so upset (sure I'd backed it up to disk, years ago, but I no longer knew where that was either), but more the idea of where it might be and who might be reading it that had me all bothered.

Let's see, if I retrace my steps, then the last time I saw it was . . . Think, Hailey! When I was sitting in first class, drinking champagne . . . right before that awful gate agent made me move . . . then there was that really cute guy . . . Oh my God, what if he read it! If he read it, I will die! Seriously. But wait. Wouldn't he just hand it over to the crew? And since I'd just spent the last five days with them, I know that didn't happen, so it must have fallen between the seat cushions. Which means it would have been found during the security check in Puerto Rico and then promptly thrown out (after scanning it for terrorist threats, of course). So that means it's probably resting on a trash barge, enjoying a long, leisurely cruise toward its final destination, a landfill. . . .

"Um, excuse me, miss?"

Oh, God, this was the worst part of riding the jump seat. People always assumed you were being lazy by not serving them, when clearly my beige linen pants, cream-colored camisole, and beige wrap sweater were a far cry from the ugly polyester uniform Atlas made us wear.

I remained sitting there, bent over my stuff, hoping she'd go away.

"Miss? I'm sorry to bother you, but I think something's wrong with my dad."

I looked up to find a terrified teenage girl standing before me, hands shaking, eyes wide with panic, and I was out of my seat, in the aisle, and checking her dad for vital signs before I'd even had a chance to think. "Go get those flight attendants on the cart up there and tell them to call for help," I told her. But when I reached for the first aid kit I saw that she was still standing behind me, completely frozen. "It's gonna be okay," I said softly. "But please go now!"

The guy sitting at the window helped me lay the sick passenger in the aisle, and as I bent over him, lowering my ear to his nose and mouth, I was filled with dread when I realized he wasn't breathing. Ripping into the first aid kit, I grabbed the pocket mask, slapped it on his face, and immediately breathed two slow breaths into his mouth, watching his chest softly rise and fall. Then I pressed two fingers to his neck, desperately searching for his carotid pulse, but there wasn't any.

Oh God, oh God. I looked frantically up the aisle. The young girl was just now telling Clay, and I knew there wasn't enough time to wait for him to arrive with the defibrillator. I had to start CPR now! But was it still trace, space, and place? No, that was outdated. Now it was something like, imagine a line across the nipples, estimate the middle, and start pushing. But what if I broke a rib?

I glanced down at him, noticing his face had gone completely white and his lips were taking on a bluish tinge. And knowing it was probably already too late, I took a deep breath, and let everything I'd learned about first aid instinctively take over until Clay and Jennifer arrived.

Since I was already on the floor, I stayed put when Clay got there, helping him cut open the man's shirt, shave his chest, and attach those sticky pads to the designated spots while Jennifer ran to page for a doctor and tried to calm the terrified young girl.

Over the years I'd had plenty of onboard minor medical emergencies, but there always seemed to be a doctor, nurse, EMT, or paramedic on board. But now that it was a life-or-death matter, it was just Clay and me. And we remained crouched in the aisle, desperately trying to breathe air into his lungs and shock him back to consciousness, until we returned to the San Juan airport and the emergency medical team stormed on board and rushed him away on a stretcher.

We stood in the aisle, dazed and sweaty, and I looked at the girl just as the Atlas reps were taking her away. "My dad!" she cried. But I had nothing for her. It was already too late when I'd found him.

When we finally landed at Kennedy Airport, there was the usual gaggle of supervisors waiting to meet us.

"Are y'all okay?" asked Dotty, a Southerner with bleached blond curly bangs and a tight, purple suit that hadn't fit since 1987.

"I need you to fill out some paperwork," said Shannon, our overanxious and underqualified base manager.

"You haven't talked to any media, have you?" This one came from Lawrence, my very own supervisor, whom, quite frankly, I could not stand.

I rolled my eyes and kept walking. There was no way I was even going to answer that. What was he thinking? That I'd called CNN from the in-flight phone? That my agent was fielding bids on an exclusive story? I mean, some kid's dad had died right in front of me, and that was the best this bozo could come up with?

I glanced over at Clay, who was surrounded by suits. But he was part of the working crew, which meant he had no choice but to stick around and answer questions. Whereas I, on the other hand, was on my own time. And right or wrong, to me, that little fact made all the difference.

I dragged my bag up the jetway, determined to shake Lawrence.

"Hailey, I know you've had a traumatic flight, but you *cannot* walk away," he said, tailgating me. "We *must* debrief."

"I'm going home. I'll e-mail a report tomorrow," I called over my shoulder as I entered the terminal and beelined for the exit.

There was no way I was "debriefing" with him. This was the same overzealous clown who wrote me up for wearing Ugg boots from my apartment to the airport during one of the worst blizzards the city had ever seen. Never mind that I'd promptly changed into my airline-approved pumps before I signed in. Apparently I'd done great harm to the Atlas image by allowing the crackheads loitering at the bus stop on the corner of 125th and Lex to peek at my non-regulation snow boots at four o'clock in the morning.

But Lawrence didn't just limit himself to footwear infractions. Oh no. During the last several years he'd busted me for:

1. Wearing earrings bigger than a quarter.
2. Recklessly allowing my hair to fall past my collar.
3. Sporting opaque hose instead of silky sheer during foul weather.
4. Wearing two silver rings on the same hand and on different fingers.
5. Using a nonapproved piece of luggage when my roll-aboard suffered a severe blowout during a three-day trip. (Apparently I was supposed to have a backup bag on hand. Never mind that this went against the strict two-bag policy that even we were forced to adhere to.)
6. Not wearing the blazer during boarding. (Uh, let's not even mention that it was 105 degrees outside and 110 in the cabin, as the Atlas suits, intent on saving money, forbade us from using the air conditioner.)
7. Chewing gum in uniform.
8. Using a "designer" lanyard to hold my ID rather than the Atlas-issued chain/clip one. (Even though it wasn't really designer, but a Burberry plaid knockoff.)

He'd even gone so far as to drag me over to the mirror early one morning, directing me to gaze at my reflection while contemplating the sign overhead that read, "Image is everything" and "This is what your customers see."

Well, if that's what they were forced to look at, then I was truly sorry for them. Because not only was there an overworked and underpaid flight attendant with early-morning eye bags, an ugly uniform, and frizzy hair fighting to break free from its company-

approved French twist, but next to her stood a vertically challenged imbecile with a bad attitude, overplucked brows, sketchy
man makeup, and a textbook case of Napoleon complex the likes
of which I'd never seen.

No wonder they keep him down here, in the bowels of JFK, I
thought as he pointed out the "wispies" that had spontaneously
sprung loose from my hair clip.

"Wispies are frowned upon," he'd reminded me. "Maybe you
should try a stronger hair spray."

And now he wanted to take a meeting? Not a chance. Didn't
this guy have papers to push, bucks to pass, lightbulbs to change?

I pushed through the filthy glass door and headed for the bus
stop, wondering if he'd follow.

He didn't.

9

By the time I made it back to Kat's I was frantic. *Just how many bodies have I left in my wake?* I wondered, making my way down the hall and bracing for whatever horror I might stumble upon. Would I find three emaciated Persians splayed across the kitchen floor, starving eyes staring at me accusingly? Or would Kat be waiting rigidly at the head of the table, flanked by a team of lawyers, ready to charge me with gross negligence?

I hesitated in the doorway, not sure if I had the guts to go through with it. Then, taking a deep breath, I walked into the kitchen, and just like in a clip from *When Animals Attack*, Harold, Conrad, and William came charging toward me, their tiny white paws scraping furiously against the stone floor while their blue eyes remained fixed on their intended prey—*me*. I froze in horror as I watched them closing in, and for a brief moment I considered fleeing down the hall toward the safety of my room. But in the end, I just dropped my bags and stood there, knowing that whatever vicious act they had in mind, surely I deserved it.

But instead of leaping for my throat and going straight for the jugular, they skidded to a stop at my feet. And then, arching their backs and lowering their heads, they sidled up against my legs, meowing in a way that was more greeting than protest. And as a lifelong, dedicated "dog person," I gotta admit, I was impressed.

Relieved that all they seemed to want was a little love and nourishment, I busied myself with filling their bowls. Then I got down on the floor with them, and cried while they ate.

When the alarm rang at seven, I was already wide awake, having spent the previous half hour rubbing my itchy, watery eyes and battling through intense sneeze attacks brought on by "the kids." And by the fact that I'd felt so guilty about their desertion I'd actually let them sleep with me.

I reached over, silenced the clock, and wandered into the kitchen in search of coffee, some paper, and a pen. Yesterday's tragedy was still fresh in my mind, and I knew that eventually I'd have to deal with it, since I could only dodge Lawrence for so long. But for now, I had the whole day off, and I was determined to use it for more pressing issues.

I had promised myself that as soon as I returned from Puerto Rico I would begin rebuilding my life. And the best way for me to do that is always by making a list. Otherwise I tend to get side-tracked and drift way off course.

So I grabbed a notepad from a hotel in Barcelona and a ball-point pen advertising a Dublin pub and wrote:

To Do Today:

1. Pick up stuff from Michael's.
2. Find apartment to put stuff in.

Okay, this being New York City and all, I knew what a seemingly impossible task the second item would be. It can take people with

far more money and resources than I months to find a decent place
to live. But this was one of those rare cases when being a flight attendant could actually work in my favor. Since our irregular sched-
ules rarely keep us in one place for more than a few days at a time,
we are known to occupy the tiniest apartments in large quantities.
So surely, somewhere on this twenty-five-mile island there was a vacant bunk bed waiting for me. I mean, as nice as it was in the Fifth
Avenue penthouse, there was no way I could survive the rest of the
week with three fluffy Persians and their collective dander. Besides,
it was time to reclaim my life and start paying my own way.

So after feeding the felines, and brewing some coffee, I fired up
my laptop and logged onto the Atlas Airlines Web site, heading
straight for the employee swap board, which serves as a sort of
craigslist for flight attendants, offering up everything from unwanted trips to gently worn uniform items and rooms for rent.

Since the majority of New York–based flight attendants and pilots are commuters, flying in to work and then heading back home
as soon as their trip ends, there was a long list of available space in
Kew Gardens (which due to its airport proximity and apartments
chock-full of airline employees is also known as Crew Gardens).
But that's mostly a "twenty people to a two-bedroom" commuter
crash pad, hot bed (bring your own sheets, first come first served)
situation. And since I was a newly single, noncommuting, full-
time New York–dwelling gal, I really preferred to live in the city.
And I really preferred to have my own bed.

But after reading through countless listings I knew would never
work, I was just about to give up when I read the very last one:

WANTED—

1 F, N/S, F/A, 2 SHARE 1 BDR, IN CITY.

CALL LISETTE JOHNSON.

Since I didn't know anyone named Lisette, I immediately tried
to research her schedule, hoping I could glean something about

her from the type of trips she liked to fly. But when I typed in her name, RESTRICTED INFORMATION flashed on-screen, and I immediately assumed that, like me, she too had suffered a bad breakup with a fellow Atlas employee, and was determined not to be tracked.

So, feeling a common bond, I picked up the phone and dialed her number, keeping my fingers crossed that the apartment would still be available.

By the time I reached the fifth-floor walkup I was sweaty, gasping for breath, and vowing to join a gym as soon as I got settled in. Then, combing my fingers through my long, curly hair, I knocked on Lisette's door, and blinked in surprise when I was greeted by Lisa, whom I vaguely remembered from flight attendant training all those years ago.

"Oh, hey," I said, wiping my hand across my sweaty brow, hoping the room hadn't been rented before I'd even had a chance to see it. "I'm here to see Lisette."

"That's me," she said, stepping aside and revealing a tiny, cluttered apartment with no discernible natural light.

"Wait. You're Lisette?" I asked, pausing in the threshold and squinting at her, feeling more than a little confused. I mean, sure her hair had changed from its former brown ponytail to a jet black, flat-ironed, chin-length bob, and her formerly bottle-tanned skin was now a pale, creamy white, but I definitely remembered her as being Lisa, the girl who'd pulled me into the raft during the "Unanticipated Ocean Landing" class held in the Atlas swimming pool.

"I passed the French language exam. I fly only to Nice, Lyon, and Paris now," she said, as though that somehow explained it.

I just nodded, frantically trying to recall anything more about her from our six weeks in the South, six years ago. But unfortunately, the memory bank was empty.

"So, this is it," she said, with inexplicable pride. "Kitchen there, bathroom with tub/shower through that door, and my bedroom through that one." She pointed, her index finger hitting all the important landmarks in the small, rectangular space. "What do you think?" she asked, obviously anticipating a compliment.

"Well . . ." I stalled, focusing on the dying houseplant in the far corner; the hideous, pockmarked, parquet wood floors; and the peeling, bubbled, yellowing walls, all the while trying to convince myself that this would be, at most, a temporary situation. "Can I see the room we'll be sharing?"

"Oh, we're not sharing," she said, shaking her head emphatically. "The bedroom is *my* room. This pull-out couch is where *you'll* sleep. I'm told it's very comfortable," she said, running her short red nails along the armrest like a game show model.

Seeing that ugly, dismal, sagging, brown corduroy couch made my eyes threaten to fill with tears; but determined to get through it, I wiped my hand across my forehead, shook my head, and said, "Okay. So how much are you asking?"

She stood there regarding me carefully. "Well, since you'll be sleeping on a couch, I've decided to ask for less than half the rent." She smiled.

"And how much is that?" I asked, determined to get to the bottom of it. I was in no mood for games.

"One thousand dollars a month, plus half the utilities." She didn't even flinch.

"For the *couch*? Are you kidding?" I said, staring at her in disbelief.

"The total rent is twenty-two hundred! I'm paying more than you!" she argued.

"Yeah, but you have a *door*! While I'm just winging it in the middle of the living room here," I said, feeling deeply depressed that I was actually bartering over a *couch*.

"*D'accord,*" she sighed, rolling her eyes and slipping into French. "Nine hundred and fifty."

"Nine even," I countered, narrowing my eyes.

"Done, *fini*." She clapped her hands together twice, bringing an end to the bartering.

Shaking my head, I settled onto the crappy, lumpy couch, which would now double as my bed, and wrote her a check for the first and last months' rent, secretly hoping the first month would be the last.

"I'll come by later with my stuff," I said, exchanging the check for a set of shiny gold keys.

And as I headed for the door I stopped and turned, glancing from Lisette to the couch, knowing I'd just been completely had. But I also knew that if I was going to find my own way, I'd have to start here.

STERILE COCKPIT

Flight attendants are prohibited from engaging in any activity that could distract the pilots from their performance.

10

My first night on the couch had not gone well. Never mind the lumps, the bumps, and the creaky springs, not to mention my own germ-phobic paranoia about its murky origins and sexual history. The main reason I hadn't slept was due to the constant sound of Lisette and her pilot boyfriend going at it so loudly that two earplugs, two pillows, and a thick down comforter thrown over my head couldn't drown out the noise. And by the time it was finally, mercifully over, well that's when the snoring started (both his and hers). And before I knew it, it was 3:45 A.M. and my clock radio was blasting the oddly appropriate "All Out of Love," which would play in my head for the rest of the day.

I stumbled into the bathroom, turned on the taps, and peered in the mirror as I waited for the water to warm. My hazel eyes had bags the size of checked luggage, my hair was a frizzed-out mess, and if I wasn't mistaken, my chin held the promise of what by day's end would surely be a freakishly large zit. And as I opened the glass shower door and cautiously stepped inside, I asked myself,

once again, why I always traded my afternoon trips for ones that
signed in early, when clearly I was not a morning person.

Yes, it was true that all I had to do was survive two quick yet te-
diously boring round trips to Washington, D.C., and back, but if
the small gash I'd just made while shaving my legs was any indica-
tion, my hand-eye coordination was severely hindered. And as a
person whose secondary responsibility is to get piping hot coffee
swiftly and safely into the hands of the politicians and newscasters
who frequent the shuttle (even though they think it's my *only*
responsibility), my early-morning handicap would surely work
against me.

But the flip side was that a 5:00 A.M. sign-in often made for an
early-afternoon return. And I knew that once I'd choked down a
few cups of that brutal airplane brew, I'd be just coherent enough
to get through the first flight of the day bomb check that was now
required of me.

Freshly showered, with one towel coiled around my head and
another tucked tightly around my body, I was bent over the sink,
spitting mouthwash into the bowl, when a pale, paunchy, middle-
aged man, unfortunately clad in a pair of tighty whities, threw the
door open and demanded, "Have you seen my bag tag?"

I turned to face him, mouthwash bubbles racing a speedy
slalom down my chin. "Excuse me? Don't you knock?" I grasped
my towel against my chest while narrowing my eyes at Dan,
Lisette's creepy captain boyfriend, who also happened to be half
the reason why I'd barely slept.

"Have you seen it?" he demanded, peering around my shoulder
and barreling his way into the tiny bathroom. "I need to get out of
here. I have a 5:00 A.M. commuter flight home, and I can't find it
anywhere."

"Wait. You can't fly without your bag tag?" I asked, clutching
my towel and standing my ground, refusing to be pushed around.

"Would you please just start looking!" he yelled, glaring at me and shaking his head in exasperation as he rifled through my makeup bag. "It's just a plain gold band. You can't miss it."

I stood there, growing increasingly confused as I watched him manhandle my eyelash curler. "Uh, I'm a little lost here. Didn't you just say you were looking for a bag tag?" I asked, yanking my Nars Multiple stick out of his hand and staring at his Adam's apple, determined to focus from only the neck up.

"It's my *wedding ring*." He lifted my blow dryer and peered underneath. "And if I go home without it, my wife will *kill* me!"

"Wait—*you're married?*" I asked, eyes darting toward the bedroom door, wondering if Lisette knew. Oh, who was I kidding? Of course she knew.

But he didn't answer. He just shook his head, pushed past me, and headed into the living room.

"I don't get it," I said, tailing him, determined to get to the bottom of this. "What's with the 'bag tag' bit?"

"The. Old. Bag. Tagged. Me." He enunciated slowly. "Now could you get crackin', and help me out here?" he said, peering behind some framed photos of Lisette posing in front of all the usual French landmarks.

I just stood there, my wet hair making a sizable puddle on the ugly wood floor, watching him desperately try to locate the symbol of his everlasting love that he'd apparently removed before spanking the symbol of his everlasting lust. And it was pretty clear that the only thing he really cared about saving was his own saggy ass.

Then I shook my head, grabbed my uniform pieces, and carried them into the bathroom. This time making sure to lock the door behind me.

The best part of working the Washington, D.C., shuttle was the half-hour breaks we enjoyed between flights. We were lounging in the blue leather passenger seats, in the fully reclined position, and enjoying our breakfast of leftovers when I said, "It went on and on and on." I rolled my eyes at the memory. "I didn't get any sleep. Not to mention that I'll never get those five hours back." I shook my head and struggled to break off a piece of the rock-hard bagel we serve our passengers.

"Is he living there?" Clay asked, peering at me from over the top of his mini carton of orange juice. Everything we served on the shuttle was miniature—well, except for all the oversized egos we catered to.

"No. He commutes from Atlanta, where he lives with his wife and kids. God, it is just so *wrong*. And she's so *loud!*" I said, taking a sip of my coffee.

Clay's eyes lit up. "Any particular fetish? Or just a random screamer?" He leaned toward me, on high alert for the juicy details.

"Well," I whispered, wiping my mouth and glancing around, making sure the pilots and air marshals were well out of earshot. "She likes him to spank her. She says stuff like, 'That's it Daddy, give me a red-hot ass.'" When I looked at him I started laughing in spite of myself.

Clay's eyes went wide with pure joy. "You're making that up!"

"I wish. And this morning, when I was in the bathroom trying to get ready, he just barged right in and asked if I'd seen his bag tag."

"His what?"

"That's what he calls his wedding ring. You know, the old bag tagged him," I said, shaking my head and feeling disgusted all over again.

"Charming." Clay rolled his eyes.

"On my way out I found it lying next to the kitchen sink. I guess she makes him take it off and wash his hands before he spanks her," I said, reaching into my bag and retrieving the slim gold band.

Clay reached for the ring. "No diamond?" He shook his head. "Cheap bastard. So what are you gonna do with it?"

I shrugged and took a sip of my coffee. "You can keep it if you want," I told him, watching as he slid it onto his left ring finger.

"It's a little loose, but I think I can make it work." He held up his hand and admired it. "Maybe he and I can move to Vermont and make it official." He smiled. "But seriously, I think this will come in handy. Peter's been doubling up on his abs class, and you know that can only mean *one thing*." He looked at me, shaking his head ominously.

"Uh, you might have to fill me in here, because your Hamptons summer share is about the most sinister reason I can think of," I said.

"It means he's up to no good. It means he's trying to *impress* someone. And this might be just the thing I need to make him jealous," he said, raising his eyebrows and wagging his newly accessorized finger at me.

"That sounds very healthy, Clay." I shook my head.

"You guys, guess who's in the boarding area?" I looked up to see Sydney, the head flight attendant and our good friend, rushing down the aisle. She was the one person out of all fifteen thousand of us who somehow managed to look amazing in the uniform. But at five feet ten, with the body of a Brazilian supermodel, the face of a Russian supermodel, and the gorgeous straight blond hair of a Swedish supermodel, it's not like she had a choice. "I just saw, like, *a bunch* of supervisors," she said, stopping to catch her breath.

"Oh great," I said, giving up on my stale bagel and tossing it back into the cardboard box it came in. "What's going on?"

"Apparently, they just got back from some meeting. They're all carrying these white coffee mugs with black letters that say 'OO.'"

"They finally cloned Oprah?" Clay asked, crushing his empty OJ carton, and opening another.

"It's what we're supposed to call them now. It stands for 'Occupational Overseer.'"

"You're joking, right?" I looked at her.

She perched on the armrest across from us and shook her head. "'Using a less-threatening name is the first step in mending the unfortunate gap of distrust that has grown between labor and management,'" she quoted.

"Where'd you get that?" Clay laughed.

"I was sideswiped by four of them on my way to Starbucks. They couldn't wait to unveil the new OO strategy and introduce the softer, friendlier supervisor of the future." She rolled her eyes.

"Does that come with a side of softer, friendlier attitude?" I asked.

"No. Their primary function is still writing us up. But now when they do it as OOs we won't feel as resentful as we did when they were supervisors. What's this?" she asked, reaching for Clay's hand.

"Clay got engaged, to an Atlas captain," I told her.

"And I had such high hopes for you." She dropped his hand and took a sip of her latte. "So how's the couch working out?"

"Total nightmare." I shrugged.

"I can't believe you didn't know," she said, reaching over to break off a piece of Clay's bagel. "It's an unwritten rule on layovers that only the most junior flight attendants get the rooms next to theirs."

"Well, it's been a while since I've flown international," I said, lifting my Styrofoam cup and taking a sip. "I guess I'm a little out of the loop."

"Learn a language; then you can fly to Europe all the time." Clay nodded. "They always need Greek speakers."

"Well, on the flight down here I gave George Stephanopoulos two bottles of water; does that count?" I laughed. "Anyway, she has no idea what a mistake she's making. I mean, look what happened to me. It was bad enough being in the same San Juan hotel with Michael; just imagine if I had to actually *fly* with him. I swear, I will never, *ever* date another Atlas employee again. Seriously. And that includes the CEO."

"Hailey, please. *Especially* the CEO! Have you *seen* him?" Clay shook his head and took a sip of juice.

"Ready to board?" I looked up to see my favorite gate agent coming down the aisle. George had been around for nearly forty years and had the inside story on everyone at Atlas. He was also quite a flirt, and a bit of a perv, but at his advanced age he easily got away with it. But what we really loved about him was how he always gave us the heads-up whenever Atlas management or FAA check riders were coming onboard. "There's a whole gaggle of supervisors out there, so make sure one of you stays at the exit row the entire time," he warned.

But today I was way ahead of him. "Hey George, they're not supervisors anymore; they're OOs now," I called after him, watching as he headed back up the aisle.

"OOs my ass," he grumbled.

I'd never understood how someone standing in the middle of an airplane, dressed in a hideous polyester uniform, could be so invisible. But after ten minutes of holding my position next to the exit row, I'd already had my foot stomped on twice, my left leg broadsided by a renegade garment bag, and my head nearly decapitated by a sleek aluminum roll-aboard being hurled into the overhead bin.

I turned and waved until I got Clay's attention. Then I gave him the exaggerated eye roll/headshake combo that served as our prearranged evacuation signal, meaning it was now time to switch places.

I headed into the galley and fixed myself another cup of coffee, then leaned against the bank of beverage carts, acting as though I was keeping a close eye on the cabin, when really I was flipping through the latest issue of *People* magazine that a passenger from the last flight had so thoughtfully left behind. Angelina Jolie was on the cover, and I could hardly wait to read all about it.

"Can I get a bottle of water?"

I looked up to see one of the supervisors, er, OOs, standing before me, wearing a beige, "heavy on the shoulder pads" suit with suntan nylons, cream-colored, sturdy-heeled pumps, and bangs that swooped and curled like a forehead awning. Her darkly lined lips were arranged in a thin, grim line, and her eyes were fixed on my magazine.

"Uh, certainly," I said, smiling my heart out while pushing the magazine aside, as though it hadn't even occurred to me to actually read it, but that it might come in handy a little later if I decided to wipe down the galley or something.

"Do you think I could get, like, twelve? Everyone's *really* thirsty," she said, eyes still ogling Angelina.

I smiled even brighter and opened the beverage cart. I guess the fact that we're only catered with twenty bottles of water for the 138 passengers we were expecting didn't really concern her. I mean, after all, there were twelve dehydrated OOs out there, and it was my job to serve them.

Not to mention that I'd just been caught partaking in the most heinous of all personal pastimes. The reading of a magazine during any phase of flight, especially boarding, takeoff, and landing, was strictly forbidden. And now, with the advent of camera phones, I'd heard of more than one sorry stewardess being photographed in the act and promptly marched into her supervisor's—I mean OO's—office for a major browbeating.

Besides, this latest title change didn't fool me, since everyone knows the entire in-flight supervisor group consists of all the former flight attendants who couldn't hack it. Who couldn't handle the daily challenge of working in the air—of never knowing who you'd work with, who you'd serve, not to mention where you'd end up. These people loathed spontaneity and longed for structure, rules, and sameness. And unfortunately, they wanted you to want it too.

Oh sure, every now and then you'd get some well-meaning interloper with good intentions and revolutionary dreams of changing the system by somehow making it more equal, less inhumane. But just six months down the line, those Che Guevara wannabes always ended up right back where they started, with their idealism shattered and their spirits broken by the unbridled tyranny of Atlas office life.

Supervisors, OOs, whatever you call them, it was all the same to me. They were of a particular breed, and I knew better than to ever try to befriend them.

I dropped the dozen bottles of water into a blue plastic Atlas-logo trash bag that would serve the dual purpose of helping her transport them to her seat, as well as keeping them out of customer view so as not to incite a preflight water stampede. All it takes is for one person to go traipsing down the aisle with an amenity no one else has yet been offered to start the call lights ringing and a mad rush toward the galley.

"Here you go," I said, smiling till my face ached, praying we could just put the whole unfortunate magazine debacle behind us and return to La Guardia without anyone filing an incident report.

And just as she left the galley, I was shoving the magazine in my jump seat so I could read it during takeoff when she peeked her head back in and said, "Do you mind if I borrow that *People*? I mean, you weren't actually planning to *read it on your jump seat*, were you?" Her eyes locked on mine as I broke out in a cold, cowardly sweat.

"Oh, you mean this?" I laughed nervously, retrieving it by its edge, as though it were some foreign object I bore no attachment to. "Actually, why don't you just keep it?" I said, holding my breath as she thrust it into her little blue bag and headed back up the aisle.

And the moment she was finally seated, I leaned against the beverage carts and sighed. A softer, friendlier supervisor? Doubtful. But clearly, she had her price.

11

I was standing in front of my closet, trying to pack for my bipolar three-day trip with long layovers in both Miami and Missoula (bikinis and cowboy boots, anyone?) when my cell phone rang.

"Hailey Lane, please," said a deep, masculine voice I didn't recognize.

"This is," I said, tossing a bottle of sunscreen along with a pair of thick cotton socks into my bag.

"Hi. My name is Dane Richards. We were on the same flight recently."

I held the phone away from my ear and stared at it, wondering what he could possibly want. Was this some sort of new Atlas Airlines customer-satisfaction initiative? Were the passengers actually calling us on our cells to complain about the crappy service?

"It seems you left some papers behind and they got mixed in with mine. We almost filed them in court today. Good thing you had your name and number on the front."

"You have my manuscript?" I asked, relieved that it was no longer lost, yet horrified to think he might have read it.

"Should I messenger it to you? I can have it there by five o'clock."

"No, I'm going out of town," I told him. "Could I maybe pick it up somewhere?"

"Can you get to midtown?" he asked, sounding distracted, as there were now several other voices in the background.

"Perfect. I'm catching a ride on Forty-second Street. Just give me the address and I'll see you there."

The second I hung up I tore into the cardboard box that housed my favorite non-Atlas approved accessories. If memory served me right, then Dane Richards was a total hottie. And since during the course of our brief conversation I'd specifically heard the words "court" and "midtown," I knew I'd just been presented with an opportunity I couldn't afford to ignore.

Even though there were no shortage of hotties in Manhattan, finding an age-appropriate, unmarried hottie with a good job was like getting a really great gift-with-purchase—they were only available while supplies lasted. Whereas finding an unmarried, age-appropriate hottie with a good job *who wasn't afraid to commit* would be like locating the Holy Grail—we've all heard it exists, though we've yet to see it for ourselves.

Changing from my boring, Atlas-approved, fake pearl earrings to my favorite gold-and-emerald chandeliers I'd bought on a trip to Bombay, I released my hair from its usual headache-inducing French twist and let it fall loose and wild down my back. Then I folded over the waistband of my navy blue skirt, which hiked it up a good inch and a half, and slipped into a pair of nonapproved but supercute wedge-heel pumps. Then, looking in the mirror, I assessed my two-minute makeover from strict scary prison warden to style-conscious stewardess. And then I crossed my fingers, ran out the door, and hoped I wouldn't run into Lawrence.

But by the time I was standing in front of Dane's building, gazing up at all intimidating forty-four floors, I started to feel incredibly small and nervous. I mean, who was I kidding? Midtown was teeming with all kinds of gorgeous, chic, professional, well-heeled women, and I was gonna try to impress someone with my poly/cotton blouse, plastic wings, and flammable skirt?

Because even though the average American woman was supposedly five feet four and a size fourteen, here in Manhattan that statistic was more like five feet ten and a size two. And although I was currently one inch taller and several sizes smaller than the national average, in these parts I might as well be invisible.

I mean, in the movie version of my life, I would be played by Blossom the Powerpuff girl. And even though she might be adorable and feisty—with genuine, kick-ass, save-the-world abilities—she was still no match for all those long, languorous, Jessica Rabbit types that were currently cast opposite me in this cutthroat world of big-city dating.

Buttoning my blazer, I rode the elevator all the way to the eighteenth floor, lecturing myself the entire way for getting so excited about seeing this Dane guy, who probably wasn't all that hot, was most certainly married, and in all likelihood was a big fat jerk. Because let's face it, anyone who shows up at the last minute like that, expecting the entire plane to wait for *him* while recklessly bumping someone out of a first-class seat is obviously an entitled elitist who should be avoided at all costs. And I had so successfully convinced myself of this that by the time I reached his floor, I was determined to just grab my manuscript and get the hell out of there.

Standing in front of the shiny black quarter-moon-shaped desk, I struggled to get the attention of a receptionist with a rolling chair and a headset who for no apparent reason seemed dead set on ignoring me.

"Hi," I said, waving at her as she quickly swiveled away while an endless stream of chatter drifted into her mouthpiece. "Uh, excuse me, but I'm sort of in a hurry, and I'm here to see Dane Richards? My name's Hailey Lane?" I stood there lamely, with no way of telling if any of that had penetrated.

I watched as, with no sign of acknowledgment, she rolled her way back, punched on her keyboard, squinted at the computer screen, then reached into a cubby and retrieved a thick manila envelope with a big white label bearing the name HAILY LAIN.

I stared at it for a moment, feeling like the world's biggest idiot for wearing my coolest shoes for someone who couldn't even spell my name right. Then I crammed the envelope into my overstuffed bag and headed for the elevator.

And the second I was seated on the bus to JFK, I flipped through my manuscript, searching for coffee stains, fingerprints, DNA—any sort of clue that would show me Dane had been curious enough to at least glance through it. But the only pen markings and page creases I found were the ones I remembered making, which only proved that Mr. Dane Richards, Esq., wasn't even curious enough about the first page to flip through to the last.

And since everyone knows how nosy lawyers are, it was pretty clear I'd just gotten my first bad review.

After surviving a five-hour flight to Missoula with two nearly empty beverage carts and just twenty-four sandwiches to feed 128 passengers, I was in the hotel gym, riding the recumbent bike and reading the latest issue of *Author!* magazine when my cell phone rang. Immersed in an article titled, "Bring Your Characters to Work!" I answered without checking the display.

"Hailey? Is that you?"

Oh great. It was my mom. I promptly dropped the magazine on the floor and settled in for what I knew would be a long, emotionally draining conversation.

"I have a surprise for you!" she squealed, sounding way too excited for my comfort.

"Yeah?" I said, already dreading whatever it might be.

"I'm coming to New York! To visit with you and Michael!"

"Oh . . . that's . . . great," I mumbled, staring at my reflection in the mirrored wall, wondering how I could deter her. I mean, there was no way I could allow that to happen, since I hadn't quite gotten around to telling her about Michael and me. I'd been hoping I could put it off for, I don't know, a year? Maybe two? "Um, when were you thinking of coming?"

"Day after tomorrow!"

"Oh. Well. That really is a surprise," I said, frantically brainstorming for one very good reason why this visit could never, *ever* happen. "How long were you planning on staying?"

"Two days, two nights," she singsonged.

"But have you checked the flights? Because they're really overselling them these days, so there's a good chance you won't even get on," I warned. Just because my flight privileges extend to her didn't mean there'd be a seat.

"I already checked, and it's wide open. I get in at three, and I've even booked a room at the SoHo Grand. I didn't want you to worry about putting me up."

"You're staying in SoHo?" I asked. I don't know which was the bigger surprise, her visit or her room reservation. My mom's always been the more conservative midtown hotel type, not the hip downtown boutique type.

"Yes, and I've made dinner reservations at Spice! I hear that's the hot new place."

First SoHo and now Spice. . . . Was she watching Sex and the City *reruns on TBS?* "Well, it might just be me," I warned. "Michael's flying so much I hardly see him anymore." I laughed nervously.

"Well that will just give us a chance to catch up then, won't it? It's been so long since your last visit. What has it been, a year? Year and a half? You know, for someone who flies for free, you really don't make it home much, do you?"

I just sat there breathing in and out, determined to rise above that last little dig of hers. "Okay," I said finally. "I get in at five tomorrow. If you want to wait, we can ride into the city together."

"That's okay. I'll just grab a cab and head to the hotel. We can meet there later."

"Do you need me to put you on the standby list?" I asked.

"That would be great. And if you could list me for first class, I'd really appreciate it."

By the time I'd made it to Broadway, I was resigned to the inevitable, knowing exactly how the evening would go. First, my mom would give me a quick once-over and say, "Oh, so *that's* how you're wearing your hair these days." Then she'd smile politely and ask how I've been. And then, without any further ado, she'd plunge right into the whole point of her two-thousand-mile transcontinental journey. Touching me lightly on the arm, she'd lean toward me, and in the voice of a conspirator ask, "Have you two set a date yet?"

I shook my head and pushed through the Coke-bottle glass doors, heading straight for the noisy, packed bar and squinting in the dim light as I searched the crowd of after-work revelers, still not quite believing I'd really find her here among New York's trendiest.

Then suddenly I was enveloped in a Gucci-clad hug while a cloud of Christian Dior Addict hung over my head. "Mom?" I asked tentatively, pulling away and scanning for just one familiar feature on the face of the woman who gave birth to me nearly three decades ago. "Are you in there?" I joked, knowing I was gaping, but unable to stop.

"What do you think?" she asked, smiling and twirling like a seasoned catwalker.

"You look so . . . *different*," I said while taking in the formerly brunette bob that had somehow turned a sunny, buttery blond.

And the bright blue eyes that I could've sworn were once brown. Not to mention the shiny, full lips that used to be . . . *not quite so full*.

"I had a few things done," she whispered. "So?" She smiled, waiting for the verdict.

I continued to stare, taking in the creaseless, evenly pigmented skin and the abundant cleavage peeking out of her low-cut sweater. "Um, you look great. Really," I said, secretly wondering if I'd missed a crucial episode of *The Swan*.

"Well, I *feel* great. It's like a new beginning! And I've got so much to tell you!" She smiled, exposing shiny new teeth. "But first, I want you to meet my friends."

She led me over to the bar, where two dark-haired Wall Street types were waiting. "This is Mark," she said, pointing to a guy in a charcoal suit and pink polka dot tie that he'd already loosened in some kind of after-hours, "let's get this party started" rebellion. "And this is Daniel." She motioned toward a slightly balding version of Mark.

"Hey." I smiled, feeling like an awkward twelve-year-old, watching my makeover mom flirt with two men who were obviously much closer to my age demographic than hers.

"Can I get you a drink?" Mark asked.

"Um, what are you drinking?" I peered at my mom's glass.

"I'm having an apple martini!" she said, sounding like she might already be on her second.

"Hmm, I think I'll just have a glass of wine," I said, sliding onto the stool between them.

"So, Cindy tells me you're both from California." Daniel smiled.

I glanced quickly at my mom, who was giving me a look I couldn't quite read. And not knowing what was going on, though positive that *something* was, I answered as vaguely as possible. "Yup, born and raised in the OC." I nodded.

"We were actually roommates for a number of years, but then

Hailey got a job with the airlines and flew away." She took a sip of her drink and giggled fondly at this charming little nugget of revised history.

Roommates? Was she serious? I mean, I guess in a way it was true . . . but still. I shook my head, taking in her fluffy bleached hair, her prominently displayed cleavage, and the martini glass half full of tart fuel. . . . *Oh my God—my mom's on the prowl!*

I watched as she smiled flirtatiously, knowing there was no way I could go through with this. It was way too disturbing, and could quite possibly send me to therapy for the next twenty years. "Uh, *Cindy*, don't we have dinner reservations?" I asked, tapping the face on the Cartier watch she'd given me when I started my freshman year of college, and then threatened to repossess when I dropped out two years later.

"Oh, you're right, we should get going," she said, tossing off her martini in one hearty swig.

I watched as Daniel and Mark flung a stack of bills onto the bar and rose as though they were joining us. "Well, it was nice meeting you," I said, giving a determined little half wave and tugging on my mom's sleeve, anxious to put an end to this creepy charade.

"But I've invited them to join us," she said, smiling happily. "Won't that be fun?"

I looked at Daniel and Mark, wondering which one was supposed to be mine. Then I followed meekly behind as we exited the hotel and hailed a cab on the street.

Somewhere between the cinnamon-scented lentil soup and the cardamom ice cream it was pretty obvious that Cindy and Daniel were hitting it off. Which left me with way too much attention from Mark.

"So where to now?" my mom asked, sounding like a rebellious teenager about to break curfew.

"Well, there's this new club a couple blocks over. We can grab a cocktail and listen to some live jazz," Daniel offered, sliding even closer and tracing his finger down the length of her arm.

"Uh, if you don't mind, I think I'm just gonna head home," I said, giving *Cindy* a pointed look.

"But the night is young!" she said in protest.

"Yeah, well, I flew all day and I'm pretty exhausted," I said, yawning for effect.

"Well, I flew all day too, and I feel great!" She smiled.

"Well, you weren't exactly wearing a polyester apron and pushing a two-hundred-pound beverage cart, were you, *Cindy*?" I narrowed my eyes at her.

But she just shrugged and reached for her purse, retrieving a plastic key card from her Louis Vuitton wallet and tossing it to me. "Here. We're in suite three-oh-six. I'll meet up with you later," she said.

I sat there in shock, feeling the hard edge of that plastic key dig deep into my palm, as I watched my mom dip her head toward Daniel and laugh softly as he whispered in her ear.

Then I shook my head, grabbed my purse, and hurried for the door, pretending I didn't hear when Mark called out after me.

Heading down the hall, I felt so annoyed with *Cindy* that I actually considered going back downstairs, grabbing a cab, and traveling uptown to my sickly little pull-out couch. But as I slid the key card into the lock, opened the door, and took in the hip, clean, well-appointed room, I realized that going back to my meager apartment would only serve in punishing *me*. And really, hadn't I been through enough already?

I kicked off my heels, climbed out of my jeans, and tossed my top over the back of a chair. Then I padded into the bathroom, eager to try all of the high-end amenities that now, in my single-income existence, I could no longer afford to buy. And after washing my face, slathering myself with lemon-scented lotion, and spritzing on some of my mom's cool new perfume, I slipped between the luxurious high-thread-count sheets and watched the hotel-provided goldfish swim laps in his chic, minimalist bowl.

Then I rolled over, looked at the clock, and waited.

If a stowaway is suspected, do not attempt to collect a fare.

12

"You're still asleep?"

I opened my eyes to find my mom shaking my shoulder and peering down at me.

"What time is it?" I asked, rubbing my eyes and squinting at her.

"Time to get up!" she sang, opening the drapes and inviting the cruel morning light into the room.

I blinked at the clock next to the bed, not believing it was really ten thirty. I hadn't slept that late since I'd flown international last spring. Then I shook my head and looked at her again. Was she just now getting back?

"I've got big plans!" she said, smiling excitedly and tweaking my foot through the thick cotton duvet.

I glanced at the other bed—the one she should have slept in—and saw that the sheets were still pressed and tight. Then I turned back toward her, noticing she was dressed in last night's clothes, with last night's mascara faded softly across her cheeks. And then it dawned on me: *Oh, my God! My mother just completed the morning-after walk of shame!*

"Are you just now getting in?" I asked, gaping at her.

"Hurry up and get in the shower," she said, deftly avoiding my question. "We're booked for brunch at Tavern on the Green in less than an hour. And then I thought we'd spend the day shopping!"

I watched as she busied herself with the flower arrangement at the far end of the room. "Mom, I think we should talk," I said, determined to get to the bottom of her bizarre behavior and even more bizarre appearance.

"There's plenty of time to talk over brunch," she said, concentrating on the flowers and refusing to look at me. "Now go get ready."

Before I could even swallow my first sip of cappuccino my mother looked right at me and said, "I want to know what's going on with Michael and you."

"What do you mean?" I asked, stalling for time, wondering how I could avoid this altogether.

"Hailey, please. I know something's wrong. I just wish you'd trust me enough to tell me."

"Oh, well, should I confide in you as my former roommate Cindy? Or as my mother?" I asked, giving her an accusing look as she took a sudden interest in the hashbrowns she normally avoids. "Well, you'll have to forgive my confusion," I continued. "I mean, last I heard we weren't exactly related." I glared at her, willing her to look up. But when she finally did, something about her expression made me regret everything I'd just said.

"Oh Hailey," she sighed, giving me an embarrassed look. "There's no way you could ever understand."

"Try me." I took a sip of coffee and waited.

She pressed her lips together and shook her head. "You're young, and you've got your whole life ahead of you. I'm not sure you can comprehend how differently things can turn out from how you expected."

"Oh really? Well, for your information, I've had a few surprises tossed my way lately. Why, just the other day I got home early and caught Michael in bed—*with a man!* There, how's *that* for a little life detour?" I said, realizing too late that I'd just played right into her well-manicured hands.

"Oh, honey, I'm so sorry." She reached across the table and grabbed my arm.

But I just shrugged and took a swig of mimosa.

"Why didn't you mention this before?" she asked.

I shook my head and looked at her. "I couldn't," I whispered, hearing my voice crack.

"But you can tell me anything!"

"Mom, please. That's so not true. You've disapproved of practically every decision I've ever made! In college, when I decided to major in English, you said I should major in business. When I took the job with Atlas, you said I was wasting my life. And you pretty much stood by that until I met Michael. Then suddenly everything was great, because I was dating a man whose office was a *cockpit!*" I shook my head. "It's like, Michael was the only thing in my life that ever met with your approval. So excuse me for not rushing out to share the news!"

"But you've always made me proud," she said, squinting like she does when she's about to cry but doesn't want her mascara to run.

"And would you like to know what Michael said?" I asked. I was on a roll now; there was no stopping me. "He said he'd *never* considered marrying me because I was *too old!*" I sat back and folded my arms across my chest. *There, whatcha gonna say about that?*

But my mom just shook her head. "Alan got remarried," she said, then busied herself with her white linen napkin.

"What? When?" I leaned toward her. Alan was my on-again, off-again stepdad. My real dad passed away when I was little, and my only memories of him came from old photographs.

"Last month." She shrugged, looking away.

"And who's the lucky bride?"

"His thirty-year-old personal trainer." She sighed.

"Tell me this is a bad joke," I pleaded.

But she just looked at me.

"I thought you guys were talking again, trying to patch things up?" My mom and Alan had divorced years ago, but they'd never fully let go. They were like Liz Taylor and Richard Burton, miserable alone but toxic together.

"We had a few dinners, played a little golf; then I decided to have some work done, and during my recovery, I guess he found a better deal."

I reached across the table and grabbed her hand. "Okay, you win," I said, smiling awkwardly.

"Hailey." She sighed, shaking her head. "I felt so lost when your father passed, and when Alan came along, well, marrying him seemed like the safe thing to do. Then you left for college, we divorced, and I had no idea what to do next. So I spent the last ten years clinging to the past." She looked at me and shook her head. "I guess I'm trying to make up for it now."

"So what about Daniel?" I asked. "What was that about?"

She gazed down at her plate. "I wanted to see what it was like to be with someone other than your father or Alan."

Oh God! Oh no! I stared at my napkin, terrified she was about to tell me *just exactly* what it was like.

"It was different." She shrugged.

"So how far is your apartment?" my mom asked, one arm loaded down with shopping bags, the other outstretched, hailing a cab.

"Um, not far. Why?" I asked nervously.

"I thought we could swing by. I'd love to see your new place." She smiled, opening the door and motioning for me to climb in.

I slid across the seat, imagining my mom walking in to the sound of Lisette getting a red-hot ass spanking. "Um, that's proba-

bly not such a great idea. My roommate might be there and . . .
she's a little strange," I admitted.

"Hailey, do you need money?" my mother asked, face full of
concern.

"No!" I said, shaking my head vehemently. Jeez, I already felt
weird about all the stuff she'd just bought me, not to mention how
I'd spent the last four years being fed, clothed, and sheltered cour-
tesy of Michael, so there was no way I was gonna let her take over
where he'd left off. I mean, it was time to go it alone. Cold turkey.
No benefactors, no handouts, and definitely no withdrawals from
the Bank of Mom.

"It's nothing to be ashamed of," she said.

"Mom, I'm fine. Really. I have a job, and if I need more money,
I'll just fly more hours."

She shook her head and looked at me. "You're so independent.
Just like your father." She sighed.

But I just smiled and looked out the window, hoping that would
someday be true.

Though no matter how self-sufficient I was determined to be, I
had to admit I was really gonna miss bunking at the SoHo Grand.
We'd just spent two surprisingly nice days together, and now it was
time for my mom to head back to California and her life without
Alan. I felt sad for her but, like Michael ditching me, I knew she
was better off.

"Make sure we didn't leave anything behind," she said, searching the drawers for the fourth time. "And did you check under the
bed?"

"All clear," I said, getting up from the floor and gazing at the
fishbowl. "But what are you going to do with Jonathan Franzen?"

"Who?" My mother turned and looked at me.

"The goldfish. That's what I named him," I said, running my

finger along the rim of the round glass bowl while Jonathan swam in determined circles, never seeming to tire of the sameness.

"Is that after a friend of yours?" she asked, applying one firm layer of lipstick and then blotting it lightly with a tissue.

"He's an author," I told her, remembering how the E! channel had always been her primary news source.

"Well, now that you've named him, I think you should keep him," she said, calling the front desk and asking that a large Ziploc baggie be sent up right away.

13

Now that I had a pet, I was really feeling the push to get better digs. I mean, there was no way I could properly raise Jonathan Franzen in such a chaotic, promiscuous environment. And with Lisette temporarily out of work with a sprained ankle (which basically translated to even more time spent in bed), the only way I could accomplish any writing was by grabbing my laptop and heading out to the nearest Starbucks, leaving Jonathan behind to witness all kinds of unholy acts.

I was hunched over my computer, caught in a fit of creativity and typing like mad, when I heard someone say, "Hey, how's the book coming along?"

Assuming the comment was meant for one of the other aspiring authors that crowded this place, I continued typing.

And then I heard that same voice say, "Sorry, I thought you were Hailey."

With my fingers paused in midair, I looked up to see that Dane guy standing before me, looking even cuter than I remembered. "Oh. Hey," I said, brushing a renegade curl off my face. "Uh, it's coming." I nodded at the computer screen and cringed at my response. *"It's coming?" Oh God, lame, Hailey, so lame! And you call yourself a writer?*

"What's it about?" he asked, smiling as though he really was interested.

"Um, it's about this girl . . . and . . . well . . . it's fiction," I said, unwilling to divulge the plot since he'd already had his chance to read it.

"Ah." He nodded. "Is this your first, or do you have others?"

I glanced around at all the other hacks and felt like the ultimate wannabe. "Um, first." I shrugged.

"Well, good luck," he said, smiling and heading for the counter.

I watched as he got in line to order his coffee, and then tried to get back to my story. But all I could think about was what a great smile he had . . . and how nice he seemed . . . and how cute he was. . . .

Get a grip, I thought, shaking my head. *If he was into you, he wouldn't have left you hanging in reception like some common courier.*

But then again, he did stop to say hello. And it's not like he had to, since I hadn't even seen him. He probably still feels guilty for evicting me to coach. I bet that's it.

I looked up, sneaking a quick peek as he paid for his coffee, then quickly looked away before he could catch me. And as my eyes settled back on my screen, it occurred to me that for someone who'd just spent the last four years shacking up with a guy, I still didn't understand a single thing about them.

Going over the page I'd just written, I was at the part where my protagonist confronts her mother when I heard, "Hi again. I promise this is the last time I'll interrupt, but there's this party I thought you might be interested in."

I just sat there, fingers resting on the keyboard, thinking, *Is he asking me out?*

"Well, it's actually a book launch."

I nodded and smiled encouragingly, waiting for him to pop the question.

"It's for Harrison Mann's latest. Are you familiar with him?"

Am I familiar? Uh, didn't he have a couple Pulitzers under his belt? Hadn't I worshiped practically every word he'd ever written? "Yeah, I've heard of him." I nodded, trying to appear cool and casual like these kinds of parties were de rigueur *pour moi.*

"Great, well it's this Friday at the Kasbah, starts at eight."

"I think I can make that," I told him. Knowing full well that this Friday, like all my Fridays, was wide open, and wondering if I should risk having him pick me up at my place. It'd been so long since I'd had a date I felt completely out of practice. But with Lisette home all the time, it was probably better to just meet him there, I decided.

"Great! So I'll put you on the list, plus one if you want. I've got another engagement, but I'm gonna try to pop in for a quick hello." He smiled.

"Oh. Well. That'd be great! Maybe I'll see you there," I said, trying to act casual, like I never, ever, not even for a second, thought he was asking me out. And I stayed like that, smiling and red-faced, until he was gone.

Then I reached for my cell and called Clay.

I was waiting outside the Kasbah, watching as one chic New Yorker after another stepped out of a cab, limo, or town car and made their slinky, black-clad way to the door. Then I gazed down at my colorful, sequined, boho skirt, gold wedge sandals, and tight white tank top and sighed. No matter how long I lived in this city I could never manage to shake my California look. Then I glanced at my watch and rolled my eyes. Clay was now more than fifteen minutes late, and I was just about to call him when he called me.

"Hailey, thank God," he said, sounding out of breath.

"Where are you?" I asked, watching as a slim, gorgeous, perfectly turned-out *Vogue* magazine protégé who'd recently written the chick lit book of the season snaked her way toward the entrance.

"Listen, I'm really sorry, but I'm not gonna make it."

"What? Why?" *This had better be good.*

"I'm in the middle of something, and it's taking a little longer than planned," he said cryptically.

"Why are you whispering?" I whispered, turning my back on the door and giving the phone my full attention.

"I'm observing Peter," he said. "And I can't risk being seen."

"Please tell me you're joking," I said.

"This is not a joke. Oh my God, I knew it! Carson just walked in, kissed Peter on the cheek, and took the seat across from him!"

"Where are you?"

"I'm outside Canteen, but don't worry; he can't tell it's me."

"Why? Are you in drag?" I laughed.

"Hailey, this is so not funny," he said ominously.

"Clay, really. Don't you think you're being a little unfair? I mean, you flirt with everyone!"

"That's different."

"Why?"

"Because that's *me,* and this is *him.*"

"Gotcha," I said, shaking my head.

"Oh my God, Peter just got up and headed for the bathroom. Listen, I gotta go," he whispered urgently, ending the call before I could even respond.

I shook my head and dropped the phone in my purse, thinking that of all the crazy behavior I'd witnessed since I'd known Clay, I'd never seen anything quite like this. But then again, he'd never been in love before either. And now that he'd jumped the shark, I knew there was no going back.

I turned toward the door and watched as a stunning, blond, bestselling novelist and her equally gorgeous husband went inside. Then I took a deep breath, ran my hands through my hair, and tried to psych myself up about going in alone.

After getting over the initial relief that I really was on the guest list, the first thing I did when I stepped inside was scan for Dane. But not seeing him anywhere, I headed straight for the bar and grabbed some champagne, thinking that even though I had no one to talk to, at least my hands would stay busy holding on to something.

And as I wandered around the room, checking out all the faces I recognized from book jackets, magazine articles, and TV interviews, I tried to look approachable and interesting too. But after completing two full laps without so much as a single hello, I knew I'd be better off just finding a nice cozy corner to lean in before cutting my losses and heading home.

I sipped my champagne and gazed down at my outfit, wishing I'd worn my Atlas uniform instead of this loud gypsy getup. I probably wouldn't have stood out any worse than I already did, and there was something about being in my flight attendant garb that erased all shyness. It was like, the second I put on that navy blue suit I became this authoritative person who could direct a planeload of passengers to shut off their electronic devices, stow their baggage completely underneath the seat in front of them, and raise their seatbacks to the full and upright locked position. It was almost as though that poly-blend suit afforded me special powers, like Superman and his cape, Popeye and his spinach, Dr. Jekyll and his potion.

But this was ridiculous. Everyone around me was laughing, talking, making the most of the free booze and food, while I just stood there, chugging my drink and staring longingly at the door, wondering if I should make a run for it.

"If you go, I go."

I looked up to see this craggy, yet ruggedly handsome older man smiling at me. "Oh!" I stared at him, feeling my face go all warm. "You're Harrison Mann!" I said, as though he didn't already know that. *Real smooth, Hailey.*

"I am?" His face curved into a warm smile. "Well, now that we know who I am, who might you be?"

I looked into his eyes, which were dark blue, deepset, and surrounded by crow's-feet, thinking how unfair it was that wrinkles make some men sexy and most women panic. "I'm Hailey." I smiled nervously, extending my hot, trembling hand for him to shake, and feeling ridiculous about how nervous I felt considering the countless rock stars, movie stars, supermodels, newscasters, ambassadors, royalty, world leaders, CEOs, artists, heiresses—just your everyday assortment of *Vanity Fair* cover models—I'd served during my six years of flying.

Releasing my hand, he took a hearty sip of his scotch, gazed around, and said, "So what do you think of my party?"

"It's great!" I smiled enthusiastically.

"Then why were you staring at the door, debating whether you should run toward it?"

"I guess because I don't really know anyone here," I admitted, shrugging with embarrassment.

"Are you a crasher?" he asked, eyeing me with renewed interest.

"No! It's strictly legit," I said, taking a nervous sip of champagne.

"Well, that's a relief. I'd hate to have to evict you. You're the only one here with any color. You caught my eye immediately," he said, motioning to my skirt and winking.

Oh my God! Was Harrison Mann flirting? With me?

I just laughed, feeling completely flustered, and way out of my league.

"So, what do you do?" He moved toward me. "Are you in publishing? A writer, perhaps?"

"No and yes. I mean, I'm working on something right now, but . . ." I trailed off. Oh who was I kidding? I was talking to a critically acclaimed, Pulitzer-winning, literary god! There was no way he wanted to hear about my small-time scribbling.

"And when you're not writing?" he asked.

"Well, in my other life I'm a flight attendant for Atlas Airlines,"

I said, feeling ashamed for being embarrassed by that. But over the years I'd been made painfully aware of how more than a few well-schooled New Yorkers were surprised by the fact that we could even read, much less write. Which was pretty uninformed when you consider that nearly everyone I flew with had college degrees and managed to maintain separate lives outside the airport, where they worked as lawyers, CPAs, authors, psychologists, opera singers, actors, models, photographers, artists, teachers, brokers, financial analysts, personal trainers, small-business owners—you name it. I mean, being a flight attendant was a lifestyle choice, *not* an act of desperation.

"You're a stewardess?" he asked, eyes lighting up.

"Well, yeah," I said, inwardly cringing at his use of the word "stewardess." But then again, he was kind of old. Not to mention much celebrated for his word choices. So who was I to judge?

"Let me get you a refill; then I want to hear all about it," he said, grabbing my glass and heading for the bar.

I watched as he walked away; then I glanced around the room, noticing how a number of people were suddenly looking at me with renewed interest. It was amazing how in such a short amount of time I'd gone from being embarrassed about not blending in, to hobnobbing with the guest of honor because of it. And if Harrison and I could actually become friends, then maybe, somewhere down the line, he'd be willing to read my work and share some of his wisdom. *Just imagine, Harrison and I meeting at the local Starbucks, sharing broken biscotti and talking about books.* . . .

"Hailey!" I looked up to see Dane with this completely stunning woman hanging on his arm.

"Glad to see you could make it." He smiled. "This is Cadence," he said, nodding toward the exquisite being with the long, straight black hair, smooth olive skin, large innocent doe eyes, infinite legs, and abundant breasts that in her current braless state seemed to fall naturally into the fully upright and locked position.

"Hi." I smiled, feeling suddenly frumpy and frizzy while wondering if that was her real name or stage name.

"We're just dropping by for a bit. We're meeting with Cadence's agent soon," he said.

Agent? Would that be model or escort? In call or out? Okay, I know it was bitchy, immature, and envy-based—but it's not like I said it out loud. I just smiled and glanced around nervously, wondering what was taking Harrison so long. Seeing Dane with his dream girl was making me anxious for a little social validation of my own.

"Are you alone?" he asked, giving me a concerned look.

"No!" I said, eyes searching frantically for Harrison. "I mean, yes. But I've met someone, and he's just gone off to fetch me a drink." I nodded, wondering what was worse: The fact that I'd just sounded incredibly insecure? Or that I'd unwittingly used a British accent?

We stood there looking at each other, awkward and silent, and just as I was about to say something, anything, Harrison appeared. "I see you've met my stewardess friend," he said, handing me a flute.

"You're a flight attendant?" Dane asked, his features arranging into an expression I couldn't quite read.

Well, at least he used the modern, more politically correct term, I thought, shrugging and running my free hand through my long, unruly, anti-Cadence hair.

"How's the book coming?" Harrison asked Cadence while sliding his arm around me.

Book? What book? I watched her closely. *Please let it be a how-to book. Please let it be a beauty tips book. Please don't let life be so unfair as to give her genuine talent and a great mind in addition to all of her other obvious gifts.*

"Advance reviews are starting to come in, and so far it's being really well received," she said, smiling modestly with perfect white Chiclet teeth.

"Cadence wrote a book of short stories," Dane explained. "She's being touted as the next Jhumpa Lahiri."

Oh, is that all? I smiled weakly. I was being eaten alive by envy.

"Well, it's been great meeting you, Hailey. But we really should be going," she said, glancing quickly at her gold Bulgari watch.

Dane nodded and extended his hand. "Harrison," he said, and then turning to me, "See you around, Hailey." He smiled.

I watched as they weaved their way through the cocktail-toting partygoers, stopping frequently for a quick hello as Dane kept his hand pressed firmly in the small of Cadence's silky back. And just before they left, I could've sworn he turned and looked at me, with the weirdest expression. But before I could confirm it, Harrison said, "What do you say we go grab a bite?"

And by the time I looked back, they were gone.

"But, it's your party!" I said. "I mean, you can't just walk out on your own party. Can you?"

"We'll find out," he said, slipping his arm through mine and leading me toward the door.

The last time I'd been to Elaine's was nearly six years before, after I first moved to the city and couldn't wait to visit all the places I'd only read about. And knowing that it was supposedly a big, glitterati, literary hangout, it was at the very top of my to-do list. But after squeezing into the overcrowded bar and spending the next ten minutes attempting to order a drink from a surly bartender who seemed hell-bent on ignoring me, I quickly crossed it off my list and doubted I'd ever return.

But going to Elaine's with Harrison Mann was a whole new experience. Suddenly every member of the waitstaff was my new best friend, as a glass of red wine, a scotch on the rocks, and a table full of appetizers appeared within seconds of our being seated.

Ignoring the significant buzz I was already feeling from the two glasses of champagne I'd just quaffed at the party, I lifted my glass and smiled at Harrison. "Do you own this table?" I asked, taking a sip of cabernet.

"It's an illegal sublet, and I was lucky to get it." He smiled, raising his glass and tossing back a hefty amount of scotch.

I gazed around the crowded room, then leaned toward him excitedly, still not quite believing we were actually sharing a table. I mean, I had so many questions I didn't even know where to begin. But deciding not to waste any time, I cleared my throat and said, "Harrison, I was wondering—"

"Harrison! Darling!"

I looked up to see a Very Famous TV Interviewer whom I'd recently served on a New York to L.A. nonstop (and who'd been so rude and demanding that the flight had seemed twice as long as usual) puckering her bright pink lips and veering toward Harrison's cheek. Then, using her thumb to erase the faint tattoo she'd left behind, she planted herself right next to him, glanced briefly at me, and, instantly calculating that I was *no one special,* placed her hand on his forearm and proceeded to monopolize all of his attention.

I just sat there, picking at the appetizers and drinking my wine, as the table began to fill with famous faces. And even though it might seem fascinating and exciting to be surrounded by celebrities, the fact that I was being so systematically ignored made it no different than when I was forced to serve these exact same people on an airplane. So after five pieces of shrimp cocktail, a bowl of linguine with clam sauce, a glass and a half of cabernet, and a complete lack of attention from Harrison, I decided to leave.

"Excuse me, Harrison?" I said, reaching for my purse. "I'm taking off."

"Wait, I'll walk you out," he said, rising from his seat and leaving the literary bad boy, the newscaster, the Broadway star, and the political pundit to fend for themselves.

"Sorry about that," he said, holding the door and rushing to hail a cab.

"Oh, I can walk," I said, knowing my wallet was down to its last twenty and that the ATM definitely wouldn't cooperate between now and payday.

"Don't be ridiculous." He motioned me into the backseat, and for a brief moment I wondered if he was planning to come along. But then he closed the door between us and said. "How about dinner? This Saturday? Somewhere quiet." He raised his heavy eyebrows and waited.

"Okay," I said, reaching into my purse and scribbling my number on the back of a Rite Aid receipt, wondering if he really would call.

Then I watched as he tossed the driver a twenty, waved goodbye, and headed back to Elaine's.

"I know that guy," the cabbie said, peering at me through the rearview mirror as he pulled into Second Avenue traffic. "What movie was he in?"

"He's not an actor," I told him, leaning back onto the slick vinyl seat. "He's a writer. A Pulitzer prize winner." I smiled.

14

I was sitting in my usual Starbucks at my usual table, next to the window, just north of the condiment counter, waiting impatiently for Clay, who was now more than fifteen minutes late even though he was the one who'd initiated this whole early-morning, emergency summit.

"Hey," he said, striding through the front door, a little too casually for someone so late. "Where's Kat?" He removed his Gucci sunglasses and tossed them on the table between us.

"She's in Greece," I told him. "Again."

"Must be love." He shrugged, reaching over and breaking off a piece of my biscotti.

"Is that why she's always going there?" I asked, curiosity fully peaked. "She's dating someone?"

"Probably," he said, covering his mouth while he chewed. "But she's acting all hush-hush, so who knows?" He shrugged.

"So, what's going on with you?" I asked.

He looked at me and shook his head sadly. "Peter and I are over."

"Oh Clay." I reached across the table and squeezed his hand. I'd never actually met Peter, but he seemed like a decent guy. "When did this happen?"

"Well, I haven't exactly told him yet, but trust me, it's over."

I dropped his hand, leaned back in my seat, and looked at him. "Okay, so when do you plan on giving him the good news?" I asked.

"Soon," he said, taking my recycled paper napkin and folding it down to a small, neat square. "I should have this case wrapped up in a week; then I'll just lay out all the evidence, and that will be it." He shrugged.

"Evidence? Who are you? Charlie's fourth Angel?"

"Very funny." He rolled his eyes. "For your information, this is serious. Ever since I accidentally said 'I love you,' he's started acting really strange. I'm telling you, it's the worst thing you can ever say in a relationship." He shook his head sadly.

I watched him unfold the napkin, smooth it out, then start all over again. This time making triangles. "But do you love him?" I asked.

"No," he said, sounding like a two-year-old.

"So let me get this straight. You just spent the last four days slinking around town, spying on him?"

"If you don't mind, I prefer the word 'observing,'" he said, rolling his little paper triangle awkwardly across the table.

"Oh, so it's really more of an *anthropological* study, rather than a crazed, psycho boyfriend stalking kind of thing," I said.

"I sense that you're not taking this seriously." He dropped his little origami project in the center of the table, leaned back in his chair, and gave me "the look."

But I ignored it. "Because it kind of seems like *you're* the one who's been freaking ever since those fateful words were spoken. You're the one who's flirting with everyone, dressing up in drag, and spying on your boyfriend."

"I wasn't in *drag,* Hailey. I was in *hetero.* I was wearing baggy jeans, a flannel shirt, and a backward baseball cap."

"New York Yankees?"

"Fire Island. I lost the Yankees on a layover."

"Oh yeah, real hetero." I laughed. "So tell me, after all this *observing,* what exactly have you come up with? A chaste kiss on the cheek? A clandestine meal at the most overlit restaurant in Chelsea?"

He just shrugged and looked away.

"Which leads me to conclude that maybe *you're* the one with intimacy issues, not Peter." I leaned back in my chair and smiled triumphantly, wondering why I never had that kind of clarity in my own romantic disasters.

But Clay refused to look at me. "I will consider your opinion, but I make no promises," he said, and I watched as he got up from the table and headed for the counter.

And then, just as I popped the last piece of biscotti in my mouth, Dane walked in.

"Hey, how's it going?" he asked, combing his fingers through his wavy brown hair and smiling.

"Great!" I mumbled, covering my mouth and chewing furiously while feeling for any random crumbs that might've gotten stuck in my lip gloss.

"How was the party?"

"Great! Thanks for inviting me. I mean, for getting me in." *God, why am I always so verbally challenged around him?* I wondered, taking in his charcoal gray suit, lavender shirt, and blue tie, and thinking how I might start coming here every morning around this time, since it seemed to be part of his normal routine.

"And Harrison?" He raised an eyebrow at me.

"Harrison was great!" I said. Ugh, why did I keep saying "great"? Surely I knew other descriptive terms. I mean, what kind of hack writer was I?

But he just nodded.

"We left shortly after you guys, and then grabbed some dinner at Elaine's," I said, wondering why I'd just divulged that.

"Elaine's, huh?" His face wore an expression I couldn't quite read, though I would definitely rule out surprise.

And was that an amused nod? Or just a regular nod? Jeez, where was Clay when I needed him to dissect my own romantic dilemmas? I looked toward the counter and saw Clay flirting with the guy behind it. *Figures.*

"In fact, I'm supposed to see Harrison this weekend," I informed him. *Tourette's. Could I possibly have Tourette's?*

But Dane just smiled. "Well, I'm gonna grab some coffee and run. Good seeing you, though."

"You too." I smiled. "And say hi to Cadence!" I added, to my own dismay. Then I spent the next five minutes obsessing over our dialogue, and cringing every time I came to my part.

"Hailey?" Clay slid onto the seat across from me with coffee in one hand, barista's screen name in the other. "Who was that?" he whispered, watching Dane leave.

"That was Dane, the guy that got me into the party." I shrugged, avoiding his eyes.

"You've been holding out on me." He gave me an accusing look.

"No, I haven't." I gazed down at my scattered biscotti crumbs.

"I can't believe you went out with him. He's gorgeous."

"Okay, first, I'm not quite sure how to take that. And second, I didn't 'go out with him.' He had a date. And believe me, she is overgifted in every possible way. You should have seen her: shiny, glossy, and word has it completely brilliant, too."

"But you *like* him," he said, as though it was fact.

"I do not!" I said, sounding like a seventh grader.

"You do too!" he said, sounding like a bully.

"Clay, are you not listening? He has a girlfriend."

"How do you know it's a girlfriend? How can you be so sure it wasn't just a hookup?"

"Because *I* saw her and *you* didn't. Believe me, there's not a straight guy on the planet that wouldn't want to live happily ever after with her."

"Don't be so sure." He shook his head.

"Clay, trust me. She's a Triple Crown–winning thoroughbred, and I'm—" I hesitated, searching for just the right words. "I'm a Shetland pony forced to work the kiddie carnivals."

"Yeah—cute, stubborn, and a helluva ride."

Just because Harrison Mann was a Pulitzer prize–winning author didn't mean I wanted him to know where I lived. So after agonizing over what to wear (I was so desperate I even asked Lisette's opinion), I settled on a colorful Diane vonFurstenberg wrap dress I'd bought on sale two years ago but still loved, a pair of strappy gold stiletto sandals, and my trusty Bombay chandelier earrings. Then I hurried uptown, narrowly avoiding a death-by-taxi situation, until finally arriving at Elaine's short of breath, wobbly of heel, and with a forty-dollar blowout that was threatening to strike.

And just as I was about to step inside and head for our designated meet spot, I heard someone say, "Ms. Lane?" And I turned to find a tall, thin man dressed in a somber black suit and chauffeur's hat motioning toward a long, shiny black limo, where Harrison Mann held court in the back.

"Do you always travel by limo?" I asked, attempting to climb inside without hitting my head, breaking my heel, or flashing my panties.

"Ever try to grab a cab on a rainy Saturday night?" He reached for two champagne glasses and proceeded to fill them up.

"That's where my MetroCard comes in," I said, taking my glass and smiling.

"Did you fly today?" he asked, settling back against the seat and crossing his long legs.

"Nope." I shook my head and sipped.

"Yesterday?" He looked hopeful.

"Yesterday I flew back from Scottsdale, via Salt Lake City," I told him, watching his eyes light up. *Bingo.*

"Is that your usual route?" He leaned toward me, his interest obviously piqued.

"Not really. I pretty much go everywhere." I shrugged, taking another sip.

"Any international?"

"Sometimes." I smiled, thinking how nice it was that he, the big famous author, was trying to show a little interest in my job.

"But which do you prefer?" he asked, sliding so close I could make out all the clogged pores on his nose and the shiny gold filling in his far left molar.

"I like international, but it's hard to get," I said, leaning against the door and wondering where we were headed.

"What's the craziest thing you've ever seen someone do?" he asked, staring at me in anticipation.

Inwardly, I rolled my eyes. People always asked this question. It was right up there with, "What city are we flying over?" As though I could identify it simply by glancing at the landmass from thirty thousand feet. Or, "Are you showing a movie?" which invariably came just after we showed the preview.

The truth was, I'd pretty much seen it all in the last six years, and I had no idea what qualified as the craziest. Could it be the breast-feeding seven-year-old who paused long enough to order an orange juice? The inebriated movie star who mistook the first-class coat closet for the bathroom? The businessman who stood in the aisle, changing into a matching set of flannel pajamas, sleeping cap, booties, and eye mask during an overnight flight to Europe? The guy who rang his call light during the safety demo to ask if he could sample some of that oxygen he just saw on-screen? The philandering husband who snuck into the lav with another passenger, renewing his mile-high club membership while his angry wife screamed obscenities from the other side of the door? Or maybe it was the blind man who announced he was on his way to a Klan meeting?

And it's not like the passengers held the patent on outrageous behavior, because some of the flight attendants I'd worked with were just as weird. Like that Dallas-based guy who insisted on sharing photos of his pet cow's red, swollen udders. The thirty-year veteran who insisted on wearing elbow-length white gloves and adding a list of "specials" to the first-class menu with food she'd brought from home. The animal lover who brought her three pet turtles on all of her trips. The girl in training who wanted the job so bad she photocopied someone else's hire forms, whiting out the other person's name and putting hers in its place.

I looked at Harrison, who was patiently waiting for a response, and I knew I wasn't about to tell him any of those things. I mean, who's to say I wouldn't write my own book about it someday? So instead I just smiled and said, "This one time, I saw a man kick off his shoes, and then go into the lav with just his socks on."

Then the limo came to a stop and the driver slid open the little window and said, "Mr. Mann, we've arrived."

WHEN CONFRONTED WITH A MEDICAL EMERGENCY

Check responsiveness

Obtain consent

Reposition the person if
   necessary

15

As we headed for our table I prayed I wouldn't trip, since it seemed like the entire restaurant was focused on us. And even though I was used to being stared at by planeloads of bored passengers, this kind of scrutiny was all new to me.

"Does it annoy you?" I asked, placing my napkin carefully across my lap and smiling at him.

But Harrison just shrugged. "They won't bother us," he said.

I watched as he scanned the wine list, and hoped he was right. I'd been so excited about this night, I couldn't bear the thought of being ignored again, as I'd spent every free moment during the last week Googling the details of his amazing career. Yet somehow everything I'd learned only seemed to spawn more questions.

So when the wine was finally ordered and the whole twirling, sniffing, sipping scenario was over, I leaned toward him and said, "Did you always know you wanted to be a writer?" I gazed at him eagerly, watching as he sipped his wine and nodded thoughtfully, waiting for a little elaboration that never came.

Okay, maybe that wasn't the most inspired question, but I'm just getting started, and I have plenty more where that came from.

"So tell me," he said, resting his forearms on the table and leaning toward me. "What made you decide to become a stewardess?"

I knew I couldn't answer that with a simple nod like he had, so I just shrugged and said, "Um, well, it was purely by accident. I mean, I like to travel, I heard they were hiring, and I thought it would allow me plenty of free time to work on my writing." There, I'd brought it back to writing, the perfect segue into my next question.

"So tell me about training. What was that like?"

"Are you serious?" I asked, feeling my shoulders droop and my heart sink as I looked into his deep blue eyes.

"Very." He nodded, reaching for his wine. "I want to know everything."

By the time we left the restaurant, the sky had cleared, and deciding it was too nice of a night to drive, Harrison dismissed the limo and we made our way down the smaller, cobblestone streets of SoHo while my already compromised heel came dangerously close to snapping off completely.

"So let me get this straight," he said. "You're not actually getting paid during boarding, since you're only paid for actual flight hours. Am I right?"

"Yes," I said, rolling my eyes, not even trying to hide my annoyance. We'd been having this same boring conversation for nearly three hours now, and I was beginning to think that this celebrated author was just another creepy bore with a stewardess fetish. "Door close to door open," I repeated, for the third and final time.

"But isn't boarding the worst part of the flight? All those passengers screaming about their seats and baggage?"

Boarding *was* the worst part of the flight, but I was totally over discussing it. "Harrison? Do you think we could maybe talk about something else? Like, I don't know, books, publishers, agents, Pulitzers? Basically anything other than the Atlas Airlines employee handbook?"

But he just looked at me and smiled. "This is home," he said, motioning to a beautiful four-story building. "Would you like to come up for a nightcap?"

Like all New Yorkers, I had an insatiable curiosity for how other city dwellers lived. Especially those with glamorous careers, who made loads of money and occupied four floors all to themselves. "Sure." I shrugged. "But just one drink and then I have to go," I said, not wanting him to get the wrong idea.

"Are you flying tomorrow?" he asked, inserting his key and opening the door.

And even though I was, I shook my head no. I mean, there was no way I would encourage any more airplane talk.

Leading me through his enormous, multistoried home, we entered room after endless room, with Harrison pointing out the ceremonial tribal masks, ancient family photographs, and abstract paintings by artists I'd actually heard of that seemed to fill every square inch of wall space. And as we entered his study, my breath actually caught in my throat as I gazed upon the beautiful, old, scarred wood desk and worn leather chair where he'd crafted all of his novels. I trailed my fingers along the well-oiled, pockmarked wood, thinking how it looked exactly like the picture I'd seen in *Architectural Digest* a few years back. And now I was standing here, touching it. Unbelievable.

"May I use your bathroom?" I asked, still fondling the desk.

"Down the hall, last door on the left. I'll go pour us a drink. Do you have any preference?" he asked.

Not being big on nightcaps, I just shrugged and said, "Surprise me."

Harrison Mann's guest bathroom was a large, cavernous room that reminded me of those found in grand old hotels. Not that I'd actually stayed in many of those, as most of my hotel experience was limited to the lower-end, Atlas-contracted, chain hotels they provided for layovers. But every now and then, they'd throw us a bone and book us somewhere nice, mostly in Europe where they liked to project a false image.

I washed my hands with almond soap, and dried them on a plush red towel. Then I peeked in the cabinet under the sink, searching for a clue into the private world of this celebrated author. But other than the usual array of expensive hand soaps and extra toilet paper rolls, there really wasn't much to see. So I sat on the edge of the old claw-foot tub, reapplied my lip gloss, and evaluated the evening so far.

Other than Harrison's obsessive curiosity about my job I guess it really wasn't so bad. For all I knew he was writing an airplane scene and just wanted to nail the details. And who was I to mess with his creative process? Besides, wasn't that a valuable trait in a writer? The ability to really listen and learn about others? And since years of mind-numbing passengers had left me jaded and all too willing to tune people out, it was obvious I could learn a thing or two. And really, wasn't that the whole point of being here?

I gazed into the Venetian mirror and ran my index finger gently under each eye, feeling thankful that he hadn't tried to kiss me or hold my hand. I mean, even though it might be cool to say I made out with a Pulitzer prize winner, it's not like he looked like Michael Chabon.

The second I left the bathroom I was enveloped in darkness. And other than the faint, flickering glow at the end of the hall, all I could see was black. "Harrison?" I called, squinting as my eyes adjusted, nervously groping my way along the wall.

"I'm in here," he answered, in a faraway voice.

He's a famous author, not a serial killer. He writes literary fiction, not horror, I reminded myself as I tried to remember where the front door was located, just in case.

"Um, are you still on the third floor?" I asked, stopping to peek over the banister, thinking about making a run for it.

"I'm at the end of the hall. Just head toward the light."

Okay, now I was officially creeped out. "Is everything okay?" I asked, hesitating just outside the doorway, on high alert, ready to bolt.

"Everything's fine, Hailey. Please, come join me."

And even though he sounded pleasant enough, I still glanced longingly toward the stairway, assuring myself that with his heavy drinking and mounting birthdays, I could definitely outrun him if I had to.

Then I took a deep breath and stepped into the large candlelit room, where the critically acclaimed, Pulitzer prize–winning, *New York Times* bestselling author was splayed across his bed, snifter of brandy in each hand, completely naked.

"Ready for takeoff?" he asked, rising to hand me my drink.

I stood there in shock, watching all of Harrison's various body parts *move and sway* as he approached. Then, shaking my head and averting my eyes, I said, "Um, I think I should be going."

Oh my God, this was so not what I meant when I told him to surprise me, I thought, racing down the hall.

"Hailey? Are you sick?" he asked, chasing after me.

"Um, yeah," I mumbled, taking the stairs as fast as I could while still favoring the nearly broken heel on my sandal, noticing he was moving surprisingly fast for someone in such an advanced state of atrophy.

"What happened? Was it the shrimp?" he asked, so close now I could feel his breath on the back of my neck.

I grasped the door handle and pulled, feeling a flood of relief as the cold night air hit my damp, panicked face. "Yes," I nodded, catching my breath and turning to face him. "It's definitely the shrimp."

And as I stepped outside, I felt his rough, callused fingers press firmly into my shoulder. "I'd love to read your novel," he said. "Feel free to send it anytime."

Then I ran down the stairs, onto the street, and all the way to the corner, where I hailed myself a cab, feeling totally relieved I wasn't nearly desperate enough to take him up on that offer.

By the time I made it to my door, all I wanted was a glass of wine, a hot shower, and a memory erase like the one I'd seen in *Eternal Sunshine of the Spotless Mind*. And now that Lisette was healed and back at work, I was really looking forward to having the place to myself.

I walked in, kicked off my shoes, and was just about to untie my dress when I noticed Lisette's hairy, married captain dozing on my couch/bed, clad in nothing more than some ill-fitting tighty whities and a pair of black dress socks.

"What're you doing?" I asked, dropping my purse and narrowing my eyes. I mean, two visual assaults in one night was truly cruel and unusual.

But he just grabbed the remote and turned up the volume.

"Where's Lisette?" I asked, approaching him, determined to get an answer.

"Paris," he mumbled, still not looking at me.

But I was looking at him. And was growing increasingly agitated at the sight of his half-naked body enjoying such close proximity to my bed. "This is not your apartment," I said, folding my arms across my chest. "You don't live here, you don't pay rent, and you're not allowed to stay here without Lisette."

"She knows I'm here. So if you have a problem, you can take it up with her," he said, giving me a smug look.

I glanced at his ring finger, noticing that the simple gold band had yet to be replaced, and suddenly I was so completely over this sloppy loser who made over ten times my salary yet insisted on parking his flabby ass on my bed. "For your information, I pay nine hundred dollars a month to sleep on that couch. So unless you want to reimburse me for the portion you're currently occupying, I suggest you move it to the bedroom. Or better yet, take it home to your wife and kids."

And I stood there glaring at him, arms crossed and face burning, as he unplugged the TV, carried it into Lisette's room, and locked the door behind him.

16

When I woke the next morning, the first thing I noticed was that the TV was back in its usual spot and the captain was long gone. And after crawling out of bed, I headed straight for Jonathan Franzen's tank, tapping on the glass in a desperate attempt to get him to notice me. "Who's the one that feeds you? Who's the one that rescued you from that overly slick downtown hotel?" I asked. But he just hovered in the corner, bulging eyes staring off to either side, completely ignoring me. I continued tapping on the glass, hell-bent on getting just a crumb of acknowledgment for all of my efforts, when suddenly it occurred to me that as far as pets go, he was turning out to be pretty aloof and unsatisfying.

I headed to the kitchen and poured some cereal into a bowl, realizing I'd have to eat it in dry fistfuls since *someone* had taken liberties with my milk, polishing off all but the last two drops and leaving the empty carton in the fridge to avoid suspicion. And as I carried my dry goods back to bed, I knew that this phase in my life had definitely run its course, and it was time to start socking away some money so I could find a new place to live.

"I wish we could just skip the flight and go straight to the layover," I told Clay, gazing at a completely stripped car on the side of the Van Wyck Expressway that'd been there for over a week now.

"Sing it, sister." He nodded, inspecting his cuticles.

We were on the New York Airport bus, making our slow, traffic-clogged way toward JFK, where by some stroke of unprecedented luck (not to mention a whole lot of schedule swapping), we would be working a seven-hour-and-forty-five-minute flight to France. To be immediately followed by a nice, long layover in Paris.

"So what are you gonna do about your author friend?" Clay asked, glancing at me briefly, then back at his nails.

"Uh, nothing?" I shrugged, not interested in any further discussion on this particular topic.

"You want my opinion?" he asked.

"Not really," I said, still looking out the window.

"I think you should take him up on his offer."

"That's because you're not the one who suffered the full frontal assault. 'Cause I guarantee you would not be singing that tune if you saw what I saw. I'm telling you it was bad. Very, very bad." I cringed at the memory.

"My point exactly," he said, giving up on his nails and focusing on me. "Critiquing your manuscript is the least he can do after subjecting you to that."

"Forget it," I said, shaking my head. "I saw the price of admission, and I'm not paying the cover charge. No such thing as a free lunch, my friend."

"But see, that's the whole point. You've already *paid* the tab, so now it's time to head for the counter and pick up your happy meal," he insisted.

"No cover charge, no lunches, no happy meals, no critiques, and no more metaphors." I unzipped my bag and retrieved my manuscript, along with the red pen I use for corrections. "Harrison

Mann is like a literary casting couch. And I'm not auditioning," I said, settling into chapter fifteen.

The second we walked into the flight attendant lounge I knew something was up. Normally the room was full of navy-clad people hurrying into briefing rooms, gossiping with friends, cursing at the computers and their forever-malfunctioning printers, or heading for the "sleep room" to catch a quick nap before the long day ahead. But today seemed quieter, less busy. Or at least on the surface. Because if you looked closer, you'd notice a whole lot of whispering and eye darting going on.

"Did you hear?" I looked up to see Kat striding toward us. "Over eight thousand employees are being furloughed. Pilots, flight attendants, gate agents, mechanics, ground crew." She shook her head.

"What about the supervisors?" Clay asked, eyeing one of the laziest ones eating the last few pieces of popcorn from the machine they'd bought us a few months back, in an attempt to boost morale. So far I'd yet to get a single kernel. Now I know why.

"The OOs stay," Kat said, directing a withering glance at the corpulent popcorn stealer. "Apparently shuffling papers and sniffing out uniform infractions is what keeps this airline afloat."

Well, that explains it, I thought, looking at all the worried, angry faces. Our last CEO had just been awarded over twenty million dollars for bringing us to the verge of bankruptcy before saying his final "Buh-bye." And now the rest of us would be taking the heat for the declining revenue in the form of threatening memos and pink slips.

If I thought I had it bad now, sleeping on an overpriced couch with only an antisocial fish for company, I couldn't begin to imagine how I'd feel if I lost my job. Because even though I didn't really like working for Atlas anymore, that didn't mean I was ready to stop.

And now, with a possible layoff approaching, I had good reason to panic, since I'd spent the last few years cruising through life in an extended holding pattern, going around and around in circles but getting nowhere. And now, like it or not, I was being forced to land. And I wasn't so sure I could bring it in safely.

"I think it's time to retire," Kat said, nodding her head firmly, as though she'd already put some thought into this and it wasn't just some random statement.

"Are you serious?" I asked, waking from my own private thoughts, and looking at her in shock.

"Who am I kidding? The fun died years ago." She shrugged.

Clay and I just stared at her, speechless. She was right about the fun—it *had* died years ago. Although Clay and I had never experienced the kind of fun she was referring to. Kat had flown in the days when air travel was considered a privilege, when people actually dressed up to get on a plane and being a stewardess was a much-sought-after, highly glamorous career choice.

By the time Clay and I came along, the entire industry had morphed into nothing more than a flying bus service—just a necessary evil to get from point A to point B. The glamour was gone, and the party was over—making me feel like that last, annoying guest who ignores the blinking lights and refuses to move on.

But before either of us could respond, the PA squawked, "Hailey Lane and Clay Stevens, please report to room number four immediately. You are late for briefing."

"Where you off to?" I asked, grabbing my bags and following Clay.

"Athens," Kat said, smiling as she took her place in the computer line.

I hadn't flown to Europe in over six months, and hadn't dated a passenger during the last six years. But the cute guy in 2B was about to become the exception.

"So what's going on?" Clay asked.

We were working in the "Business Select" galley, with Clay plating the meals as I delivered them to passengers. "Nothing," I said, watching as he plucked a curled-up, overcooked piece of meat from its tinfoil container and carefully placed it on a plate of navy-edged Atlas china, then added a flourish of limp parsley for garnish. "Do you think they'll ever catch on that we're serving them TV dinners?" I asked, setting it on my linen-lined tray for delivery.

"Don't change the subject," he said, wiping his hands on a towel and looking at me.

"He's cute." I shrugged. "But you and I already made plans, remember?"

"You have my full permission to ditch me if he asks you out."

"Seriously?" I asked, balancing the tray with one hand while reaching for the bottle of Châteauneuf du Pape with the other.

"Yup. Now go dazzle him with your home-cooked meal," he said, pushing me out of the galley.

As I approached Mr. 2B, I thought about what I might say if he really did ask me out. Over the years, I'd kept to a strict policy of never dating a passenger. Which in light of the fact that four of those years were tied up with Michael, not to mention the fact that the majority of men I served weren't exactly datable, really hadn't been all that hard to keep.

But now, everything was different. And clearly the old rules no longer applied, as I was out of a boyfriend, and soon maybe even out of a job. So who was I to turn down an interesting diversion?

"You ordered the steak?" I placed it in front of him and tried not to cringe at how awful it looked. "Would you like more wine?" I offered, trying to distract him with the label.

He stared at the curled-up piece of meat, flanked by soggy, yellowish baby carrots and some kind of crispy beige starch that was either rice, potatoes, or cream of wheat. Then he looked at me and smiled. "Please tell me you're not the chef," he said, lifting his glass for a refill.

"Sorry, I can't take credit for that. Though I have to admit, I probably couldn't do much better," I said, twisting the bottle at the finish, just like I'd learned in the Atlas-sponsored wine course I'd taken several years ago.

"So what are you doing for dinner?" he asked, still gazing at me with his gorgeous brown eyes.

"Hanging in the galley, fighting the crew for leftovers." I shrugged.

"No." He laughed. "I meant in Paris. How long will you be there?"

"Twenty-seven hours and thirty-two minutes," I said, noticing how his sweater was cashmere, his dark hair was freshly cut, and his teeth were very white, but most likely real.

"Would you like to have dinner with me? I'm staying at the Ritz, over on the Place Vendome. But I have a car and driver, so I can pick you up anywhere." He smiled.

The Ritz? A car and driver? I was beginning to feel like Cinderella. "Sounds great," I said casually, trying not to skip on my way back to the galley.

"What took?" Clay asked, glancing at me briefly. "These plates are getting all backed up."

I looked at the cart, piled precariously high with plated meals that I no longer cared about serving. *I mean, why am I still working in the galley when I've just been invited to the ball?* "He asked me to dinner!" I smiled, struggling to balance the tray that now held three plates. "Hey, this is getting heavy," I whined as he added a fourth.

"You're way behind. In case you haven't noticed, the other aisle is two rows ahead, which means we're losing." He shook his head and retrieved another meal from the oven, lifting the paper lid and watching the steam escape. Clay took his galley duties very seriously.

"Oh, I didn't know we were racing," I told him, feeling awful about being the weakest link.

"We're *always* racing."

"Well just wait till we get on the ice cream carts," I told him. "I really kick ass on the sundaes."

But by the time we were on final approach, passing out the coats and preparing to land, most, if not all, of my excitement had died. Mr. 2B had spent the last six hours in a deep, nearly coma-tose sleep, which meant our dinner plans were never finalized. And as I flipped down my jump seat, buckled my seat belt, and gazed out the tiny porthole at the early-morning Parisian land-scape, I suppressed my disappointment, stifled a yawn, and fought to stay awake during landing.

"So what's going on with dinner?" Clay asked, retrieving his bag from the closet and slipping into his coat.

"You wanna go to that little quiche place in Saint-Germain?" I asked, heading down the aisle, dragging my bag behind me.

"What're you talking about? I thought the prince was sending his carriage?"

"No prince, no carriage." I shook my head sadly. "It all turned into a big fat pumpkin."

"But I thought you liked him?" he said, rushing alongside me.

"I did. He was the perfect passenger. Cute but didn't act like he knew it, nice but not overly ingratiating, witty but not obnoxiously jokey. And he never rang his call light, never took his socks off, never attended to any highly personal grooming needs, never stuck his foot in the aisle for me to trip over, and sadly, never woke up in time to get my name and number." I shrugged. "But it was good while it lasted."

We stopped in the first-class cabin and waited for the rest of the crew; then we all headed into the jetway, anxious to get through customs and onto the hotel van, where we would break out the wa-ter bottles we'd filled with screwdrivers, galley-blend sangria, and

mimosas, and enjoy a brief second wind before arriving at the hotel and falling into bed with exhaustion.

I released my hair from the tight ponytail that had been giving
me a dull headache for the last three hours and ran my fingers
through it, letting it fall loose around my shoulders.

"Wow. You have beautiful hair." I looked up to see Mr. 2B waiting by the door, smiling. "I completely passed out. That's so unlike
me," he said, shaking his head sheepishly and falling in step beside me.

"You missed dessert," I scolded, noticing Clay had gone on
ahead.

"Well, I'm hoping I can make it up to you. Are we still on for
dinner?"

I nodded, noticing the rest of the crew already making their
way through customs, and knowing I needed to catch up with
them, quick.

"Is seven good?"

"Seven's perfect," I said, already rushing away.

"And where should I go? Who should I ask for?" he called.

"Hailey Lane, at the Grand Hotel," I said, smiling as I ran toward customs.

READY POSITION

Flight attendants must sit on their jump seats with feet apart and hands placed under their thighs, palms up.

17

At 6:55 I was standing in my room, naked and nervous. I mean, I knew nothing about this guy except for the few facts I'd pieced together from the passenger manifest list, combined with good old-fashioned observation. Like, I knew his name was Maxwell Dunne, and that he was an Atlas regular, having earned himself Platinum status—which meant he spent more time on a plane than I did. I knew he was really cute, liked red wine, didn't like mystery meat, and was supposedly staying in one of the best hotels in Paris. Though his reason for being in Paris was unknown. And now I was about to get in a car with him and head out for God knows where in a city I'd explored many times before but that was nonetheless still foreign to me.

Glancing at the clock, I slipped on my silky off-white cami, shrunken black blazer, Citizens for Humanity jeans, and gold stiletto sandals. Then I reached for my purse and headed out of my room and toward the elevator.

Was I crazy for going out with this guy? I wondered, pushing the down arrow. I mean, just how much faith could I really put in the Atlas passenger-screening process anyway? It was like, our conversation had been so brief that the only reason I was going out with him was because of his gorgeous eyes and great smile. And yet, wasn't that the basis for all first dates?

As the elevator doors slid open, I nervously ran my hands through my hair and double-checked my outfit. *Get a grip,* I thought, heading toward the lobby. *I'm just a girl, he's just a guy, and we're just having dinner.*

And when I looked up, I saw Maxwell Dunne striding through the glass doors, dressed in khaki slacks, a crisp white shirt, and a brown leather jacket flung over his shoulder.

"I got us a table at Jules Verne," he said. "Have you been?"

I gazed at him and shook my head. Le Jules Verne was the restaurant at the top of the Eiffel Tower—well, the second level to be exact. And the high-priced menu, along with the hard-to-get reservation, didn't exactly make it a layover staple.

"We're in luck; it's such a clear night that the view should be spectacular." He smiled. "I mean, if that's okay? Because we could go somewhere else if you'd rather," he said, stepping outside and leading me to a black Mercedes-Benz.

"Sounds great," I said, smiling as the driver opened the door, and I slid across the tan leather seat.

The thing about the Eiffel Tower is that it can be seen from just about everywhere in Paris, which means you always think it's a lot closer than it really is. So by the time we finally arrived, I couldn't believe how long it took.

"Should we take the stairs?" Max asked. "At last count there were only one thousand six hundred and sixty-five, give or take a few." He smiled.

"Well, I would, except I happen to have the inside scoop about a private elevator, that's reserved just for restaurant patrons," I told him. "There's a sign over there." I pointed.

"Lead the way."

We rode the south elevator all the way up to the restaurant level, and the climb was so quick and steep that my ears actually popped along the way. And when the doors finally opened, I felt my shoulders sink with disappointment as I took in the dark, angular space that looked more like a nightclub than one of the world's most romantic restaurants.

But after Max palmed the maitre d' with a fistful of euros, we were led to a cozy window-front table with such a stunning view of Paris that my earlier impression was all but forgotten.

"This is amazing," I said, gazing at the city below.

"Glad you like it," he said, gazing at me.

"Do you come here a lot?" I asked, opening my menu and wondering if he was in the habit of picking up flight attendants and showing 'em a good time. Not that I cared, as long as he showed me one too.

"Just once," he said, reaching for the wine list. "A long time ago."

Leaning back in my chair, I gazed at the lights of Paris, thinking how awesome Max was. He was interesting, smart, well traveled, and even more important, he had a great sense of humor. And we'd just finished a three-hour food orgy that left me happy, sated, and more than a little curious about what would happen next.

"Where to now?" he asked, signing the check and finishing his wine.

I looked at him and shrugged. I was willing to follow him just about anywhere after a meal like that.

"Have you been to Temple?" he asked, sliding his wallet into his pocket and looking at me.

"Um, I'm not Jewish." I squirmed, wondering why he asked.

But he just laughed. "It's a club," he said. "C'mon, it'll be fun."

I followed behind, not entirely convinced about clubbing being "fun." The last time I'd gone out like that in New York, I'd ended the night feeling too old, and terminally unhip. But maybe things would be different in Paris.

We found our driver, Jean Claude, leaning against the Mercedes, smoking a cigarette and chatting on his cell phone. And after twenty minutes of weaving in and out of Parisian traffic, we stopped in front of a newly renovated three-story building with a small, unmarked entrance.

Max checked in at the door, then led me upstairs to a small private booth lined in soft suede upholstery with sheer, filmy drapes on either side. "Not a typical club like you were probably thinking." He smiled, browsing the drink menu.

"Is this one of those private members-only clubs?" I asked, glancing around at the sexy, sleek décor and even sleeker patrons and feeling like some all-American, milk-fed farm girl with my curly hair and jeans.

"Yeah. And I hear there's even a wait list now." He smiled.

I knew that he lived in Boston and traveled to Paris often, but I hadn't realized it was that often. "You must spend a lot of time here," I said.

"For the last six months it's been one to two weeks every month." He shrugged, squinting at the menu. "How does brandy sound?"

Brandy sounded great, but suddenly remembering my flight the next morning, the ban on drinking within eight hours of sign-in, and Atlas' penchant for collecting our urine into little plastic cups and testing our breath for alcohol in a supposedly random manner, I shook my head and said, "I should probably just stick with soda."

But Max just smiled and slid even closer.

Here comes the kiss, I thought, fiddling nervously with my earring and wondering if I should go through with this. On the one hand I hadn't kissed anyone but Michael in over four years, so the whole idea of making out with someone new seemed a little awkward. Not to mention that I was leaving tomorrow and would most likely never see him again.

Yet, wasn't that also a very good reason for why I *should* kiss him? I mean, so far everything about the night had been perfect, so why not try to make it even better?

I glanced up to see Max gazing at me with his gorgeous, heavy-lidded, sexy brown eyes, and I felt myself being drawn to him as though by some undeniable, magnetic force. And as he leaned in and pressed his lips against mine, all I could think was *Bermuda Triangle* as I drifted into oblivion.

Weaving his fingers into my hair, he cradled my face and continued to kiss me so passionately and so fully, and so well, I was completely lost in him. Then he unbuttoned my blazer and slid it slowly down my shoulders, taking my camisole straps along for the ride. And as he lowered his head, I closed my eyes and enjoyed the feel of his lips nipping at my earlobe.

But when his hands began to migrate from my shoulders to my breasts, I stopped and pushed him away. I mean, I was all about a nice little public display of affection. But breast cupping? Not so much. Even if we were in Paris.

"Are you okay?" he asked, leaning toward me and tilting my chin, forcing me to look at him.

"Yeah, but I should go. I have to fly back to New York in the morning."

"But it is the morning," he said, displaying the face on his watch. It was 1:00 A.M. Paris time.

"Well, then I really gotta go," I said, leaning in to kiss him again.

"Wow, it must've been good, 'cause you look like hell," Clay said as we walked down the hall and headed toward the elevator.

"It was all right." I shrugged, remembering every amazing moment.

"Are you kidding? Your skin is inflamed and you have a sex beard!"

"We did not have sex," I whispered, touching my tender, raw

chin and cheeks and smiling at the memory. "We just kissed a little, that's all."

"And?" he asked, clearly hoping for something more.

"*And,* it was pretty amazing." I smiled, watching the elevator door close before us. "So, what did you do?" I asked, anxious to change the subject. I'd had a great date with Max, but the odds of seeing him again were zero. A fact that I wasn't so eager to dwell on.

"Ate, did some shopping, ate again, slept a little." He shrugged. "Picked up that Louis Vuitton wallet that Peter's been lusting after."

"I thought you two were through," I said, glancing at him as I dragged my bag into the lobby.

"I decided to withhold judgment, and give him a second chance." He shrugged.

"I think that's a very wise decision," I said, stopping at the front desk to drop off my key and pay for the pot of coffee I'd ordered from room service.

"Are you Mademoiselle Lane?" asked the tall, slim receptionist.

"Uh, *oui,*" I answered, using up just about all the French I knew.

"We have something for you. Wait right here."

I watched as he disappeared into a back room, wondering what it could possibly be. Had I inadvertently left something in the lobby while we were waiting for our rooms?

But when he returned he was carrying a beautiful bouquet of flowers, in a cut-crystal vase, and I knew immediately they were from Max. He was a class act, and definitely the grand gesture type.

"What does the card say?" Clay asked, peeking over my shoulder.

"'Thanks for a wonderful time. Bon voyage. Max.'"

As I climbed the stairs to my apartment, I was completely exhausted. My late night with Max, the endless glasses of wine, and the lack of sleep had definitely caught up with me. And as magical as the first half of the trip was, the way home was a whole other story.

You can really tell a lot about a person by the way they treat the people who serve them, and I'd just spent the last eight hours serving a planeload of people who'd somehow gotten the idea that I was their personal servant. I was yelled at when I ran out of newspapers, berated when I ran out of pillows, insulted when I ran out of chicken, and threatened when we had to wait for a gate. I'd had an underage pop star try to trip me when I refused to serve her alcohol, a movie star who insisted on communicating only through her assistant, and a famous newscaster who became completely enraged at the gate when it was her turn for a random security search.

But these days, it wasn't just the passengers doling out the abuse; it was coming from Atlas management too. As they expected us to work overbooked flights with half the staff, search the airplane for bombs before boarding, defend ourselves against violent passengers with dialogue learned in a Verbal Judo seminar, and act as an unarmed human shield for pilots who, securely locked in their cockpit, were now packing heat. They had cut my pay, cut my benefits, scheduled longer workdays with shorter layovers, demanded a doctor's note for every sick day taken, and basically deleted any last crumb of dignity ever associated with the job. And for my efforts I received weekly e-mails from smug OOs admonishing *me* for the drastic drop in revenue, on-time departures, and customer satisfaction.

But now that they were laying off thousands of employees and forcing the pilots into drastic pay concessions (while top-level executives stuffed their pockets with bonuses, stock options, and secured pensions) I found myself fearing the loss of something I didn't even particularly like. Because for every horrifying moment during the course of a flight, there were still times like Paris, and the glaring fact that no other job that I was currently qualified for could provide that kind of perk.

So after dumping my bags and climbing out of my uniform and into my favorite flannel PJs, I poured myself a glass of Lisette's duty-free wine and sat on my couch, gazing back and forth between Jonathan Franzen and Max's flowers.

And when I got up to refill my glass, I saw a note lying next to the phone:

> *Hailey—*
> *I'm sorry, but this isn't working.*
> *You have two weeks to find a new place to live.*
> *Lisette*

18

Kat was serious about retiring. Just days after mentioning it, I was sitting at her kitchen table staring at my computer screen while she filled out all the necessary paperwork. And to say I was envious would be putting it mildly. I had just one week to find a new place to live, and no idea how I could possibly sign a lease when I didn't even know if I'd still be employed three months from now. Not to mention that it'd been well over a week since I said *au revoir* to Max, and I'd yet to hear from him.

"What are you doing?" Kat asked, signing the very last document.

"Looking for a place to crash," I said, squinting at my laptop. "But everything is either completely out of my reach, or in Kew Gardens."

"So why don't you stay here?" She removed her Chanel reading glasses and placed them on the table between us.

"We've already been through this," I said. "I'm allergic to the cats, and I don't want to impose."

"You wouldn't be imposing; you'd be house-sitting," she said.

"Where're you going?" I asked, cringing as I remembered the last time I was in charge of the cats' well-being.

"Greece." She smiled.

"What?" I stared at her, my mouth hanging open.

"It's time for a change," she said. "And Yanni has the most beautiful homes in Athens, Mykonos, and Spetses."

"Are you getting married?" I asked, while actually thinking, *Again?*

"Who knows?" She shrugged, reaching for her coffee mug. "All I know is that I'm ready for the next chapter in my life. How about you?"

I gazed at Kat sitting across from me. She was well into her fifties, and still beautiful, vibrant, and full of excitement. Not to mention that her life already held so many chapters it read like an intricately crafted thousand-page saga. Whereas mine felt as sparse and unplotted as *Baby's First Bathtub Book*. "Look, that sounds great and all, but eventually, when you return, I'll still have to find somewhere to live. So wouldn't that just be delaying the inevitable?" I asked.

"Hailey," she said patiently, eyes focused on me. "I need someone to stay here. I'm not selling, and I'm not bringing the cats just yet. And you're the best choice I can think of."

I looked down at the three cats lying at her feet. Well that's what allergy medicine was for, right? "But what about Jonathan Franzen?" I asked, still holding out.

"What about him?"

"Well, wouldn't that be like, jeopardizing his safety? Making him share a space with three cats?"

"He can have his own room." She shrugged. "So, what do you say?"

I glanced around the beautiful kitchen, with the granite-topped island and gourmet stove. *I can save money, finish my novel, and it wouldn't be freeloading since I'm doing her a favor. . . .* "Okay," I agreed. "But on one condition. You promise to kick me out the second you return."

"Deal." She smiled.

It's amazing what you can accomplish when you live in a quiet Fifth Avenue penthouse with a glorious park view, plenty of Allegra-D, and no skanky roommates to distract you. Kat had wasted no time saying good-bye and heading to Greece, and I, no longer burdened with paying rent, became very choosy about the trips I'd fly. No more thirty-hour Podunk layovers for me. I now had the freedom to fly only the fun trips, or I wouldn't fly at all. And even though, technically, I'd only migrated a few avenues west, the difference between Lexington and Fifth was like a whole different world.

So after three weeks of shutting myself in, leaving just long enough to indulge my daily latte habit, I'd finished my manuscript. And hoping for a fresh perspective when I returned, I left it behind and headed out for what was advertised on the Atlas trip list as a nice twenty-four-hour layover at the St. Francis hotel in San Francisco, but which, because of inclement weather in Atlanta and a mechanical in Cincinnati, had quickly deteriorated into a barely legal seven-hour *lean-over* in some dingy Kentucky motel with lumpy mattresses, questionable sheets, and no hot water. And by the time I returned from that hell trip, I was determined to tackle my novel with renewed enthusiasm, polishing it up and going over it again and again until it was the very best I could make it.

And just as I was putting six printed copies into six different envelopes to be mailed to six major publishers, my cell phone rang.

"Hailey?"

"Yeah?" I mumbled, sealing the final package and adding it to the top of the stack.

"It's me, Max. How are you?"

I dropped onto the nearest chair and stared at the phone. I'd completely given up on him, thinking he was like one of those socks you put in the dryer and never see again. But here he was, calling as though seven weeks hadn't really passed. "I'm great," I said. "You?"

"Well, I'm leaving for Paris tonight, and I was hoping I could see you."

"Uh, you mean in Paris or at the airport?" I asked.

"Paris." He laughed. "There's this new restaurant I'm dying to show you."

"Well, that sounds great, but France isn't exactly part of my normal route. Getting a trip like that involves a lot of bribing, and one or two death threats, you know."

"I'll be there for the next two weeks. I'm staying at the Ritz. Call me if you can make it?"

"Okay. Sure," I said, logging on to the Atlas swap board well before I'd even pressed END.

On my way home from the post office, I stopped in at my local Barnes & Noble so I could see just where my book would fall on the "new releases" shelf. Pushing through the revolving glass door, I went straight for "new fiction," gazing at the competing titles while imagining mine among them. I mean, how cool would it be to see "a novel by Hailey Lane" placed next to my favorite authors?

I noticed a slim book with a beautiful gold cover and ran my hand over the front, then quickly flipped it over to check out the back. And when I glanced down at the author photo, my breath caught in my throat.

There, in the far left corner, was a small, square photo of Cadence, looking gorgeous in a crisp white blouse and jade earrings, while her glorious dark hair fanned out around her as though she'd just been caught in a random, yet very flattering, breeze. And then, only out of curiosity and *not* because I cared, I quickly scanned the first few pages, curious to see if she'd mentioned Dane in either the dedication or acknowledgments.

"It's a pretty good read, but you don't have to buy it. I can get you a copy."

I turned to see Dane standing beside me. "Oh, hey, I was just . . ." I trailed off, placing the book back on the shelf and shrugging lamely. "I guess that's one of the perks of knowing the author, huh? Lots of free copies." I laughed nervously.

He ran his fingers through his floppy brown hair and smiled. "I was just heading upstairs to grab a bite. Care to join me?"

Let's see, I was living on Fifth Avenue, I'd just mailed out my manuscript, and now two cute guys in one day had offered to share a meal with me. As far as days went, this was definitely one of my best.

Sitting at the small, square table, I watched while Dane ordered at the counter and thought how strange it was I kept running into him. But New York City was weird like that. You could have the same roommate for five straight years and hardly ever see them. But then every time you went to the corner deli you'd run into the same three random faces.

"I know you said you weren't hungry, but I got you this," he said, placing a vanilla/almond biscotti next to my latte.

"So is this your usual lunch spot?" I asked, already breaking into the biscotti. "Seems a little far from midtown."

"I live nearby," he said, biting into a turkey sandwich.

"So that explains it," I said, sipping my coffee and looking at him. "You know, the whole stalking thing."

He looked at me and laughed. "Well, now that you mention it, I haven't seen you around Starbucks lately. Did you finish your book?"

"Yup, I just mailed out six copies," I told him, still amazed that my manuscript was finished, printed, and on its way to six editors' desks.

"Where'd you send it?" he asked, reaching for his water bottle and twisting the cap.

"Some big-name publishers," I said, unable to keep from grinning as I took a sip of my latte and waited to be congratulated.

"Any agents?" He tilted his head back as he sipped his water.

"Agents? Um, no." I shrugged. Jeez, I hadn't even considered sending it to an agent. I didn't think an agent would even want me unless I'd been published. But maybe I was wrong? I mean, should I have tried to get an agent?

"Well, did you at least check their submission guidelines?" He looked at me, his eyes full of concern, and lips pressed all tight together.

"Um, no. I guess I didn't do that either," I said, shaking my head and avoiding his eyes, my mood turning as quickly as a carton of milk left in the sun.

He shook his head, his face bearing a dire expression. "Well they have pretty strict rules, and they won't so much as glance at anything that doesn't adhere. They'll either trash it, send it back, or let it languish in the slush pile for the next year and a half," he informed me, finishing his sandwich and using his paper napkin to wipe the crumbs from his mouth.

I stared at the tabletop, feeling like a birthday balloon that had just gotten popped by a big bully with a long, sharp pin. "Well, before I saw *you*, I was feeling pretty darn good about just having finished it," I said, my throat all tight and choked with anger, and maybe even, God forbid, the possible threat of tears. "I mean, that alone felt like a pretty big accomplishment." *Until you came along, you buzz-killing, dream-stomping sadist!*

"Hmmm," he mumbled.

Hmmm? That's it? Just "hmmm"? I mean, excuse me for not being a critically acclaimed literary genius like Cadence. But would it kill you to give me a little high five? Or even a halfhearted "atta girl!" I mean, what's with you? And why did you even ask me to join you anyway?

"So how's Harrison?" he asked, immediately segueing into new conversational territory, since obviously there was no reason to waste any more time on my poorly executed, ill-advised, mass-mailing blunder.

I took a sip of coffee and shrugged. "Harrison's great," I lied. "He's a really cool guy." *There, let him think Harrison advised me to bypass the submissions guidelines.*

"Really?" He looked surprised.

"Really." I nodded, finishing my coffee. All I wanted was to say "adiós" and get the hell out of there. This guy was toxic. And he was totally dragging me down.

But he just shrugged and said, "Well, I have to get to the office. But I was wondering, are you free this weekend?"

I stared at my recycled-paper coffee cup that I had unconsciously bent and folded until it was completely misshapen. *Is he serious? I mean, why would I want to go out with him? So he could give me a point-by-point synopsis on just how much I didn't know about the world of publishing? Jeez, what an ego! I mean, he's a lawyer, not a writer, and just because he's dating an author doesn't make him one. This guy's a total creep, and it's time I find another neighborhood to buy my coffee and books in.* "I'm spending the weekend in Paris," I said finally, narrowing my eyes as they met his.

"Lucky you," he said, holding my gaze for just a fraction too long, considering he had a girlfriend. And considering how much I hated him.

Then, without another word, we grabbed our things and headed for the escalator, with me standing in front so I wouldn't have to look at him. And when we got to the bottom, he rushed to the door and held it open. Then we headed out into the sunshine, each going our separate ways.

19

Flying to Paris without Clay wasn't nearly as much fun. The eight-person crew was unfriendly and cliquish, having instinctively divided themselves into three sharply defined groups well before we'd even finished briefing. And even though I'd been in similar situations before, I'd always been lucky enough to have at least one fellow outsider to hang with. But this time I was on my own, with everyone unanimously agreeing that I would be the odd girl out. And as we headed for the gate with them all happily paired off, and me lagging behind, I knew I was in for a long flight.

First there were the Atlas Pioneers, comprised of those who began their careers back in the days when flight attendants were stewardesses and Atlas was just a small-time regional airline. They're convinced that their place in the Atlas family is an exalted one, and that behaving like good, obedient children can only result in management responding like a fair and trusted parent. Yet this seemingly loyal, unquestioning commitment to their kin also fuels a deep, dark animosity toward any new recruits, especially the Foster Children, whom they've resented since their arrival.

The Foster Children are a group of multinational, multilingual, multisexual flight attendants adopted by Atlas when their original airline went bust several years ago. But even though they've been successfully placed in a new, more conventional and stable home doesn't mean they've assimilated. Because having spent their formative years with a more worldly, glamorous, globe-trotting airline, they are way more sophisticated, far more jaded, much more urbane, and deeply disdainful of their provincial Pioneer siblings. And like tourists on a cruise ship, they tend to stick together.

Then there were the French Speakers, consisting of two recent Berlitz school graduates who with only three and a half years of flying between them are allowed to skip the usual seniority trip-bidding rules and fly to all the foreign destinations falling within their corresponding language skills. This alone makes them the object of resentment by the Pioneers, the Foster Children, and oddly enough, each other.

And then there was me. With no clique identity, and a seniority number ranking well below the others (except perhaps the French Speakers), I was promptly relegated to all of the duties no one else wanted to perform. And a few more that were invented purely for my benefit.

You're going to Paris, where you'll have dinner with Max, and hopefully get to kiss him again became my mantra as I picked up trash in the aisles to avoid the backstabbing in the galleys.

And just as I was shoving my third overstuffed trash bag into the already full garbage cart I heard someone say, "Who wants to feed the pilots?" And desperate to get away for a while, I was the first (and only) to volunteer.

"Mind if I hang out?" I asked as I handed Bill and Ted their meals.

"Must be pretty bad out there, if you're seeking refuge in here." Ted laughed.

I just rolled my eyes and shook my head. I wasn't about to elaborate.

"Got any layover plans?" Bill asked, sipping Diet Coke from a Styrofoam cup with a plastic lid, a sort of Atlas-mandated sippy cup for pilots, so as not to spill on the instrument panel.

"I have a date." I smiled. I'd known Bill for years, as he was a good friend of Michael's; but he was also a really great guy, so I didn't hold that against him.

"Who's the lucky guy?" he asked, cutting into his steak and looking up at me.

"Maxwell Dunne. I met him on a flight a while back," I said, gazing out the window as we flew high above the clouds.

"Is he French?" Ted asked, cutting into his chicken.

I shook my head. "Nope, but he sure knows his way around the city." *And a girl's neck,* I thought, feeling myself blush at the memory.

"Sure we can't talk you into joining us for dinner?" Ted asked. "I was thinking of taking everyone to this little place over on the Left Bank."

"I should warn you, it's like a civil war out there," I told him. "But if you're up for knocking down borders and building bridges, then more power to you." I smiled.

"That bad?" he asked.

"Worse." I nodded.

"Well still, it may be one of the last times I treat, especially if management gets that fifty-five percent pay cut they're after." He shook his head.

"Jeez, we really are going to hell, aren't we?" I said, watching as he buttered his dinner roll.

"No doubt." Ted nodded.

Bill looked up then and, wiping his mouth with his linen napkin, said, "You sure you're okay, Hailey? I mean, without Michael and all? It's a hell of a time to be out there on your own. Especially in New York City."

But I just shrugged. While it was nice of him to be concerned,

I didn't take the city comment seriously. I knew very few pilots who had a good word to say about Manhattan.

"Ever think about moving back home and commuting? Could be the best thing for you." He looked at me, nodding his head while chewing his food.

Going back home? To live with my mom? Was he kidding? He was looking at me, waiting for a response. And even though I knew he meant well, I still couldn't resist saying, "Well, right now I'm living in a Fifth Avenue penthouse and looking forward to nothing more than my date in Paris, who happens to be completely amazing." I shrugged. "But other than that, I'm just taking it one day at a time, Bill, just one day at a time."

Then I grabbed their empty trays and headed back into the cabin, wondering how much of that would get back to Michael.

Before I'd headed out to JFK, I'd tried calling Max at the Ritz. But when he didn't answer, I left a brief message on the machine informing him of my arrival and accepting his dinner invitation. So by the time I made it to the front desk at the Grand Hotel, I was hoping for a note of confirmation, if not another bouquet of flowers.

"Is this it?" I asked, staring at the lone key card. "Because I'm expecting a message."

"*Non,* no message," the clerk said, already moving on to the next in line.

Clutching my key, I headed for my room, scolding myself for feeling disappointed. *Get a grip. You're in Paris,* I thought, unlocking the door. *It's one of your favorite cities* and *you're being paid to be here! And if Max blows you off, so what? You know your way around! You don't need him. You can buy your own dinner!*

I dropped my bags on the floor and peeled off my uniform, anxious to grab a short nap before heading out to explore the city. *Forget Max. Don't even think about him. Just sleep.*

Rolling over to set my alarm, I noticed the red telephone message light was flashing. And trying not to feel overly hopeful, I held my breath and lifted the receiver.

"Hailey, the front desk said you just checked in, so you're probably on your way up. Anyway, I'm glad you made it, and if it's okay with you I'll pick you up at seven. If that doesn't work, leave a message at the Ritz. Otherwise, I'll assume we're on. À *bientôt!*"

I listened to the message again, and then reset my alarm to go off much, much later. I was going to dinner with Max! And I was hoping for another late night.

When I got to the lobby I found Max thumbing through a magazine, waiting for me. "Am I late?" I asked, taking in his antiqued jeans, untucked striped shirt, and tan suede loafers, feeling relieved that he really was as cute as I remembered.

"I'm early." He smiled, leaning in for a brief kiss on the cheek, and leaving me to enjoy the lingering scent of minty fresh breath, recently washed hair, and his own natural, sexy muskiness. And as he led me outside to his car and driver, I slid onto the leather seats and thought how easy it would be to get used to this.

"Have you been to the Latin Quarter?" he asked as the Mercedes merged into traffic.

"Many times." I nodded. "It's my favorite part of the city."

"Well, there's this little restaurant I saw last time. It's fairly new, and I haven't eaten there yet, so I don't know if it's any good. In fact, I'm not even sure I can find it again. But I thought I'd have Jean Claude drop us off and then we could go exploring on our own. How does that sound?"

"Great," I said, gazing into his gorgeous brown eyes and feeling my stomach go all weird when he smiled at me.

●   ●   ●

Jean Claude left us on the boulevard Saint-Germain, and Max grabbed my hand as we headed into the maze of narrow, lively streets. "If I'm not mistaken it should be right up here on the left," he said.

"Well, if it's not, then there's always those sidewalk crepe vendors." I smiled, thinking how I'd enjoyed a Nutella-filled crepe for dinner on more than one occasion.

"Sorry, no crepes tonight. It's right over there."

We walked into a small, dim, noisy space that was filled to capacity. And as we sat in a booth along the wall, I thought how very Parisian it was, with the cloth-covered tables, red leather seats, and chalkboard wine list. Not to mention the adorable white terrier at the next table, waiting patiently while his owner enjoyed a leisurely meal.

"It's perfect," I said, lifting my menu and feeling dismayed when I realized I couldn't understand a word of it. "But I may need a little help with the ordering part. My high school French doesn't stretch as far as you'd think."

"No problem," Max said, quickly scanning the entrées. "Do you like traditional bistro food?"

"If you mean steak frites and French onion soup, then the answer is *oui*." I smiled.

When the waiter arrived, Max spent a good deal of time conversing in rapid-fire French that I didn't even try to follow. And when he left, Max leaned in and smiled. "I hope you're feeling adventurous."

"Escargot? Yes. Monkey brains? Not so much."

"Oh well, more for me then." He shrugged, leaning back in his seat and winking.

But as our table began to fill with carafes of wine, bowls of mussels, plates of pâté frisée salads, and terrines of foie gras, I was relieved to see there were no monkeys, no simians, and no primates anywhere in the vicinity—just an amazing display of food that I couldn't wait to taste.

"True bistro cooking is about taking the simplest ingredients and elevating them to excellence through preparation and technique," he said, spooning some marinated olives onto my plate.

"You really know your stuff," I said, taking a bite of caviar on toasted brioche with crème fraîche. "Do you cook like this at home?"

But Max just shook his head sadly. "I can't even boil water without setting off the smoke alarm," he said. "I'm strictly a restaurant guy."

By the time we finished our dessert of little individual lemon tarts, we were feeling so full we decided to take a leisurely walk through the pedestrian-filled streets. And turning onto the boulevard Saint-Michel, we made our way toward the Seine.

"I love this city," I said, gazing at the beautiful old buildings, and the lively corner cafes. "You're so lucky to spend so much time here."

"I am," he agreed, sliding his arm around my waist and guiding me across the street and over to the Pont Neuf, which despite its name translating to "New Bridge" was actually the oldest in Paris. We walked about halfway, then stopped and leaned against the concrete rail, gazing down at the dark, moody river, the gargoyles of Notre Dame, and the flickering city lights beyond. And just as I leaned into him thinking, *Kiss me*, he pulled me even closer and pressed his lips against mine.

Like the last time we'd had dinner together, I'd drunk a fair amount of wine. But the feelings I had when I was wrapped in his arms had nothing to do with alcohol and everything to do with good old-fashioned lust. The kind I hadn't experienced for a very long time, and certainly not for the bulk of my relationship with Michael.

I ran my hands over Max's body, feeling the taut muscles of his

shoulders, arms, and chest through the soft cotton of his shirt.
And then, gripping me even tighter, he pressed his body hard
against mine while his lips drifted down to my neck.

"Come back to the Ritz with me," he whispered.

And I opened my eyes and looked deep into his. "I can't."

"Why?" he asked, nipping at my neck again, which almost suc-
ceeded in changing my mind.

But then, thinking of all the logistics, like us getting to the Ritz,
me getting back to the Grand Hotel in time for pickup the next
morning, and then having to work the flight home with the nasty
crew and little to no sleep, I shook my head and said, "Really, I
can't. I have to fly back in the morning."

"But when can I see you again?" he asked, gazing into my eyes.

"I don't know." I shrugged, thinking how his real home in
Boston was actually just a short plane ride away.

"Come back to Paris. Tomorrow."

"What?" I squinted at him. I mean, was he serious?

"You land at JFK before the evening flight to Paris takes off,
right?"

"Well, yeah," I said, with more than a little hesitation.

"And you fly for free?"

I nodded slowly.

"So, you go through customs, turn around, and come right
back. You told me over dinner you have the whole week off, right?"

"Well, yeah, but—"

"Then it's perfect. I'll have Jean Claude pick you up, and you'll
stay with me at the Ritz."

"But—what about my clothes? I mean, I won't have time to go
home and repack," I said, realizing that as far as excuses went, it was
pretty lame. But even though I was really tempted to go along with
his plan, I was still in need of a little more convincing.

But he just waved it away. "This is *Paris*," he said. "We'll go
shopping."

And even though I'd never been one to beg off shopping, I knew I was in no position to buy a new wardrobe. And if Max was planning to pick up the tab, well then, that was awkward too. I mean, I just didn't know him well enough for that. But just as I was about to decline, he kissed me. And as my lips yielded against his I went over everything he'd just offered: Paris, shopping, the Ritz, and the blatantly unspoken but definitely understood—S-E-X—and most likely the amazing, toe-curling kind.

I pulled away for a moment, taking in his dark eyes, strong nose, and soft, moist lips. Life was short. So wasn't it better to regret something you did, rather than something you didn't do?

I pressed my mouth hard against his. "Yes," I told him. "Yes. I'll do it!"

20

The second I got through customs, I ran down to the flight attendant lounge, hoping I could brush my teeth, change my clothes,
and try to freshen up a little before I got back on the plane and
headed to France.

"Hey, where's the fire?" Clay asked, grabbing my sleeve as I
rushed past him.

"Oh, I didn't see you," I said, stopping to catch my breath. "I'm
headed to Paris for a few days."

"I thought you just got back?" He gave me a suspicious look.

"I did, but it's a long story and I'm outta time. Can we talk
later?" I asked, shifting my purse and looking around nervously.

"Where you staying?" he asked, knowing something was up and
refusing to let it go.

"The Ritz," I admitted, feeling myself turn every shade of red.

"You little vixen!" He smiled. "For how long?"

I just shrugged.

"Hey, I just picked up this two-day Amsterdam layover, gets

there Friday leaves on Monday. You should meet me there from Paris, and we'll fly back together."

Friday would only give me four days with Max, I thought. Which would either be far too much time together, or not nearly enough, depending on how things went. "I don't know," I told him, looking anxiously toward the bathroom. I was running out of time and really needed to get in there.

"Fine, I'll call you at the Ritz. Whose room should I ask for? Yours or his?" he teased.

"Ask for Maxwell Dunne," I said, giving him a quick hug before I grabbed my bag and ran down the hall.

The fact that I'd just spent the previous eight hours dishing out food from the same menu I was now being offered meant I was pretty uninterested in any of it. So after ordering a glass of red wine from a flight attendant I'd hung out with on a Prague layover several years before, I retrieved a squashed strawberry-yogurt Zone bar from the bottom of my bag and reminded my thighs how they'd thank me later.

I was seated at the window in our Business Select cabin, which was a sort of hybrid between a downgraded first class and a marginally better business class. And even though I had a choice of eight movies and four trivia games at my disposal, my goal was to go straight to sleep the second I'd quaffed down my food and drink.

I glanced at the guy sitting next to me, who was rumpled, unwashed, and looked to be well into his sixties. But he seemed friendly enough as he raised his wineglass high in the air and smiled in a sort of *toast to us*. Lifting mine as well, I smiled back, took a sip, and then broke out my iPod so he wouldn't get any ideas about talking to me.

As I listened to Gwen Stefani singing "It's My Life," I tore into the wrapper of my protein bar, taking a bite and marveling at how well that sweet, artificial strawberry taste blended with my wine.

And just as I was about to take another, the old guy next to me extended his footrest, removed his socks, and propped up his crusty bare feet for the entire cabin to view.

The skin on his left foot was yellow in some spots, red in others, and dry and flaky like I'd never seen. And as he reached down to scratch it, I covered my dinner in horror as I imagined the trillions of funky skin particles that were now being driven into the cabin air only to be recycled over and over again as we made our way across the Atlantic.

Oh sick! It doesn't get worse than this, I thought, burrowing deeper into my corner. And just as I was shielding myself with my blanket, getting it all tucked in around me, he crossed his right leg over his left, proudly displaying his big toe with the thick, warped yellow nail, the shrunken crooked pinky toe that had no nail, and the big empty space in between, where the other three toes should have been.

I just sat there staring at that wide blank space as though it were a car wreck I couldn't turn away from. And as his meal was delivered, he lifted his glass, tapped me on the arm, and said, "Bon appétit!"

Taking one last glance at his mangled feet, I smiled weakly. "Bon appétit," I mumbled, then threw the blanket over my head and prayed for tailwinds.

The blanket trick must have worked, as by the time I was standing in front of the Ritz, gazing at the seemingly never-ending stone façade, I wasn't feeling the least bit tired. And by the time I got to Max's suite and took one look at the stone fireplace, gilt mirrors, crystal chandeliers, velvet settees, and larger-than-large marble bathroom, I was tempted to jump up and down on the opulent, oversized bed in pure joy.

But instead, I just stood there, awkwardly fumbling through my purse, looking for something to tip the bellhop with.

"Mademoiselle, it is not necessary. Monsieur Dunne has taken care of everything. But please ring if you require anything else," he said as I watched him leave.

Then I stripped off my clothes, dropped them in a heap in the middle of the floor, and headed for that large luxurious bathroom, looking forward to a nice long bubble bath in the huge marble tub.

Dressed in the same boot-cut jeans I'd worn to dinner the other night, and a clean(ish) white cotton tank top under a turquoise sweater, I headed out of the Ritz and into the city, wanting to pick up a few things while I enjoyed the day in Paris. And since I was more familiar with the area on the Left Bank, I made my way toward the Seine, intent on visiting some of the little shops I knew of on the other side.

The day was bright and warm, and the streets were busy with people rushing about, and as I removed my cardigan and tossed it into my black, duty-free, Longchamp tote bag, I thought about how much my life had changed since my birthday, and how I couldn't help but think there'd be more of this.

I mean, in just a few short months, I'd finished my manuscript and mailed it out, moved to a Fifth Avenue address (okay, so maybe it wasn't mine, and it was only temporary, but I was there now and that's all that mattered), and had started dating the most amazing, sexy, exciting guy I'd ever met in real life.

Max was perfect. He had everything I'd ever dreamed of, and the fact that he wasn't married was almost too good to be true. But single he was, since, not content to rely solely on the ring-finger test, I'd come right out and asked him in the middle of our last dinner. I mean, I knew I could fall hard for this guy, and I'd wanted to gather all of the facts before the dessert arrived.

"Jeez, Max, I fly all the way to Paris to see you, when you're just a quick forty-minute flight away back home. I mean, you're not married, are you?" I asked, followed by a nervous giggle and a gulp of wine. But he just shook his head, which wasn't exactly the verbal affirmation I was after. So I pressed a little further. "No wife and five kids, anxiously awaiting your return?" I bit my bottom lip and waited.

"No wife, no kids, no girlfriend. Look Hailey, I'm always flying back and forth between Paris and Boston, and that can make it pretty tough to sustain a relationship."

But not if you're dating a flight attendant! I'd thought.

"Of course I'd like to slow down and get married someday." He shrugged. "Though I'm not so sure about the kid part."

Even that was fine with me, since I wasn't so sure about the kid part either.

"If you want to meet up in Boston, we can do that. I just thought it would be more fun to explore Paris together," he'd said, smiling and leaning over to kiss me.

Yup, Max was perfect. And single. And deserved much better than my frayed, beige Gap bra-and-panty set, I thought as I walked through the doors of Sabbia Rosa, one of the best lingerie stores in Paris.

"May I help you?" asked a slim older woman who looked incredibly chic in that undone yet totally put-together way the French specialize in.

"Oh, I'm just browsing," I said, wishing I didn't look so blatantly apple-pie American, as just once it would be nice to fool a local, any local.

"I have a new collection of sets that would go perfect with your coloring. Come," she said, leading me to the other side of the store, where a row of delicate, elegant, whisper-soft silk underthings hung.

"Wow," I said, reaching for a deep apricot-colored bra edged in cream-colored lace. "This is beautiful." I stroked the soft, filmy fabric while nonchalantly searching for a price tag. *Three hundred euros! Are they serious?* I smiled faintly and placed it back on the rack, thinking maybe I should try to locate a Victoria's Secret or at least something more in my airline employee budget.

"And then there's this," she said, thrusting a dark, emerald green nightgown at me.

"Oh, it's gorgeous." I nodded, knowing there was no way I was wearing a nightgown. The logistics of that were just way too complex, requiring me to beeline for the bathroom immediately after dinner so I could do a quick change, and then reemerge as though I'd been secretly stowing it beneath my sweater and jeans the whole time. And as I flipped over the price tag and saw that it was nine hundred euros, I was glad I'd already vetoed it.

"I'm not really the nightgown type," I told her, heading back to the bra and panties, thinking how the apricot set now seemed like a bargain after the negligee. I picked up the matching thong and noticed it was half the price of the bra. But since it consisted of nothing more than a small silk V in the front and a piece of string in the back, you could see why it'd be cheaper.

But it was beautiful. And it's not like I was paying rent anymore. Not to mention that I hadn't brought any nice lingerie with me (probably because I didn't own any). And Max was special. And I really wanted our night to be special. . . .

"I'll just try this on real quick." I told the saleswoman as I slipped into a dressing room.

I'd told Max I would meet him at Bar Hemingway for four reasons:

1. I thought it might be really awkward to meet up in a room that centered around a bed, even if we both knew that's where we'd end up.
2. The bar had a strong literary history, with actual photos taken by Ernest Hemingway himself displayed on the walls.

3. I'd read it was the birthplace of the Bloody Mary—a drink
    I was quite fond of.
4. I was kind of hoping for a *Pretty Woman* moment. You
    know the part where Richard Gere (who oddly enough
    bore a slight resemblance to Max) walks into the hotel bar
    and finds Julia Roberts (who other than being an auburn-
    haired female bears no resemblance to me) looking radi-
    ant in her little black dress. (Let's just forget the stuff
    about her being a hooker and him paying her to be there.)

I sat at a small round table, legs crossed, index finger making
nervous laps around the rim of my wineglass, wearing a brand-
new, sexy little black dress, a new pair of strappy silver sandals I'd
bought to go with it, and of course, the very soft, very expensive
lingerie that offered no support whatsoever hiding discreetly underneath. All of it conveniently charged to my Atlas AirMiles Visa
card, as I'd convinced myself that not only was I getting an amazing new outfit, but mileage points as well, which would come in
handy if Atlas decided to pink slip me.

"Bonsoir." I looked up to see Max crossing the room, looking
amazing in a trim charcoal suit, with a lavender shirt and navy, patterned tie. "You look beautiful." He bent down to kiss me, taking
the seat next to mine. "Did you shop?" he asked, gazing at my new
dress.

"I took a walk over to the Left Bank," I told him.

"Walked? You should've used the car. I told Jean Claude to
hang around in case you needed him."

"I know. He mentioned it at the airport. But it was such a beautiful day, and I'd slept the whole flight, so I just felt like walking." I
shrugged.

"So you had a good flight?" he asked, motioning to the waiter
for a glass of wine.

I thought about my seatmate and his disgusting bare feet. But I
guess in retrospect, it had been a small price to pay to end up in a

place like this. "I slept right through it," I said, smiling and taking a sip of my wine.

I swear, dining with Max was like getting a Ph.D. in food, as each meal was like a whole new culinary experience. And even though I'd lived in the restaurant capital of America for the last six years, that didn't mean I knew what to order in any of them.

"What do you suggest?" I asked, gazing at the menu that was written in French and cursing myself, once again, for not having paid more attention to my high school teacher Mademoiselle Simone when I'd had the chance.

"Well," Max said, slipping on his reading glasses, which just made him even more perfect. I've always had a thing for men in glasses. "I thought we'd start with the pan-fried foie gras with black cherries, cacao beans, and pistachio streusel. How does that sound?"

Cacao beans and streusel? Was he talking appetizer or dessert? "Uh, sounds good," I said, reminding myself how he'd yet to order something I didn't like.

"Great." He glanced back at the menu and said, "Then I thought we could follow with the organic tomato-and-herb salad, and then I was trying to decide between the rabbit or the pigeon de Touraine. What do you think?" He looked at me.

People eat pigeons? "Uh, those wouldn't by chance be imported New York City pigeons?" I asked, laughing nervously while remembering the one that had clipped me in Central Park a few years back, and how his filthy wing feathers had left a trace of stinky, dark *ick* on my arm that took days to get off.

"No." He laughed. "And trust me, they're delicious."

Okay, I told myself, *I know people who still eat at McDonald's, even after seeing* Super Size Me, *so how bad can it be?* Plus I really liked him, I really wanted him to like me, and I was firmly committed to trying new things. Even if it meant consuming something I'd never seen in any food pyramid. "Why don't you order the rabbit, I'll get the pigeon, and then we can share?" I suggested.

"Perfect," he said, closing the menu and smiling.

He was right again. I loved every single thing I ate, but now as I sat there, feeling the sides of my new panties burrowing deep into my flesh, I was thinking that maybe I shouldn't have enjoyed quite so much of it. I mean, it was just a matter of time before I stood naked in front of Max, and now I would be all puffy and bloated. Great.

"What do you think of having roasted rhubarb tart with buttermilk ice cream for dessert?" he asked.

"I think there's no room at the inn," I said, rubbing my newly expanded waistline.

"Well then how 'bout a brandy?"

"That I could handle."

"Should we order it here, or back in our room?" he asked, gorgeous brown eyes looking deep into mine while his fingers continued to draw lazy circles up my thigh, sending me into a state of *want* so severe I wasn't sure I could finish my meal. Though of course I somehow managed.

"Let's head back," I said, taking his hand in mine and squeezing it tightly.

When we returned to the suite, Max promptly ordered the brandies, while I got busy in the bathroom, brushing my teeth, fixing my makeup, and convincing myself that he wouldn't care if I was bloated, since it was his fault for ordering all that delicious rich food in the first place. And when I opened the door, I found him sitting on the velvet settee, with two glasses of brandy and a roaring fire before him.

"Come join me," he said, then handed me a glass as I settled in next to him. I watched as he sipped his drink and set it on the marble-topped table; then I nervously took a sip of mine and set it next to his. "I'm so glad you came to Paris," he said, brushing a random curl off my face. And just when I thought I couldn't go another second without the feel of his lips, he pulled me close and kissed me.

We kissed like prisoners on jailbreak, like teenagers who've taken an abstinence vow, and I was so completely wrapped up in it, so completely lost in it, that I was no longer aware of anything other than the fact that I never, ever wanted it to end. Then, clutching me tight against him, he reached around my shoulders and unzipped my dress, sliding it all the way down until I was lying beneath him in nothing but my new underwear that had cost almost as much as my rent used to.

"Wow," he whispered as his fingertips outlined the lace on my bra and the soft, creamy V of my panties. And then, lifting me in his arms, he carried me over to the bed (with no overt signs of staggering or stress) and deposited me in the middle, where I watched him remove his tie, cuff links, and shirt. And then, kicking off his shoes, he knelt at the very edge, pulling off my thong and settling in until I could barely contain myself.

"Max," I whispered, pulling on his arms and hands, desperate to have him.

Slowly making his way up my body, he nuzzled his face in my neck while I frantically reached down, unbuckled his belt, and pushed off his trousers. Then, reaching around to the front of his briefs, I was just about to slip my hand inside when he grabbed both my wrists and lifted them high above my head.

"Hailey," he murmured, still holding my arms with one hand while removing his briefs with the other. And then, reaching over to the nightstand, he retrieved a condom and slipped it on, while I closed my eyes and waited.

"Oh, Hailey," he said, his damp forehead pressing into the side of my neck. "Oh, you're so beautiful." His breathing grew faster, more labored, as I lay beneath him, anxious to feel something too.

And just when I thought it might start, his jerky movements and high-pitched yelps told me it was already over.

Okay, so the first time is never that great, I thought, shifting uncomfortably under the deadweight of his body as he fought to catch his breath. *We had a lot to drink and eat, and we're just getting to know each other. Of course it was a little awkward. After all, we still have a lot to learn about each other.*

He heaved a long, loud sigh, and I watched as he rolled off me and onto his side. And then he got up from the bed and headed toward the bathroom. "Can I get you anything?" he called over his shoulder.

Um, how about my turn? But I didn't say that. Instead I just said, "Nope, I'm all set." And watched while the door closed between us.

THINGS TO CONSIDER WHEN DETERMINING WHETHER TO EVACUATE

What do you see?

What do you hear?

What do you smell?

What are you being told?

I'd been awake all night, feeling Max's body curled around mine while listening to his constant snoring, which had started pretty much the second he came out of the bathroom, turned off the lamp, and said, *"Bonne nuit."*

But as the morning light creeped around the thick brocade drapes, he began to stir. And I lay there quietly, feigning sleep, until he crawled out of bed and headed for the shower. Then I sat up, gazed around the spectacular suite, and wondered what to do.

Nearly everything about Max was perfect. Well, all except for one thing. And I had absolutely no idea what I should do about it. On the one hand, he was single, funny, romantic, sophisticated, adventurous, smart, attentive, generous, nice, and an awesome kisser—just your everyday Prince Charming kind of thing. But there was still that one potential deal breaker that couldn't be ignored.

I threw myself onto the pillows, rolling over so that my face was buried in their thick, soft down. And I was feeling so upset, and so frustrated, that I was tempted to tear into them and watch as the room filled with feathers.

Why? Why were things always so complicated? Why couldn't anything ever turn out as I'd hoped? And why hadn't I realized from the start that Max really was too good to be true?

And it wasn't just that the sex had gone from sixty to zero in a matter of seconds, because that I could work with. Or at least give it a few more tries to see if things improved. No, it was the *reason* why things had gone so bad. And so far, modern technology had yet to find a solution for that.

I heard him open the bathroom door and quickly turned on my side, peering at him through my lashes, just to make sure.

At first he had a thick white towel wrapped tightly around his waist, so I couldn't see anything. But after glancing at me nervously and determining that yes, I was still asleep, he dropped it to the floor. And in the ten seconds he went from being completely naked to wearing a clean pair of briefs, I'd already confirmed the worst.

Maxwell Dunne had the smallest penis I had ever seen.

"I don't know what to do," I said, shaking my head and taking a sip of the cappuccino I'd ordered from room service. I was freshly showered, wrapped in one of the Ritz robes I'd found hanging in the closet, and was curled up on the velvet settee, phone to my ear, talking to Clay. "And he left the sweetest note, saying he'd try to finish early so we could spend the day together." I closed my eyes and pressed my forehead against my terry-cloth-covered knees.

"Well, maybe he's a grower, not a shower," Clay said, laughing at his own little witticism.

"Clay, this is serious. I know what I saw."

"Fine. So tell me, on a scale of one to ten, how bad is it?" he asked.

"Zero. It's like nonexistent. I'm surprised he even found a condom to fit." I reached for my butter croissant and bit off a piece.

"Hailey, you've got to get out of there," he said urgently.

"But *how?* I mean, he's completely perfect in every other way.
And he's a really good kisser."

"That's because he *has* to be. Besides, this isn't seventh grade.
We graduated from just kissing a long time ago."

"But what kind of monster would I be for leaving a guy because he's . . ." I stopped, not wanting to say it out loud again.
"Well, anyway, men are very sensitive about these things, you
know."

"Well, it's not like you should tell him the truth! What you do is
find another reason to break it off."

"But there are no other reasons! I'm telling you he's a total catch
except for that one small thing. No pun intended," I said, hearing
him laugh.

"Okay, fine. So marry him. You can spend the rest of your life
cuddling in your suite at the Ritz. You could do worse," he said.

"Yeah, but unfortunately I want more. I want the whole toe-
curling package."

"Then you need to evacuate, like *now.* And if you feel guilty,
then just remember how men have been making women feel bad
about their bodies since the beginning of time. Think of it like
payback."

"Yeah, except Max isn't like that," I said, shaking my head and
adding more butter to my buttered croissant.

"Work it out, Hailey. I'll be in Amsterdam in a few days, if you
want to meet up."

"I'll let you know," I said, regretting the call even before I hung
up. Because now, no matter what decision I made, no matter what
happened between Max and me, Clay would always think of him
as the guy with the teeny weenie. And despite the desperate,
twelve-dollars-a-minute hotel surcharge phone call I'd just made,

the truth was, no matter how disappointing last night may have been, there was no way I could leave the most amazing man I'd ever dated just because of a certain, um, shortcoming.

I was still sitting there, phone by my side, feet on the table, staring at my half-eaten croissant when Max walked in. "Hey, glad you're still here. I'm taking the rest of the day off. I thought maybe we could head out to Versailles, visit the château, and then stop for lunch somewhere," he said, joining me on the couch and leaning in to kiss me. "What do you think?"

I wrapped my arms around him and kissed him back. *See? You can do this. He's an awesome kisser, way better than most. Not to mention that men like him don't come along every day, you know. Besides, you just spent the last four years having ho-hum sex with Michael, so what's with all the great expectations now?* I thought as he removed my robe and his mouth worked its way down my body, skillfully finishing what he'd started the night before.

By the time we'd exhausted the extensive grounds of the Château de Versailles, Parc de Versailles, and Petit Trianon, and then feasted on an amazing lunch at the Trianon Palace Hotel, I'd absolutely decided to stay in Paris with Max. Well, at least until next Sunday when I'd have to fly back to New York.

I mean, he was just way too good to toss, especially for the ridiculous, shallow reason I'd been contemplating. And it seemed like the more time we spent together the more I could feel myself falling for him. And if I wasn't mistaken, it seemed like he just might be feeling the same way about me.

It didn't take long to build a daily routine of Max leaving for work, followed by me ordering room service and then heading down to the beautiful indoor pool, where I'd swim lap after countless lap, hoping to work off some of those lavish dinners (and maybe just a tiny bit of sexual frustration as well). But it seemed to work, as I always climbed out of that clean warm water feeling shaky-legged and exhausted, and ready to spend the rest of the day ducking into shops, checking out museums, and sipping cappuccinos at some of those cute corner cafés.

Then in the evening we'd meet up at our favorite table at Bar Hemingway, where we'd share a quick drink before Jean Claude whisked us off to yet another amazing dinner.

And then after dinner . . . okay maybe the after-dinner part wasn't so hot, but I was learning to deal. Besides, I could already see how all that swimming was starting to carve some definition into my arms and shoulders.

And now, left with only three short days before I'd have to head back to New York, I found myself already dreading the thought of saying good-bye. So on Thursday when Max finished work earlier than usual and insisted we go shopping before dinner, I was feeling a little melancholy as we strolled around the city, and he pulled me into the Versace boutique simply because I'd admired a dress in the window.

"Max, I can't let you buy this for me," I whispered, gazing longingly at the dress and knowing that not only was it outrageously priced, but that it had no role in my real life back in New York.

"Nonsense. This dress will be perfect on you," he said, holding it against me and smiling.

"But where will I wear it?" I said, gazing into the mirror at the slinky black jersey knit with the sexy keyhole opening in front.

"You're in Paris! You can wear this anywhere! In fact, if you like it, you'll wear it right out of this shop! Try it on," he insisted. "If you don't like it I won't mention it again. Scout's honor." He held up his hand and smiled.

Well, of course I liked it. I mean, who wouldn't? And since the shoes I was wearing didn't quite go, he bought me a pair of those too.

"But what about you?" I said, watching the salesperson throw my old clothes into a bag while ringing up the new ones. "We should get you something too."

"How about this tie?" He reached for a colorful, wildly printed tie with gold Vs all over it.

"Kind of a wild tie, for a conservative investment banker," I said, shaking my head and laughing.

"This will be my after-hours tie." He smiled.

"Okay, the fact that you'd even have an after-hours tie just proves my point," I said, watching as he handed it to the clerk.

"What are you trying to say? That I don't have a wild side?" he asked, raising his brows.

But I just smiled and shrugged.

"Shall I prove it?" he dared.

"Knock yourself out." I laughed, leaning in to kiss him on the cheek.

"I'll show you," he said, sliding off his old tie and putting on the new one. Then he grabbed the packages and wrapped his arm around me. "Come on. I know just the place."

"Where we going?" I asked, exiting the shop and heading down the street.

"First I'm gonna leave these packages with Jean Claude. Then I'm going to give him the night off. Then we're going to hop on the metro. And then I'll show you my wild side."

22

Walking up the metro stairs, I squinted at the dingy, unfamiliar neighborhood. "Where are we?" I asked.

"This is Pigalle," Max said, throwing his arm around my shoulders as he led me past a funky mix of strip clubs, cabarets, trendy boutiques, and seedy bars.

"It reminds me of Times Square before Giuliani had his way with it."

"It used to be nothing but brothels, bars, and artists. Did you know that Picasso once lived here?"

"Uh, for your information it still looks like brothels and bars, but I'm not so sure about the artists," I said, walking past a sex shop and gaping at an all-dildo window display.

"Yeah, but you wouldn't believe what the real estate is going for these days. Still, I have considered buying," he said.

"So where are you taking me?" I asked.

"Where else? Dinner and a show." He smiled.

After another amazing meal at a trendy little brasserie, Max grabbed my hand and led me down the crowded, seedy boulevard past a steady stream of peep shows and adults-only nightclubs, which just made me even more curious about what he could possibly have in mind. I mean so far, from everything I'd seen, this place was definitely out of our usual comfort zone.

"So how about just a little hint?" I asked, leaning into him. He seemed so excited about his secret agenda that I couldn't resist trying to coax it out of him.

"No hints," he said, leaning down to kiss me. "You just have to wait and see."

We continued walking down the bright and busy boulevard de Clichy, past numerous nightclubs and bars, and the second I saw it I knew. But not wanting to spoil the surprise, I didn't say a word until that unmistakable red neon windmill was directly in front of us.

Of course! Max was taking me to one of the most famous cabarets in the world. "Oh, le Moulin Rouge!" I said excitedly. "I've always wanted to see that show." I squeezed his hand and gazed up at him. Leave it to Max to find a classy place in the midst of all this.

"Complete tourist trap," he said with disdain, pulling me right past it.

I turned back to glance at that well-known sign. "But . . . have you already seen it?" I asked, trying not to sound disappointed.

"No, and I don't want to. It's strictly for tourists, and a total waste of money. But don't worry, I'm taking you somewhere far more authentic." He nodded.

I just looked at him and smiled, thinking how he'd yet to show me a bad time. And then suddenly, we veered onto a dark, narrow alley, stopping in front of a windowless building with a single black door.

After nodding at a large, swarthy bouncer, Max slipped him some euros and pulled me inside. And as we entered a small, dim room with peeling wallpaper and a heavy red curtain acting as a divider, I searched in vain for some kind of signage that would tell me where I was.

"Have you been here before?" I asked, searching his face for some kind of clue.

"A few times." He shrugged, refusing to say any more.

And just when I thought I couldn't stand the suspense, a pale, short man in a dark shiny suit, frayed white shirt, and an old maroon tie stepped through the curtain. And the second he saw Max he smiled and said, "Monsieur Dunne! How nice to see you. Your usual table, I presume?" Then he parted the drapes and led us into a small square room where an oval stage dominated the center, while cloth-covered tables with small flickering candles were arranged all around.

As we settled at a front-row center table, I was amazed at how Max always knew the best places and got the best seats. Then I gazed around the room, watching as it began to fill with casually dressed couples, groups of rowdy executives, and a few solitary stragglers.

"How'd you even find this place?" I asked, turning back to Max and watching as he studied the drink menu. "I mean there are no signs or anything."

But he just smiled. And when the scantily clad cocktail waitress appeared at our table, he ordered a scotch on the rocks for himself and a glass of Bordeaux for me.

"Well, can you at least give me a hint about what I'm in for?" I asked, noting that the hand he had placed on my thigh was growing considerably damp despite the room being so cold.

But he just squeezed my leg and smiled. "Patience," he said.

I knew I had to stop grilling him. I mean, obviously he wanted to surprise me. So I should just do my part, sit back, and stop questioning. I mean how many guys would go to this much trouble, just to show how spontaneous and fun they could be? I looked at Max and smiled. Man, I was lucky.

Once the tables were full, the lights dimmed even lower, and the loud, hard-hitting strains of a song I'd never heard before began to fill the room. I watched as Max tossed back the rest of his drink and gripped my thigh even harder. And after leaning in to kiss him, I turned toward the stage to see an older man and a much younger woman who, except for a few strips of leather tied awkwardly around their torsos, were completely naked.

I just sat there, mouth gaping and eyes wide, as I watched them climb on top of a black leather ottoman, and then on top of each other.

Keep an open mind, I scolded, eyes glued to the stage in shock. *This is probably some kind of performance art.*

But after they *finished,* and the music changed to something softer and slower, a naked blonde with nothing more than a single white candle and a small book of matches took center stage. And then suddenly, I knew.

Maxwell Dunne had brought me to a sex circus.

"Max," I whispered, trying to get his attention as he drooled over the woman and her multitasking candle. "Max!" I poked him hard in the ribs. "Are you kidding me?"

"What?" He shook his head, then glanced at me briefly before turning back toward the stage, unwilling to miss a single moment.

"I can't believe you brought me here," I hissed, folding my arms across my chest, watching him watch her while completely ignoring me.

He was gripping my leg so tight it was beginning to hurt, so I peeled his fingers off, grabbed my purse, got up from my seat, and said, "I'm outta here." I stood there, hands on hips, waiting for a response. "I said I'm leaving!" And this time it came out much louder, judging by the dirty looks and the "Shhh!" I got from everyone but Max, who was focused on the stage.

Shaking with anger, I beelined for the curtain, no longer caring if he followed or not.

"Mademoiselle? Is everything okay?" asked the slimy host in the cheap, shiny suit.

But I just brushed right past him and stormed out the door.

• • •

The second I hit the street I calmed down just enough to realize that it was definitely not in my best interest to be wandering around this part of town all alone in a tiny, snug designer dress. "Oh, great," I mumbled, grasping my purse tightly while making my way to the corner, my eyes searching for potential muggers as well as a vacant taxi.

And I'd just made it to the end of the alley when I felt someone run up behind me. "Wait!" Maxwell shouted. But it was too late. I'd already nailed him with my purse. Though to be honest, I probably would've done it anyway.

"Hailey, stop," he said, catching his breath and rubbing his shoulder.

"What the hell were you thinking?" I yelled, blinking back tears and glaring at him under the yellow glow of the streetlights.

"I just thought I'd show you another side of Paris." He shrugged.

I stood before him, arms crossed, eyes narrowed, debating whether I should take another swing. "Showing me Pigalle is one thing. But bringing me to a sex show is totally inappropriate," I said, turning angrily and heading toward the boulevard.

"Hailey, I'm sorry. I just wanted to show you that I wasn't all fancy dinners and five-star hotels. That I could be spontaneous and wild too."

I stopped and stared at him, shaking my head in frustration. "Who're you kidding? You're a *regular!* You knew just where to find it, and the host knew you by name! You even have a *regular table,*" I said, watching him cringe and look away in embarrassment.

"So what now?" he asked.

"What now? I'm leaving. That's what happens now!"

"Hailey, please wait." He stood there looking tired and defeated. "Okay, so I've been here before. At least I'm not trying to hide it. Besides, you seem so open-minded, I guess I thought you'd enjoy it too." He shrugged.

I watched him standing there, his shoulders slumped in shame, and I had to admit, part of me felt bad for him. I mean, maybe Max had brought me here because he knew I wasn't satisfied. Or maybe he was hoping for a little understanding. Or maybe he was just a creepy pervert. But one thing was clear—he'd used really bad judgment. And because of that I no longer had a good excuse to stay.

Though I did have one to leave.

"Max, I think I should go," I said, squeezing his hand softly and letting it drop at his side.

"Go where?" he asked, his eyes searching my face.

"Back to the Ritz. And then to the airport," I said, hoping he wouldn't be too upset.

He looked at me for a moment, then nodded. "At least let's get a cab."

We made our way down the boulevard, carefully guarding against any accidental physical contact. And when he opened the cab door, I slid all the way across the seat, making sure there was plenty of room for him. But then he reached for his wallet, handed the driver a fistful of euros, and walked away without once looking back.

"Wait," I said as the driver started to pull away. "Wait just a moment." And I leaned my head out the window, watching as Max made his way down the alley, eventually disappearing through the small, unmarked door.

23

"Can you even believe it?" I asked, shaking my head. "I mean, don't you think that was a little early in the game to trot out the porn addiction?" I lifted my mug and took a nice long gulp of Dutch beer.

But Clay just shrugged. "Most of the couples I know met up *because* of their porn addictions," he said, taking a long pull on his cigarette—a habit he'd given up years ago, but occasionally regressed to whenever we found ourselves drinking in some European bar.

"Yeah, well, I'm no prude, but—"

"Hailey, please. Every prude I know starts their sentences like that."

I rolled my eyes and continued. "Listen, if we'd been dating for a little longer, and we decided to check out that kind of show just to be a little decadent, that would be fine. Maybe even fun. But since we hadn't known each other very long, not to mention that the sex *we* were having was pretty deficient, well that just made it even worse."

"But maybe that's why he took you there," Clay said, blowing a perfect smoke ring, then turning to face me. "You know, to like get a mood on. Since once you get back to the suite, he can't produce the goods."

I took another sip of my beer and shrugged.

"Or maybe he knew you weren't having a good time in bed, so he thought he'd show you some people who were."

"But do you think I'd be sitting here now, if it weren't for the other problem?" I asked.

Clay squinted at me and took another drag. "Quit beating yourself up," he said, curls of smoke escaping from his mouth with each word. "I think the reason this guy was so perfect in the beginning was because he *had* to be. And once the jig was up, well then he was free to be his genuine, low-life self."

I gazed at my empty beer mug, wondering if he was right.

"I'll buy you a beer for a cigarette."

I looked up to see this really pretty blonde smiling at us. And even though she spoke perfect English, the accent was pure Holland.

"You're on," Clay said, slipping a cigarette out of his pack as she motioned for the bartender.

"Two beers," she said. And then, slipping the cigarette between her lips, she noticed me and my empty mug. "Make it three." She smiled.

Several beers later, Clay and I, our new best friend whose name I'd forgotten even though she was still buying the beers, and several of her friends were trying to decide whether to head out to a club or just stay put where we already had a table and the drinks were promptly refilled.

"Let's go to a club," I said, feeling loose and happy and anxious to make the most of my night out in Amsterdam.

And before I knew it, I was sitting on the hump, in the back of a taxi, between two people whose names I didn't know.

And after that I can't remember.

"Wa—" I crawled out of bed clutching the sides of my head, with my tongue feeling thick and swollen and useless, as though somehow during the night it'd grown too large for my mouth. "Water," I mumbled, heading for the bathroom, where I turned on the faucet and angled my lips under the spray, drinking until I couldn't hold any more. Then, wiping my dripping face on the hem of my oversized T-shirt, I headed for my bag, desperately searching for something to stop the pounding in my head.

"If you're looking for aspirin, I have some right here," Clay said, holding up a tiny travel-sized bottle and shaking it so that the pills rattled against each other. "And there's plenty of coffee left to wash it down with." He motioned toward a silver room-service tray hosting an entire breakfast setup.

"How long have you been up?" I asked, downing the aspirin and taking a bite of cheese Danish. "I mean, what time is it?" I squinted at him.

"It's afternoon," he shrugged. "Probably around one."

"Are you kidding?"

"We didn't get back until after four," he said, lounging on the couch with his bare feet propped on the coffee table, looking fresh and handsome as ever.

"Well, did we at least have fun?" I asked, unable to recall anything more than a brief flashback.

"*You* had a great time." He smiled.

I set down my coffee and looked at him. "Oh no. What does that mean?" I asked, already fearing the answer.

"Let's just say Tara Reid's got nothing on you." He laughed.

Tara Reid? What could we possibly have in common?

"Yup, ole Jan and you were really whoopin' it up. And when you climbed up on that table, I thought I would *die*."

Table? What table? I looked at Clay, panicked.

"You brought the house down. I think you even made some tip money. Check your wallet for crumpled-up euros," he suggested, getting up and heading for the bathroom.

"But I kept all my clothes on, *right?*" I called after him, frantically reaching for my purse, desperate to get to the bottom of this. I mean, if I really had earned tip money, then not only did I want to know why, but also how much.

Spilling the contents across the duvet, I took inventory of the debris—the brand-new pack of travel tissues, Altoids the curiously strong breath mints, the M-A-C lip gloss that had somehow escaped the Canal Street Prada makeup bag I housed it in, the three black "ouchless" ponytail holders I kept in all my bags and coat pockets in case of unanticipated humidity—but nothing seemed out of place. And then underneath the Burberry wallet I'd bought myself for Christmas last year was a white business card with an Amsterdam address, and the words "Call me" written in small, neat script above the name Jan van Dijk. In the corner was a tiny hand-drawn heart.

Jan van Dijk. Jan van Dijk. Who the hell is Jan van Dijk? I wondered, trying to match the name to a face. But I'd met so many people last night, I couldn't keep track of it then, much less now. But wait—hadn't Clay said something about me and "ole Jan" really whooping it up? Table dancing even? I closed my eyes, determined to remember. *There was that girl at the bar with the cigarette who was buying the beer and smiling at me . . . and then later . . . was it her I sat next to in the cab?* Was she Jan van Dijk? And if so, why had she given me her card? Why did she write "call me"? And what was up with that little hand-scrawled heart?

I stared at the bathroom door just as Clay opened it. "Did I hook up with a girl?"

He stopped in his tracks and looked at me. "Would that be so bad?" He smiled.

"Just tell me," I said, all keyed up, unwilling to mess around. "Just tell me; I can take it. I made out with a girl, didn't I? I made out with Jan van Dijk!" I lay back on the bed and closed my eyes. So there it was, my own personal rock bottom. Not that I had anything against girls kissing girls. But it definitely wasn't part of my normal routine.

I mean, what the hell was I thinking? First I'd ditched Max for taking me to a sex show, only to end up in Amsterdam, where I got drunk and made out with a girl. Clearly I needed some kind of intervention. Clearly I needed to go home.

"Hailey," Clay said, sitting next to me.

"Just tell me," I begged, eyes still closed. "How bad was it? Did everyone see?"

"Well, not *everyone.*"

I opened my eyes to see him clutching his stomach, doubled over in laughter. Well at least one of us was having fun.

"You know what? Just forget it. I don't want to discuss it anymore," I said, starting to stand.

"Hailey," he gasped, reaching for my arm, unable to stop laughing. "Jan is a *guy.*"

"What?" I sank back down onto the bed, narrowing my eyes at him. "How can Jan be a guy? I thought you said Jan was a girl?"

"Jan is a girl, but her real name is Janice. That's who you were dancing with. But you were just dancing, nothing more. And you weren't on a table; you were on a dance floor." He smiled. "Whereas, Jan"—he pronounced it *yawn*—"is a guy. He's in advertising, lives in Amsterdam, and was quite taken with you."

"Did we kiss?" I asked as the memory of this Jan dude began to resurface—blond hair, blue eyes, slim build, milky skin, nice smile . . .

"Nope, no contact. I swear," he said, lifting his right hand. "Though he does want to take you to dinner."

I just sat there, staring at Clay. "You better be telling the truth," I warned.

"I'm serious. *Nothing* happened. But Jan is a hottie. You should definitely call him."

I shook my head and headed for my suitcase. "Forget it," I said, unzipping my bag and looking for something clean to change into. "It's time to fly home."

By the time I got back in town, there was a mountain of mail to sort through. Most of it was addressed to Kat, but some of it was for me—like the one addressed to Current Single Resident, my Atlas AirMiles Visa card statement whose heft and bulk was probably a bad sign, and a plain, white self-addressed stamped envelope that was either from my gynecologist reminding me of my yearly appointment, or one of the six publishers I'd sent my manuscript to. And like a jury coming back from a speedy deliberation, I knew that a quick reply from a publisher was not a good thing for me.

I tossed the mail aside, dropped my bag in the hall, slipped into my favorite, scruffy robe, poured myself a glass of water, and then settled in at the kitchen table with Kat's mother-of-pearl letter opener in one hand and the mysterious envelope in the other.

And unfolding a piece of stark white letterhead with the words CHANCE PUBLISHING HOUSE in black, block lettering, I read:

Dear Ms. Lane,

Thank you for submitting your manuscript. I enjoyed reading about your protagonist's adventures, and thought you captured the world of a seventeen-year-old girl in a very realistic way.

However, I was somewhat concerned by her friend's betrayal, and how her parents were never there when she needed them. It is my belief that children need boundaries, and with the chaotic household you provided, coupled with the lack of available role models, I don't think you've given your protagonist a fair shot.

And even though she manages to overcome all of her hardship by the end, I still believe you've made her work much too hard for it.

If you'd be interested in rewriting this story, with at least one supportive parent, less hardship, more defined boundaries, and nicer friends, I'd be interested in reading it again.

Sincerely,
Martina Rasmussen

After the third reading I still wasn't sure what to make of it. Because while it obviously wasn't an outright rejection of my writing skills, it was definitely a big thumbs-down to my parenting skills. I mean, was this lady crazy? Was she really calling me a bad mother? Because according to her letter, it was clear she thought I was doing a very poor job in raising my *fictional* character, making me wonder if I should expect a visit from child protective services.

I scanned the letter one last time before folding it up and shoving it back in the envelope. Clearly this Martina person was totally delusional, confusing fiction with reality and not understanding that the unstable parents and self-serving friend were the whole point. That without the struggle, hardship, and ultimate triumph, there would be no story.

Shaking my head, I headed down the hall toward my room. Martina was giving me a chance to make my biggest dream come true.

And all I had to do was change my entire story.

Flight attendants are required
to conduct a Mental Review
prior to takeoff and landing,
including but not limited to:
    Availability of equipment
    Location of nearest exit
    People who can help
    People who need help

24

I was standing in front of the full-length mirror, twisting and turning and trying to make sure the big taffeta bow on the back of my dress was tied just right. Then I leaned in and inspected my hair, plumping and fluffing the spiral curls that sprayed like confetti from the small pearl clip at the crown. And then, slipping my suntan-colored, nylon-clad feet into a pair of lacy, sea-foam green, dyed-to-match pumps, I glanced at the clock, confirming there was just enough time to grab a cab and head down to the East Village for the annual Bridesmaids' Ball that I hadn't been invited to in the last four years.

The Bridesmaids' Ball was held around the same time every year, but not necessarily at the same location. And the best thing about this group was that even though the members might come and go, nobody dissed you when you were happily conjoined, and they always welcomed you back when you weren't. All they asked in return was a contribution toward the booze and food, and that you show up wearing the ugliest bridesmaid dress you'd ever been forced to wear.

Having stood on the sidelines in my fair share of nuptials, I had no shortage of dresses to choose from. But not willing to risk actually running into one of my married friends and being forced to acknowledge that, yes, she was right, I really could wear the dress again, I chose one I'd worn just two months out of high school, when a former classmate of mine decided it was as good a time as any to get hitched.

I gazed in the mirror, amazed at how the dress still fit and that my hair looked exactly like it did back then, when obviously, so much had changed. I mean, taffeta was out, I no longer listened to Hootie and the Blowfish, and I had no idea what had become of that friend.

I slipped into Kat's Burberry trench coat, figuring I could hide beneath it, and use it as a sort of shield to get me to and from the party in peace. But after buttoning the front and tying the belt snugly around my waist, there was no denying I'd been reduced to a khaki blob of misshapen seams battling against an insurgence of taffeta, bows, and crinoline that refused to be contained. So after shrugging it off and leaving it behind, I convinced myself that the only people I'd run into would be either similarly attired or completely anonymous. Then I walked out the door and got in the elevator, hoping I could ride all the way down without a single stop.

So far so good, I thought as the car began its descent. But then feeling that unmistakable swoop as it neared a waiting floor, I quickly retrieved a book from my purse, feeling thankful that if nothing else, six years of airport delays had taught me to always carry something to read.

As the doors slid open, I held my book high, shielding my face as I peeked at the floor, noticing I'd just been joined by two pairs of Nikes, one pair of driving mocs, some black pointy-toed boots, four furry paws, and a twitching black nose that immediately started sniffing at the lacy hem of my dress.

Determined to ignore the terrier, now straining at his leash to get a whiff of my pantyhose, I focused back on my book, rolling my eyes in frustration as the elevator came to another stop just three floors down. And this time as the doors slid open, we welcomed a pair of gold Jimmy Choos I was already coveting, blue rubber flip-flops that New Yorkers use for pedicures and Californians for any event not black-tie specific, and freshly shined, black Ferragamo loafers, all jockeying for position on the small square floor.

Still hiding behind my book, I pressed my back against the wall, trying to make room for the newcomers while gazing down to see my dress moving, shifting, and sending layers of fabric rushing to the front, where it bulged out in a big, bulbous cloud of green. And as I casually tried to rein it in and make myself smaller, less obtrusive, Mr. Ferragamo loafers decided to break the international code of elevator etiquette (silence and anonymity) and say, "So how *is* that book? Any good?"

I recognized the voice immediately. Then quickly dismissed it. It was ridiculous! Insane! And I was just being paranoid. So without looking up, I simply nodded and mumbled, "Mmm-hmm."

And just when I thought it was over, he leaned in and said, "Hailey?"

I just stood there, cowering behind my book. *Oh crap. Oh no. Please, don't let it be,* I pleaded to whoever was in charge of things like elevator karma.

"Is that you?"

Staring at the floor, I watched as heels shifted, bodies pivoted, and paws scraped as all occupants of the overstuffed can turned to get a closer look at the girl in the big poufy dress who suddenly had a name. And even though the moment only stole thirty seconds of my life, to me, it felt infinite. And the worst part was, I knew I had no choice but to look up, and own up.

"Oh, hey," I said, nodding casually, and smiling politely as though there was nothing at all strange or unique about my appearance. As though dressing like one of those limited-edition porcelain dolls sold on QVC was just one of my cute little quirks.

"What're you doing?" he asked, squinting at me as the elevator reached the ground floor and the doors finally opened.

"I'm running late," I said, wondering if it would seem rude if I blocked the Nike twins, pushed the Jimmy Choo lady, and hurdled over the dog, so that I could get the hell out of there.

"I mean, what're you doing *here*?" he asked, trailing beside me like one of those customs dogs tracking a suspicious immigrant.

"I live here," I said, turning to face him. *I mean, jeez, is that so hard to believe? And like, is it really any of his business?*

"You *live* here?" he asked, obviously shocked, which made me wonder if it was just the mere coincidence of it all, or the massive mortgage that had him so dismayed.

"Yup. I'm in the penthouse," I said, turning away and heading for the lobby.

"I live here too," he said, determined to continue the small talk. "Though not in the penthouse. Apparently I'm in the wrong profession." He laughed.

"What's that supposed to mean?" I asked, turning to scowl at him.

"Uh, nothing. I guess I should've become a flight attendant, that's all." He laughed again.

But I just looked at him, eyes narrowed. "You wouldn't make it to takeoff," I said, turning on my lace-covered heel, not entirely sure what I'd just meant by that, though I felt like I had to say something. *I mean, how dare he act surprised that I live in the penthouse! Like it was so out of my reach or something! Well, maybe, technically, it is—but still, how dare he live here!* I'd changed all my routines, and was now trekking all the way across the park just to buy my books and lattes! But apparently, that wasn't good enough. Now I'd have to start taking the service elevator too! I shook my head and sprinted toward the door, anxious to get outside and into a cab.

And that's when I ran smack into Cadence.

"Oh, sorry," she said, even though it was clearly my fault.

"Um, it's okay," I mumbled, feeling flustered and ridiculous and just wanting to disappear.

"Are you ready? The car's waiting." She looked at Dane, who was once again standing right beside me.

"Where're you headed?" he asked, taking in my hair and dress and keeping his face remarkably straight for someone beholding such a view.

"Um, downtown," I said, following Cadence outside.

"So are we. Hop in, we'll give you a ride," he offered as the driver held the door open.

"Oh. But I'm going *east*," I said, assuming they were headed west, like to SoHo, or the West Village, or wherever Cadence's big-shot publishing buddies hung.

"So are we. Come on." He nodded, sliding toward the middle.

I stood there, hesitating on the curb, trying to think of another good reason for why I couldn't possibly share a ride with them. And then the light turned green, and since the car was double-parked, like a million horns started honking. And then someone yelled, "Get in da fuckin' car already!"

And before I knew it I was in the town car sitting next to Dane, who was sitting next to Cadence, who was talking on her cell phone as we weaved our way downtown.

"So, what's this?" he asked, eyeing my Malibu Barbie nylons, lacy pumps, poufy dress, and matching hair. "Prom night?"

"Not quite," I said, cringing at how prim I'd just sounded, but unwilling to give up the details. My outfit was humiliating enough when I was alone in my bedroom, but in close proximity to Cadence, with her slinky cami-and-skirt combo, I just wanted to dig a hole and bury myself.

We rode along in silence. Well, Dane and I were silent. Cadence sat facing the window with her phone pressed tight to her ear, saying things like, "Uh-huh," "Nu-uh!" and "Oh!" leaving me to hope she was better on paper.

And then before I could stop myself I looked at Dane and said,

"I'm going to a party. It's called the Bridesmaids' Ball, and you're supposed to show up in an ugly bridesmaid's dress. But other than that it's just a normal party, with good music, great people, lots of food and drink, and a contest at the end for the person wearing the ugliest dress." I paused for breath, realizing I'd just sounded like some sweaty sinner in a confessional. I guess I've never been one for the awkward, prolonged silence.

"What do you win?" he asked, looking at me and smiling.

"A bouquet," I said, gazing out the window and noticing it had just started to rain.

"Well, don't take this the wrong way, but I think you have a really good shot at it." He laughed. "Is this an annual thing?"

"Yeah, but I haven't gone for the last few years." I shrugged, glancing over at Cadence, who was still on her cell.

"Why not?"

"Well, you have to be single to attend," I said, feeling myself blush for no good reason.

"And for the last few years you didn't qualify?" he asked, leaning toward me, which was a little creepy considering the already too-close proximity.

But I just nodded, and gazed out the window again.

"Are there any groomsmen at these parties?"

"Not really." I shrugged. "It's mostly just bridesmaids and, of course, the requisite gay counterparts." I laughed.

"Very interesting." He nodded, smiling at me as I accidentally looked into his deep blue eyes. "So, have you heard from any of those publishers?" he asked.

"What publishers?" Cadence snapped her phone shut as her eyes darted from Dane to me.

Great. The last thing I needed was to have this discussion now. I mean, wasn't it bad enough that he'd caught me in the world's most hideous dress and head-banger hair? Did he really need to drag me down another notch? In front of *her*?

I shook my head and looked out the window. And when I saw

the light change to red, I knew I had to act fast. "Oh, this is me!" I said, throwing the door open and hurling myself out of the car. And then for no apparent reason other than sheer nervousness, awkwardness, and just all-around ineptness, I thrust a ten-dollar bill at him. "Thanks for the ride." I smiled as the rain poured steadily down my back.

"What's this for?" he asked, staring at the crumpled-up ten. "We're not even downtown yet."

"Oh, well, what I meant was I was headed downtown compared to uptown. I didn't mean *downtown* downtown," I lied, cringing at the sound of that while wondering where the nearest subway station was.

He just sat there, giving me a strange look as Cadence lowered her head to peer at me too.

Then the light turned green, and somebody behind us yelled, "Make up your fuckin' mind!"

And I slammed the door and sprinted toward shelter.

25

After all these years of flying, one of the best parts of the job was the ability to control my own schedule, allowing myself to work as little or as much as I wanted. One of the worst was how easy it was to get overambitious to the point of my own detriment.

Originally I'd thought living in Kat's place, rent-free, was the perfect opportunity to fly less. But now, with the gloomy memos Atlas management was dumping in my electronic mailbox on a daily basis, making liberal use of phrases like "challenging times," "unprecedented hardship," "tough decisions," "streamlining over-head," and my own personal favorite, "Pension Transformation Program," I knew that like a squirrel storing away nuts for the winter, I'd better start making as much money as possible while the big dogs at Atlas were still able to sign the checks.

Not to mention that I'd yet to hear back from any of the other five publishers I'd sent my manuscript to, which meant I couldn't quite rule out Martina's suggestions. Even though I was convinced she was completely insane.

So with nothing better to do and nowhere else to go, I threw myself into flying like never before, picking up trip after miserable trip until three weeks later, when my masochistic month ended in a showdown with Helga.

Although it had actually started six years before, back in the days when I was as green as my uniform was blue. Four of us had been huddling in the coach-class galley, leaning on the filthy beverage carts we'd just decorated with clean linens, overflowing ice buckets, Styrofoam cup towers, sleeves of gingerbread cookies, and one gray plastic pitcher filled with coffee we served as regular but was actually decaf.

"Decaf for everyone. We want to keep them tired and groggy," said Helga, who with thirty years of seniority, a thick German accent, and a mean look in her eye was someone I wasn't willing to tangle with.

And with the seat belt sign already extinguished, the plane at cruising altitude, and the carts dressed and ready, it was time to choose a partner.

Since I was new, I didn't know it was standard practice to just nod at the person next to you, grab a cart handle, and start pushing your way up the aisle. But on that particular day, with Helga at the helm, she took one long withering look at me, pointed to the flight attendant on my right, and said, "I want to work with her. The pretty one."

And that was that.

But six years had passed, and I'd learned a few things. Like,

A. You shouldn't hide out in the lav while the rest of your crew is still working.
B. You shouldn't be so vocal about wanting to work with just the pretty people.
C. Everybody hated Helga.

So during briefing, when it became clear that Helga had no recollection of me, or her earlier snub, I knew my moment had finally come.

"Why don't we work together?" I said, smiling brightly, with no real plan in mind, but confident in my ability to wing it.

But Helga just shrugged, mumbled something about being exhausted from her Frankfurt commute, and, grabbing the cart, started pushing so hard she nearly ran me over.

As we made our way up the aisle, her pushing forward, me fake-pulling backward, I decided I'd get my revenge by taking my time, by engaging in what I'd learned early on never to do—converse with the customers and actually look them in the eye while serving. I was more than willing to make the sacrifice, especially if it brought an end to Helga's reign of terror, since it would leave her with no choice but to pick up some of the slack for a change.

So I started chatting, and laughing, and treating each row of passengers as though I was hosting this fabulous party for 226 strangers. And when I saw how much it annoyed Helga, with her constant eye rolling, German obscenity muttering, and head shaking, I started making up errands.

"Oh, you'd like a celery stick for that Bloody Mary mix? Let me go see what they're hiding up in first class!" I'd said, waving good-bye to Helga and disappearing behind the mesh cabin divider.

But after returning from a long, drawn-out search for chocolate mints I knew we didn't have, Helga was gone. And the remaining passengers had turned the abandoned beverage cart into an open bar.

Maybe I carried it just a little too far, I thought as I shooed away the booze stealers and picked up the pace. But as the rows and minutes ticked by with absolutely no sign of her, I knew she was taking one of her infamous "lav naps" and wouldn't be emerging any time soon.

And that's when I learned the truth about revenge. I may have been serving it cold, but like bad coach-class lasagna, it was repeating on me.

As I continued down the aisle, I quickly regressed to my old ways of monosyllables and generic greetings. Though unfortunately the passengers I'd left in my wake were unaware of my recent reversal. And still under the impression that I'd do just about anything to ensure their comfort and safety, they started ringing their call lights and asking for refills, cookies, complementary headsets, pillows, blankets, newspapers, magazines—one even requested a scoop of palate-cleansing sorbet.

I knew I was responsible for this mess. It was just the natural consequence of pretending to care. But the truth was, I didn't care. And I was completely over it. I mean, Helga was probably deep into the REM stage, while I still had thirty rows to go.

Shaking my head, I continued pushing that two-hundred-pound beast down the aisle, tossing cookies like bread crumbs to pigeons, and flipping pop-tops till my calluses bled. And as I wiped my sweaty brow and gazed upon the endless rows of needy people, their mouths stretched open like newly hatched birds anxiously awaiting their share of regurgitated food, I cursed that horrible Helga, along with my own delusional dream of thinking I could change her when countless others had already tried.

And as I felt someone creep up from behind, tapping me gently on the shoulder, I thought, *That's it! This is the passenger who's going to suffer for the sins of the others! I may lose my job, and they may not remember my name, but like the legendary stewardess before me, who after a self-important passenger's repeated screams of "Do you know who I am?" grabbed the PA and announced, "There's a confused man in first class who doesn't know his name. Can someone please come and identify him?" they'll remember this!*

Clenching my jaw and narrowing my eyes, I slammed down a plastic cup of ice so hard I lost some cubes, and as I turned on my heel, ready for battle, I was faced with a tiny little person with Coke-bottle glasses, a shiny bald head, a withered arm, and a weird hump on his back. And he was bearing the loveliest, most genuine smile I'd seen in the last six years.

And that's when I learned about karma. Except I already knew about karma; I'd just temporarily forgotten. So I gave him the extra napkin he asked for, along with a pillow, a blanket, a sleeve of cookies, and a complementary headset he probably didn't want. I even mumbled something about sorbet.

Then I finished the service, parked the cart, and rigged the bathroom door so Helga couldn't get out.

After crawling home from the bus stop in complete and total exhaustion, I grabbed my stack of mail, sorting through it as I rode the elevator to the top. And as I opened the door and dropped my bag in the hall, I noticed the very last one was from Atlas. And something about the plain yet official look of the envelope made my stomach fill with dread. But like pulling a bandage from a knee, I knew I had to act fast. So after ripping into it and unfolding a single sheet of paper, I quickly skimmed over it.

> We've entered a time of NEW CHALLENGES that have resulted in a CHANGED BUSINESS LANDSCAPE such that we have no choice but to embark on a RADICAL CORPORATE TRANSFORMATION, which will unfortunately result in the FURLOUGH OF NINE THOUSAND Atlas employees, blah blah blah.

Then, at the very bottom, it stated:

> Be aware that seniority numbers 13,400 and higher may be affected.

I was number 13,802.

"Hailey? Hello, hello, can you hear me?"

"Oh, hey Kat," I said, rubbing my eyes and squinting at the clock, shocked to see that it was already 10:45 in the morning.

"I didn't wake you, did I?"

"Um, no. Of course not," I lied. "I'm just sitting here reading the paper." I rolled over and looked out the window, but the apartment was so high up all I could see from my bed was blue sky.

"How are the kids?"

"The cats are great, but I can tell they really miss you, especially Conrad," I said. "So how's Greece? Are you in Athens?"

"Greece is wonderful, so relaxing. We were in Athens up until yesterday, but then we decided to visit Yanni's villa in Mykonos. It's so beautiful; everything is white."

"Great," I said, debating whether or not I should get up and actually do something with my day, but then quickly deciding against it and tucking the down comforter snugly under my feet.

"And how are you? How's the writing and flying?"

"The writing? Well, I guess it's on standby since it's not really going anywhere. And the flying, well, Atlas has just informed me that there's a good chance they'll be laying me off. Though they make no promises." I closed my eyes and bit down on my lower lip.

"Sorry?" she said. "I'm on a cell and I couldn't quite hear you. Now what did you say?"

"I said I'm getting laid off!" I shouted, suddenly sitting upright with the phone clutched tight to my ear.

"Oh Hailey, that's terrible."

"Tell me," I said, no longer wanting to explain that Atlas and I were actually still in the trying-to-make-it-work stage. That we hadn't yet decided whether or not we'd split.

"Come to Mykonos," she said.

"Oh, no. I can't. I need to stick around and figure something out. Find a new job, start a new book, *something*."

"I agree. But all that will still be waiting for you when you return. So for now, you should come to Greece and let Yanni and I take care of you for a few days. Use your free passes one last time for something wonderful."

"But what about the cats?" I asked, having already decided to go and now just trying to nail down the details.

"Call Clay. I'm sure he won't mind."

"Okay, so they need to be fed twice a day, once in the morning and once at night. And Jonathan Franzen gets just a pinch of food. And I mean *just a pinch*. Any more and he's a floater," I warned.

"Hailey, jeez. I got it, okay?" Clay said, shaking his head and taking a swig of his beer. We were having a late-afternoon drink at a bar we'd both determined was located almost exactly halfway between my place and his. And since I was leaving for Greece the next day I needed to get him prepped and ready for duty.

"Oh, and when you're finished feeding Jonathan, make sure you close the door. I don't want the cats to know he's in there."

"What is he—a squatter?"

"A stowaway," I said, reaching for my wine. "You know, you and Peter should stay over. Take one of the spare rooms and turn it into a mini vacation suite, or honeymoon suite, or whatever. I mean, you guys are still together, right?"

"Five months and counting." He smiled.

"So, is this getting serious?" I asked.

"Check this out—the other day I came home from yet another La Guardia–Lauderdale hell trip, and when I walked in the door, Peter had champagne, flowers, scented candles, and a bubble bath all waiting for me."

"Wow," I said, feeling happy for Clay, but also kinda gypped that straight guys rarely did stuff like that. "You know that kind of treatment should be mandatory after a Lauderdale trip. In fact, Atlas should provide a team of massage therapists and posttraumatic stress counselors the second we get back to the gate."

Clay laughed and took another sip of his drink, but I wasn't joking. Certain routes had earned certain reputations, but the La Guardia to Fort Lauderdale route was by far the worst in the business. And it wasn't just at Atlas. Oh no. Over the years, I'd talked to plenty of other airline employees, and it was basically all the same.

Different uniforms, different logo, same exact shit.

It starts with boarding. Every other person boarding those flights supposedly needs a wheelchair—*because wheelchairs get on first*. And with as many as fifty chairs lined up at the gate, you'd better start early if you're gonna have a chance in hell of an on-time departure.

Once the chairs are emptied, wheeled back up the jetway, and everyone is more or less resigned to the fact that complaining the loudest will *not* result in a free first-class upgrade, we are free to board the remaining passengers.

And that's when the call lights start ringing. Since now that the aisles are clogged with 156 people all trying to locate their seats along with a spot for their oversized luggage, those already seated have decided it is the perfect time to indulge in their assortment of pills and medications, and thus they require water—*immediately*.

After struggling against the current of bodies making their way down the aisle, after being shoved into armrests and battered by bags, after somehow miraculously *not* spilling the entire tray of waters before they reach their final destination, the preflight water service is complete, and a brief period of relative calm overcomes the cabin during the showing of the safety demonstration.

But as the flight attendants get securely strapped into their jump seats and the plane enters one of the most dangerous phases of flight, speeding down the runway and lifting into the air, the call lights start ringing again as passengers let forth a litany of complaints about everything from the cabin temperature, to the way the pilots are flying, to the lack of legroom, to the appearance of the flight crew—and each other.

Once a comfortable cruising altitude is reached the flight attendants wheel the carts into the narrow aisles, signaling that this is a great opportunity for passengers to:

A.   Perform yoga stretches in their path.
B.   Ensure that all bags, briefcases, purses, and extraneous body parts are resting comfortably in their way so that they cannot move around them.
C.   Take a leisurely stroll through the cabin, peeking in the galleys and checking out the lavatories while following closely on the heels of the crew member working the beverage cart.

After moving the cart back and forth, over and over again, so that passengers can get in and out of their seats for various *valid* reasons, after every single person on board has complained about the food (or lack thereof), after every last bit of water, decaf, ginger ale, and tomato juice has been spoken for, it is time to stow the cart and collect the garbage.

Armed with the trash cart, the flight attendants head back into the aisle, where they are prodded in the ass with dirty fingers, half-full coffee cups, filthy diapers, sticky tomato juice cans, ball-point pens, mass-market paperbacks, CD jewel cases, coffee stir sticks, shoes, baby bottles, hairbrushes, thermoses, and one time even a small brown dachshund, as everyone assumes they are being ignored, when actually the crew is only trying to retrieve the items in the same order in which they were given.

Once the trash pickup is concluded, the cart is parked and flight attendants are back in the aisles, making themselves available for questions like:

"Did my bag make it on the flight?" *I'm not sure, but I'll be right back.*

"Am I going to make my connecting flight?" *I don't know, but I'll be right back.*

"I liked our last crew better; they all had such cute Southern accents. Why don't you have a cute Southern accent?" *I'll have to check, but I'll be right back.*

On final approach, when flight attendants are required to walk through the cabin performing the FAA-mandated safety check, suddenly the majority of passengers are all too happy to roll up their sleeves and pitch in by pointing out every infraction, real or imagined, that their seatmates may be engaging in.

When the plane finally arrives at the gate and the door is opened, all passengers swiftly leap into the aisle, engaging in a rowdy, pushing, shoving stampede toward the exit. Yet once it's their turn to step off the airplane and into the jetway, they each stop, smile, and say "thank you" to *the pilots* for providing such a wonderful flight.

When the last person has deplaned, the flight attendants make a mad dash into the terminal, running past fifty unwanted, unclaimed, empty wheelchairs—*because wheelchairs get off last*—in an attempt to purchase and consume a dinner from Starbucks in just under eight minutes flat.

And then boarding is announced, and the wheelchairs are quickly claimed, thus beginning an encore performance.

We call this "The Miracle Flight," since immediately upon landing everyone is miraculously ambulatory again. And it is always like that. And it never varies. And now I was actually feeling depressed about the possibility of getting booted from one of our longest-running shows.

"So how long are you staying?" Clay asked, waking me from my reverie.

"I don't know." I shrugged. "I have ten days off, but I'll probably only stay for a few. I'm getting kind of panicked about the layoffs. I mean, have you even thought about what you'll do if it happens?" I grabbed a handful of trail mix and looked at Clay.

"Yeah, I'm thinking about going back to school, and finishing my master's. Peter said he'd help me with the finances." He shrugged. "Do you ever think about going back to school?"

"I do now. Though in my case it would be to finish up my undergrad." I shook my head and took a sip of wine. "We've really been living in a bubble, you know? I mean, I used to think this job was so great, and I truly believed the low pay was worth it because of all the fun we were having. But now, six years later, what do I have to show for it? A passport full of stamps, a plastic key card collection from the cheapest hotels in America, some amusing anecdotes, and that's about it."

"What are you saying?" he asked, giving me a worried look.

"I'm saying that I'm right back where I started six years ago. Single, with no idea of what comes next. You know, after all that happened with Michael, I tried to convince myself that it was the dawn of an exciting new time, a second chance, a whole new beginning. But now I realize I'm just stuck. And I haven't made an inch of progress."

"Don't say that."

"It's true. And now Atlas is gonna have the last word, and I'll be out on the street."

"You'll be out on the avenue. Fifth Avenue."

"You know what I mean." I looked at him.

"Well, what about your book? What's going on with that?" he asked, motioning to the bartender for the check.

I just shrugged. I was in full-on self-pity mode now, which meant I wasn't really into talking about *possibilities*.

"You know, you could call that author guy, Harrison Whatever. Or you could rewrite it like that editor suggested."

"But I don't want to do either of those things," I said, taking a sip of my wine.

"But sometimes you don't get to choose."

"What's that supposed to mean?" I looked at him.

"Only you can decide how desperate you are. Only you know how bad you really want it, and just how far you'll go to get it."

"You urging me to sell out?" I asked, searching his face, curious where he was going with this.

"I'm urging you to explore your options and keep your mind open." He shrugged, dropping a twenty onto the bar.

26

I should have been happy. I was headed to Greece, to visit an island I'd only seen in glossy travel magazines, where I'd stay in a luxurious villa with a good friend and her new boyfriend whom I was very curious to meet. But as I headed up Madison Avenue, gazing into shop windows displaying clothes I knew I'd never be able to afford, I started to feel panicked in a way that I hadn't fully admitted to Clay.

Recently I'd read some hateful statistic stating that 75 percent of women are married by the time they reach their twenty-seventh birthday. So you can only imagine the statistics for the over-twenty-eight crowd. And it's not that I necessarily wanted to get married, or even have kids for that matter. (Dogs yes, but kids?) But something about those numbers made me feel so solitary and isolated—like that lone species, left on the dock, that all the other animals on the ark refused to mate with.

I mean, how did so many women figure out so quickly just who to spend the rest of their lives with?

It was true that most of my friends were married, and the majority of them seemed pretty happy. And even though their husbands were nice, with no glaring personality disorders or fatal character flaws, I had to admit that nothing about them struck me as all that remarkable. And even though just a short time ago I too had been all too willing to settle, now that I'd narrowly escaped a mediocre mingle, I couldn't help but wonder if merely being "nice" was really enough?

I mean, until *death* do you part?

I felt like I'd been on some crazy, never-ending scavenger hunt, like I was the only person still searching for that last, elusive item, while everyone else, pleased with their findings, had packed it up and gone home early. And if I ended up with the treasure, then clearly I'd win. But what if it didn't even exist? What if the idea of an exciting, toe-curling relationship was just another urban myth? And what if I was the last one to figure this out?

Where would that leave me?

Making my way toward the park, I crossed the street and headed for my building. And even though I had errands to run and bags to pack, I wasn't quite ready to go inside. So I leaned against the wall and watched all the people go by.

I loved living here, in this tough, annoying, grimy, wonderful city. I loved how on the surface it was rude and abrasive, until you looked closely and noticed that the guy at the deli actually smiled at you, or that your cab driver waited till you got safely inside your building. But if I lost my job at Atlas, I didn't know if I'd be able to stay. Since in a city full of overeducated, overqualified, hungry, *young* professionals, I wasn't so sure there was a place for me.

"Hailey?"

I looked up to see Dane holding a long, brown leather leash with a beautiful chocolate lab attached to the end, while Cadence and some blonde I'd never seen before walked alongside him.

"Hey," I said, patting the dog's soft brown coat and letting him sniff at my face and lick my hands.

"This is Jake." He smiled. "And of course you know Cadence, and this is her friend Evie."

I looked up and smiled at the ever-glorious Cadence, and her almost equally gorgeous friend. Then I focused back on the dog, putting my face close to his and scratching behind his ears. "Oh, I'm so jealous. I love dogs, and this one's perfect," I said, glancing at Dane and noticing that Cadence was watching me just a little too closely.

"So, remind me how you two know each other?" she asked, still looking at me.

"Long story." I shrugged, in no mood to recap. Besides, it wasn't like Dane and I were friends. I mean, I could barely stand the guy. As far as I was concerned the only thing he had going for him was this amazing dog.

"I was late for a flight and bumped Hailey from her seat. And she was in such a hurry to move she left her manuscript behind," Dane said, smiling happily and making me wonder if he'd ever stop showing up just so he could torture me, or if I should just learn to tolerate it, since obviously, this is what fate had in store.

"You're a writer?" Cadence asked, her eyes going wide while Evie decided it was now her turn to look me over.

Was I a writer? Uh, not according to Martina at Chance Publishing, and surely not next to her. "No, it was just . . . I'm not all that serious about it. I mostly just write for myself," I said, inwardly rolling my eyes at that, but there was no way I was furthering this discussion.

But she just stood there in her designer sweats, gazing at me. And then cute, blond, six-hundred-dollar-shag-haircut Evie glanced at her diamond-encrusted TAG Heuer watch and said, "Well, we should go if we want to be on time."

I watched as Cadence hugged Dane, peering at me from over his shoulder. And when they left, he turned to me and said, "Mind if we join you?" Then he settled against the wall while Jake lay at my feet, his head resting on top of my shoes. "Look at that." Dane shook his head. "He has no loyalties. I've been taking care of him for years now. But do you think he cares? The first pretty girl he sees, and it's like I don't even exist."

I just shrugged and gazed down at the lab, thinking how slimy it was for Dane to start flirting with me, like, the second his girl-friend was gone.

"Do you have any pets?" he asked.

"Well, I'm a nanny for three well-to-do cats, and I also have a goldfish. You know one of those black ones with the bulging eyes? I rescued him from the good life at the SoHo Grand, but I have no idea why. He's arrogant, aloof, and dead set on ignoring me. He's lucky I don't flush him," I said, bending down to pet the top of Jake's head.

"What's his name?" Dane looked at me and smiled.

"Jonathan Franzen."

"Jake is named after a character in *Chinatown,*" he said.

"Jake Gittes? Oh, I love that movie," I told him, surprised that he had such good taste in films.

"So, did you catch the bouquet?" he asked.

I squinted at him. What a weird question, considering what I'd been thinking before he showed up.

"The last time I saw you? The Bridesmaids' Ball? The polyester dress? The lacy shoes?"

"Oh, that. And it was taffeta, by the way, not polyester," I corrected him. "And no. Believe it or not there were several people wearing much uglier dresses than mine."

"You're joking."

"Nope, mine was definitely one of the better ones. Don't forget, I was up against dresses from the eighties."

"Oh, right, shoulder pads." He nodded.

I looked at him, eyebrows raised.

"My mom and sisters were addicted to *Dynasty.*" He shrugged.

I smiled and focused my attention back on Jake, making soft, lazy circles on his head.

"Listen, I know it's short notice, but are you free this weekend?" he asked. "There's another party I think you might be interested in. I know I should have called earlier, but I just found out about it."

"Thanks, but I can't," I told him. "I'm leaving for Greece tomorrow."

He just looked at me and shook his head. "Wow. You come up with the most exotic excuses of anyone I know."

"I'm a flight attendant." I shrugged.

"So is this a work thing?" he asked.

I shook my head, not wanting to explain how I was using my benefits one last time before I might lose them forever. "I'm just going for a few days. Visiting a friend."

"Well, what about now?"

"What?" I looked at him.

"Right now. You're still in Manhattan, I don't see any luggage—what do you say? Wanna have dinner with me?"

"Um . . ." *Crap, he's looking at you waiting for an answer, and you better come up with something quick, because there's no way you're having dinner with this guy.* "Well, I really need to get upstairs and pack," I said finally.

"Maybe so, but you still gotta eat. Besides, I promise to get you home early. Come on." He smiled.

"But what about Cadence?" I asked. *There, how you gonna get around that?*

"She's doing a signing at Border's." He shrugged, looking kind of puzzled.

I looked at him, looking at me. Well, I was hungry. And my refrigerator was empty. And I was getting really sick of takeout. "Okay," I said. "But only if you promise not to talk about writing."

"Whatever you say." He smiled, tugging on Jake's leash. "But do you mind if I drop him off first?"

I glanced from him to the dog, and while I really didn't want to swing by his place, I was also kind of relieved he wasn't going to leave him outside while we enjoyed our dinner. Those tied-up street dogs always look so sad and anxious. So I just shrugged, followed them into the building, and then completely out of habit, without even thinking, headed straight for the service elevator.

"Where you going?" Dane asked as he and Jake both stopped and gave me a quizzical look.

I just stood there, my face turning every shade of red as my secret life of service elevators and Dane avoidance was exposed. "I—"

And just as I was about to offer some lame, highly implausible, made-up excuse, Maurice, the maintenance guy, walked by and said, "Hey, Hailey. Mind using the regular elevators today? We got a mover and we need the space."

I looked at Dane, and he smiled at me, and not another word was spoken as we headed upstairs.

"So this is where Jake lives. But I'm pretty lucky, 'cause he lets me stay here too," he said, opening the door and allowing Jake to make a mad dash for the kitchen, straight to his water bowl.

I gazed around the beautifully decorated space with the gorgeous old rugs and heavy rustic furniture. "Do you cook?" I asked, noticing the hanging pots, the never-ending spice rack, and what seemed like hundreds of cookbooks arranged on a shelf along the wall.

"A man cannot live on takeout alone." He smiled, heading down a hall, with Jake following closely behind. "Make yourself at home," he called. "I'm just gonna change my shirt, and then we'll split."

I wandered around his place, peeking into nicely decorated rooms filled with interesting pieces where nothing matched, yet it all managed to be so seamless. *I could live like this,* I thought, forgetting for a moment that I was currently residing several floors up in Kat's luxurious penthouse. But even though Dane's home might lack the square footage of Kat's, it was luxurious in its own way, sort of rough-hewn, warm, and exotic.

At the very end of the hall I discovered a large den with an over-stuffed couch, an interesting coffee table, some lamps with Moroccan shades, a large flat-screen TV, and two wall-sized bookcases containing a number of titles, all seemingly categorized. I stood before it, gazing at a large group of political books that fell within my own ideology, a good amount of literary fiction—some that I'd read, some that I pretended I'd read—some signed David Sedaris, Nick Hornby's entire catalog, an autographed copy of *The Corrections,* and then right there, smack dab in the middle of it all, was the slim, gold-covered book that Cadence had written.

I glanced at the doorway, making sure no one was lurking; then I grabbed it, flipped it open, and scanned the first couple pages for an autograph, lipstick print, or any other kind of personal mark, all the while holding my breath, hoping Dane wouldn't sneak up on me like he had that day in Barnes & Noble.

And then the second I turned the page I saw it. Directly above the copyright info, in black ink and an elaborate, loopy scrawl, she'd written:

> *Dane,*
> *Thanks for <u>everything</u>! I couldn't have done it without you!*
> *Cadence*
> *XXX*

I just stood there, holding the book and staring at the words until they began to sway and blur. Okay, maybe on the surface it really wasn't all that intimate. But if you looked a little closer, this thing was like da Vinci's *The Last Supper*—chock-full of hidden meanings and innuendo.

First there were the XXXs. Well, technically I guess they were *last,* but they definitely stood out the *most,* which made them *first.* I mean, everyone knows that two Xs mean *kiss-kiss.* Hell, even grandmas put that on birthday cards. But *three* Xs? Not so much. No, three Xs definitely meant something more—like several kisses, or maybe even several *triple-X* kisses. And if that wasn't enough, then there was that *"I couldn't have done it without you"* part. What did that even mean? Was he, like, her muse or something? Not to mention that *"everything"* was underlined. And that could mean just about *anything*.

I stood there, gazing at the page, hands shaky, forehead sweaty, knowing I'd been a complete fool to ignore my instincts and get sucked into a dinner invitation by a guy who was obviously some kind of creepy, pompous, playboy predator.

"Hailey?" I heard him call as Jake's nails scraped against the hardwood floors in hot pursuit of me.

Yup, leave it to the dog to tip him off on my illicit activities. They don't call 'em MAN'S best friend for nothing.

"I was just checking out your library. I'll be right there," I said, frantically closing the book and trying to shove it back where it had come from. Watching in dismay as it slipped from my hands, fell to the ground, and landed hard at my feet.

"Ready to go?" he asked, smiling as he leaned in the doorway, dressed in a dark blue V-neck sweater with a crisp white T-shirt underneath.

The book is on the floor! What are you going to do about the book? You can't just leave it there; he'll know you've been snooping! He'll think you're obsessed with that damn book! Just lean down, pick it up, and put it back on the freakin' shelf!

"Do you like Italian?" he asked. "'Cause there's this great little place not far from here."

The book, Hailey! Hel-lo? Do something! "Um, about that," I said, giving the book a swift kick and glancing down just as it slid all the way under the couch. "You know, I actually have way too much to do between now and tomorrow. So, I think I'm gonna pass."

"Oh." I watched his shoulders sink. "Are you sure? 'Cause we can just grab something quick."

"No, I really should be going," I said, making my way around the couch.

"Okay. Well, maybe when you get back," he said as I headed for the door.

And then, leaning down to pet Jake one last time, I gazed up at Dane, and in my artificial, overanimated, Atlas-trained, "welcome aboard" voice said, "Well, see you later!"

Then I walked out the door and headed for the elevator, knowing full well there wouldn't be a "later."

27

By the time the ferry pulled into port, I'd been traveling for more than eighteen hours straight. But having gotten a decent nap on the plane and a little rest on the boat, I wasn't feeling nearly as bad as I could have.

I grabbed my bags and made my way to the dock, where I scanned the waiting crowd for Kat and her boyfriend, Yanni, whom I was very anxious to meet. But there were so many faces and so much activity that it wasn't until I nearly gave up that I spotted her.

"Kat!" I yelled, hurrying toward her and struggling to keep my balance as the ship swayed against the strong Meltemi winds.

"How was your flight?" she asked, giving me a quick hug before leading me to an old white Jeep she'd parked nearby.

"Good," I said, tossing my bags in the back and gazing at the town's waterfront, noticing how sleepy and quaint it seemed, despite the crazy, winding streets that lay behind.

"Did you sit in business?"

"Not a chance," I said, opening the door and climbing into the passenger seat. "It was overflowing with upgrades, mostly newly-weds and nearly deads. Besides, Atlas seems pretty serious about keeping my expectations low." I laughed. "So tell me, where's this Yanni guy I'm dying to meet?"

Kat pulled onto a paved road with no lines, no stop signs, and no streetlights. "Yanni is out diving for octopus, so you won't be meeting him until later. I thought we'd just head up to the villa and relax," she said.

"Diving for octopus? Is that, like, one of your new hobbies?" I glanced at her, noticing how beautiful she looked with her tanned skin, sun-bleached hair, all-white outfit, and beautiful lapis earrings, the same blue as her eyes. "Island life agrees with you," I said, frantically gripping the sides of my seat as she suddenly, without warning, threw the Jeep in reverse and backed up a narrow, steep hill to make room for a passing car. "And the way you handle these roads is amazing." I hoped I didn't sound as shaken as I felt.

But she just laughed. "It's like life, Hailey. Sometimes you have to back up a little so that you can move forward again," she said, throwing the Jeep into first and heading back onto the road.

We drove for a while, slowly winding our way up a long, narrow road until finally reaching the summit. "Oh my God, is this really it?" I asked, squinting at a spectacular white villa built in the traditional Mykonian style with its flat roof, smooth walls, and bright blue painted shutters and doors. Limestone walkways led to the front, while a profusion of potted geraniums and climbing bougainvillea bloomed all around.

"Turn around and check out the view," she said.

I climbed out of the Jeep and gazed at the wide swath of deep blue Aegean Sea, the colorful waterfront cafés of town, the port I'd just sailed into, and the profusion of small white houses dotting the landscape. "It's like a postcard," I said, reluctantly turning away. "You must love it here."

She smiled. "Come inside, and I'll show you your room."

Dragging my bag across pristine white marble floors, I hoped I wasn't leaving a trail of scuff marks as I followed Kat past a living room that was bigger than most Manhattan apartments.

"I hope this will do?" she said, opening a door to a large sumptuous room done in various shades of white.

"It's perfect," I said, leaning my scruffy black bag against the smooth white wall then heading for the window that opened to the same amazing view I'd seen from the driveway. "But I'm warning you. I may never leave."

Kat smiled. "There's a bathroom through there." She pointed toward a door in the corner. "And you can nap if you want, since I didn't plan anything until tonight. I thought you might be tired after traveling so far."

"Well, I wouldn't mind a shower," I admitted.

"Just call if you need anything," she said, closing the door behind her.

When I woke up, all I could see was white—white walls, white floor, white flokati rugs, white cotton sheets, and transparent white mosquito net fluttering all around. *I'm either in heaven or Greece,* I thought, stretching my arms above my head and glancing at my watch on the glossy white nightstand. *Let's see, it's just after one o'clock New York time, plus seven hours . . . oh my God, I slept until eight o'clock?*

I jumped out of bed and ran for the bathroom, hurriedly rubbing a washcloth over my face while brushing my teeth. Then I unzipped my bag and put on the first things I saw—a pair of white linen drawstring pants, a tight black tank top, and a pair of flat gold sandals. Then I ran my hands through my hair, tore down the hall, and hoped I wasn't holding up dinner.

But when I stepped onto the patio, I found Kat and a very

handsome Greek lounging comfortably and enjoying a cloudy-looking drink. "Sorry I overslept," I said, feeling like the world's worst houseguest.

But the Greek just laughed and motioned for me to sit. "We eat much later than you're used to, which makes you just in time for cocktail hour. I'm Yanni." He smiled, extending a large strong hand, and sparing me one of those limp, wimpy shakes some men give you just because you're female. "What can I get you?"

"What are you having?" I peered at their glasses.

"Ouzo," Kat said. "On the rocks with a splash of water."

"Oh, I don't know. I drank that at some bar in the Plaka once, on an Athens layover, and I can still remember the headache I suffered the next day."

"I have retsina; it's a sort of resinated wine," Yanni offered.

I hesitated, because truth be told, I didn't want either. But I also loathed Americans who traveled the world drinking nothing but Budweiser and Coke. "I'll start with an ouzo," I said, hoping they had plenty of aspirin on hand for later.

"So, this is your first visit to Mykonos?"

I nodded, taking a tentative sip of my drink, surprised that I actually enjoyed the cool, licorice-like flavor. "I've had a few Athens layovers, but I've never been to the islands."

"Well, you're in luck. Because even though Mykonos is one of the smaller islands, it's definitely the most beautiful."

I watched as he smiled and reached for Kat's hand. With his wavy, silver-streaked hair, tanned skin, and beautiful dark eyes, he was undeniably handsome, though there was nothing vain or smarmy about him. In his beat-up Levis and bare feet, he could easily pass for just another local, and not the politically connected real-estate mogul he was.

"Here's hoping your time in Mykonos brings you new friends and plenty of adventure!" he said, smiling wide and raising his glass for a toast. "*Stin iyia sas!*"

I looked to Kat for translation.

"To your health!" she said, tapping her glass against mine.

By ten o'clock all of the guests had arrived, so we headed inside for dinner. And as I followed behind a group of people I'd just met, I realized I'd already forgotten their names.

"Hailey, why don't you sit between Adonis and Eleni," Kat suggested as she headed for the kitchen.

I gazed at the supersized dining room table, knowing I was handicapped by more than just jet lag, ouzo, and an empty stomach. I'd always been bad with names. *Which one's Adonis and who the heck is Eleni?* I wondered. *Did I even meet an Eleni?*

"Pssst! She means me. I'm Adonis."

I looked up to see this gorgeous guy waving at me from one of the middle seats. "Then where's Eleni?" I whispered, taking the seat next to his.

"Which one? There are three."

"Oh. Well, I'm Hailey," I said, smiling nervously, wondering if we'd already met between ouzos.

"I know. You're the reason I'm here."

"What?" I just stared at him. Had I really traveled all this way so Kat could set me up on a date?

"Relax." He laughed, taking a sip of his wine. "You're the reason all of us are here."

I just nodded, feeling even more awkward and stupid.

"So what do you think of our island?"

"Well, from what I've seen it's beautiful," I said, noticing a plump redhead—*Athena? Anastasia? Aphrodite?*—take the seat next to mine.

"Have you been to town yet?" Adonis asked.

"No, but I definitely plan to check it out tomorrow," I told him, noticing how his English was kind of formal, with just the slightest trace of a British accent. "How did you learn such good English?"

"CNN, MTV, *Desperate Housewives.*" He shrugged. "That's how most of us learn it. Your culture is exported to us, and we can't get enough of it."

"You're joking," I said, observing how his green eyes contrasted so nicely with his thick long lashes and smooth dark skin.

"And I also studied in London." He smiled, displaying straight white teeth and nice full lips with dimples on either side.

And the view was so overwhelmingly good that I lifted my glass and finished my drink in one nervous gulp. Wishing immediately afterward that I hadn't just done that.

"Man that's strong," I said, cringing as the ouzo scorched its way down my throat.

But Adonis just smiled. "It's an acquired taste. But if you stay here long enough, you'll learn to love it."

And just as I was wondering how to respond, Yanni and Kat carried in countless dishes of food, and everybody clapped and yelled *"Kali oreksi!"* Which I assumed was Greek for "bon appétit."

I was peering at all of the heaping platters filled with things so foreign, I couldn't identify them if I had to when Adonis asked, "Need a translator?"

"I'm afraid so," I said, gazing at a pile of purple tentacles that could only be the freshly caught octopus from Yanni's earlier diving expedition.

"What you're staring at is *ktapodi salata,* or octopus salad as you might call it; and don't turn your nose up like that, because they're very difficult to catch, but somehow Yanni always manages to bring home the very best ones. And trust me, it's delicious."

I just looked at him and nodded.

"Okay, and this is pasticcio, which is basically a meat-and-macaroni pie," he said, already scooping some onto my plate. "And this is *kalasouna*, a cheese-and-onion pie." He held the platter in offering, and I watched as he served me a generous portion.

"Maybe you should slow down. You know, leave some for the others," I suggested.

"Don't worry; we'll never run out of food." He smiled, reaching for another platter.

He wasn't kidding. By the time he was finished, my plate was piled high with such delicacies as *psari psito,* which translated to grilled whole fish with lemon, olive oil, and oregano; *arni riganato,* which were braised lamb chops in olive oil, garlic, and lemon sauce; *tzatziki* and dolmades, which I actually recognized from my previous forays to Athens tavernas; and some local cheeses that looked a lot like feta but tasted entirely different. And it seemed every time a platter was empty, a new one quickly replaced it.

And even though everything was delicious, my favorite, oddly enough, was the octopus salad. "This is wonderful," I told Yanni, filling my plate with a second helping. "It's so tender. I've only had octopus once before, and it tasted like a Michelin tire."

"Yanni employs a top-secret technique," Kat told me.

"Any chance of getting you to divulge it?" I asked, fork poised in midair.

"Never!" he said, smiling as he opened another bottle of wine. "Though it does not involve hanging it on a line in the hot noonday sun. Whenever you see someone using that dreadful method, you must leave immediately. Run the other way!"

"Sounds like you take your octopus pretty serious," I said, taking a bite of mine.

"*Ktapodi* is a very serious business." He winked.

Food in general seemed to be a serious business, because no sooner had we finished dinner when we were ushered back to the patio for baklava, *melomakarona* (walnut-stuffed honey cookies), and the best fresh watermelon I'd ever tasted. I looked over at Kat and smiled. Man, she was living the good life.

"So what are your plans?"

I looked up to see a tiny woman with long dark hair, heavily made-up eyes, thin red lips, and a classic Greek nose wearing a high-necked dress that seemed better suited to a board meeting than a dinner party. And since I'd grown more familiar with the names, I knew there was a pretty good chance that hers was Stavroula.

"I don't really have any," I said, wiping watermelon juice from my chin. "I just want to relax, hang with Kat and Yanni, go to the beach, see the windmills, explore the town." I shrugged.

"Sounds good," Adonis said, smiling as he approached, and sliding so close I could actually feel the warmth of his body crowd the small space between us. "Let me know if you need a tour guide." He smiled, gazing at me with those gorgeous green eyes.

"Adonis, I'm sure she has Kat and Yanni for that," Stavroula said, her dark eyes darting between us as she laughed in a way that wasn't at all genuine.

But Adonis shrugged. "Just keep it in mind. If they're not up for the job, I'm available," he said, still smiling at me while completely ignoring her.

I glanced at Stavroula sitting before me; her face remained placid while her eyes traveled over me, investigating every square inch. "How long are you staying?" she asked, her voice sounding harsh and pinched, though her English was perfect.

"Just a few days," I said, squirming under her relentless gaze, feeling like a suspicious bag trying to sneak past security.

"Are you visiting any other islands?"

Jeez, she's still staring, and I have yet to see her blink.

"Don't be ridiculous!" Adonis said, shaking his head and laughing. "There are no other islands."

I glanced nervously at Stavroula, wondering if she'd lighten up enough to get the joke, but she just sat there, lips pressed tight, eyes darting between us. Then suddenly, without another word, she got up and left.

What was that about? I wondered, watching as she joined one of the Elenis at the far side of the terrace, where they both turned to glare at me while whispering to each other, reminding me of the time in eighth grade when I inadvertently couple-skated with the crush of the most popular girl in school. I'd paid dearly for that little indiscretion in the form of name-calling, dirty looks, nasty notes and prank calls, and was even challenged to a bathroom brawl where hair pulling was permitted but scratching was strictly forbidden.

And to this day I couldn't listen to "Wicked Game" without an overwhelming feeling of dread.

But when I looked at Adonis, he just smiled as though everything was fine. And even though he seemed really nice, and was indisputably cute, my shin-kicking days were over.

"I'm gonna go inside and help Kat," I said, rising from the bench and moving away from him as quickly as possible.

28

The next day, after enjoying a breakfast of crusty bread slathered in homemade butter and honey, along with two and a half cups of thick, sludgy Greek coffee to wash it all down, Kat, Yanni, and I climbed into the Jeep and headed out to Agios Sostis.

"This is one of the most remote, most quiet beaches on the island, as it can only be reached by boat or car. No busloads of tourists here," Yanni said, smiling as he adjusted his diving mask and gathered his gear while Kat and I spread our towels onto the clean, beige sand.

"Do you ever go with him?" I asked, watching as he headed out for his daily octopus hunt, retrieving a wide-brimmed hat from my bag.

"Are you kidding?" Kat laughed. "No, that's definitely his thing. He finds it relaxing to hunt for dinner; I find it relaxing to lie on my towel."

I looked at her and smiled. "I gotta tell ya, Kat, I'm pretty impressed. I mean, Yanni is wonderful, Mykonos is beautiful, the villa belongs in *Architectural Digest,* the food is abundant—is there a downside?"

"Well," she said, making sure Yanni was out of earshot, even though he was long gone. "His children aren't exactly crazy about me. But they have families of their own now, so it's not like we see them all that often. And sometimes the cultural differences can be . . . a bit of a challenge. But you know, it's always going to be something, Hailey. The trick is deciding if the return is greater than the investment, if all those little annoyances are worth the trouble. And in this case, it definitely is." She smiled.

"Do you think you'll get married?" I asked, remembering how much I hated it when people used to ask me that about Michael.

But Kat just laughed. "I've been married. Three times!" she said, shaking her head and looking at me. "And I'm just not sure I see the point anymore. Besides, I'm perfectly happy with the way things are, so why change it?"

I had nothing to say to that. I mean, not only was she right, but at this point in my life, I had no business doling out advice. So I just looked at her and smiled. Then I lay back on my towel, closed my eyes, and enjoyed the sun.

After a long afternoon at the beach, Kat and Yanni were looking forward to a siesta. But with only a few days left to explore the island, I couldn't afford the nap.

"Are you sure you don't want us to show you around?" Kat asked as they dropped me off in town. "The streets are built like a maze and can be very confusing. It took me weeks to learn my way around." She gave me a worried look.

"I'll be fine," I said, climbing out of the back. "And when I'm ready to head back, I'll just grab a taxi."

"But you have our number in case you get lost, right?" she asked while Yanni smiled and shook his head behind her.

"Yes, *Mom*. Now go get some rest," I said, waving good-bye and heading toward the waterfront cafés, where I grabbed a front-row seat, ordered a frappé, and indulged in a little people watching.

It didn't take long to figure out that Mykonos was an island of contrasts. A place where old-timers on donkeys posed for pictures with jet-setters, where men in thongs rubbed shoulders with the "sixty-five and over" cruise-boat crowd. I watched as two tourists in bikini tops and shorts bought fruit from an old Greek woman clad in head-to-toe black; then, finishing my coffee, I left some euros on the table and headed straight for Matoyianni Street, which according to my map was the main drag in the maze of streets that made up the town.

I was walking along the charming, narrow, whitewashed path when I noticed a sign for a trendy boutique on a little side street. And never one to resist an interesting display and an open door, I stepped inside. And when I was finished in there, I wandered into the one across from it. And then there were two more just a little farther down and to the left. And by the fifth one I found myself so completely lost and turned around, I had no idea how to get back.

Oh well. Eventually I'll find my way out of this maze, I thought as I meandered through the tiny pedestrians-only streets, flanked on either side by smooth white walls housing small apartments, trendy bars, hip boutiques, and a profusion of little jewelry shops displaying gold copies of ancient Greek and Byzantine designs.

Noticing a particularly beautiful pair of hoop earrings, I stopped and gazed into the window, thinking they were so yellow in color they had to be at least twenty-two karats.

"Come inside. You must to try them," said an older dark-haired man leaning in the doorway and smiling at me.

"Oh, no. I'm just looking," I said, eyes still glued on the earrings.

"So you look from inside. Please. Come," he said, waving me in.

And before I knew it I was gazing into a small handheld mirror, with a beautiful pair of intricate gold earrings dangling from my lobes. But when I finally found the nerve to ask the price, I knew they were never gonna happen for me.

"You should get them," said a voice I recognized from the night before. And when I turned, I saw Adonis.

"Oh, well, I was just trying them on," I said, quickly removing them while wondering how he'd found me.

"But they're perfect on you," he urged.

"Yeah, well." I shrugged, thinking about my impending layoff and knowing there was no way I could splurge on a pair of earrings that resembled something Cleopatra might have worn.

"So how was the beach?" he asked, following me out of the store.

"Good," I said, heading down a street so narrow we were forced to walk single file.

"Agios Sostis, right?"

I stopped to lean against a smooth white wall, allowing an old woman with a basket of eggs to pass. "How'd you know?"

"The island is small," he said, looking right at me. "Everyone knows everything about everyone." He smiled.

I gazed at him for a moment, unable to tell if he was serious or joking, and just as I started to move away, a group of mangy-looking cats ran directly across my path.

"Isn't that bad luck?" I asked, watching as they scurried under a gate.

"Only if they're black." He laughed. Then reaching for my arm he asked, "Would you like to have lunch?"

I looked at him, and he was so cute, and I was kind of hungry, but I shook my head no. I had too many places to see, and I didn't want to get sidetracked. Besides, I just didn't see the point. I mean I was leaving in three days, and I'd already seen *Shirley Valentine*. "I'm headed over to Paraportiani," I said. "I want to see it while the light's still good."

"I can show you the way," he offered.

"No thanks, I have a map," I said, holding it up as proof. Then, waving over my shoulder, I headed down a street I hoped would lead me to the famous old church.

After taking over twenty photos of Paraportiani, having my sales resistance severely tested by two pushy salesmen and half a glass of ouzo, and barely surviving a very embarrassing and not so charming encounter with the island mascot, Petros the Pelican, I finally found my way to Little Venice, the area on the very edge of town where the whitewashed buildings butted right up against the water.

"This is supposed to be the best spot for viewing the sunset," I overheard a couple of tourists say, and since that sounded good enough for me, I followed them into the Caprice Bar and out onto the patio, where I grabbed a seat.

I ordered a glass of wine and retrieved the travel journal I'd been dragging around the world for the last six years. Though to be honest, it was really more a grocery list of names and places than an actual account of my experiences. And just as I wrote *Pelicans are only cute from a distance,* I heard someone ask, "Are you using this?"

And I looked up to see a blonde in a tank top and shorts, clutching the back of the empty chair.

"Um, no, you can have it," I said, watching as she dragged it over to a crowded table where Adonis sat.

Well he certainly doesn't waste any time, I thought, sneaking a peek at his date before turning my back on him. *He's probably one of those player types Kat warned me about, the ones who spend entire summers chasing tourists. What did she call them? Greek kamaki?* I shook my head and concentrated on my journal, feeling pleased that I hadn't fallen for his tired old lines. All I wanted now was to finish my wine and enjoy the sunset, and hopefully without being seen.

By the time I'd filled a few pages with thoughts and illustrations and emptied my glass, the sun was reduced to a faint orangey glow at the edge of the sea. And still conscious of the sound of laughter and chatter drifting from Adonis' table, I gathered my things and took a wide, circuitous, yet wholly necessary detour around them, determined to do whatever it took to escape undetected.

I wandered through the labyrinth of streets, amazed at how the town had transformed. Those same narrow alleys that just a short time ago had seemed so quiet and tranquil were now packed with trendy tourists, eager for a fun night out. And even though it seemed like a great town for staying out late, I knew Kat would really start to worry if I didn't return soon. So I weaved my way through the crowds of people as I headed for the waterfront, and the end of the line at the taxi stand.

"Need a ride?"

I looked up to see Adonis standing there, smiling at me.

But I just shook my head, rolled my eyes, and moved up a spot. "You know, back home we have a law against that. It's called stalking," I informed him.

But he just laughed and moved right alongside me. "So, how was Paraportiani?" he asked.

"Even better than the postcards," I said, barely glancing at him. No way would I fall for this *kamaki* crap. It was pathetic the way he lurked around town, preying on tourists.

"And how was the Caprice Bar? Did you enjoy the sunset?"

When I glanced at him, I saw he was giving me an amused look. And I have to admit, it really bugged me. "The sunset was great. And how was your date? Over already?" I asked, smirking as I moved up in line and closer to escape.

But he just laughed. "Did I do something to offend you?" he asked.

"Nope," I said, staring straight ahead. I had just two people in front of me now, and I was hoping they were together.

"Then let me buy you a drink."

I rolled my eyes and turned to face him. "Adonis, I—" And just as I was about to say no, we were joined by his friends from the Caprice Bar. Only the girl whom I'd thought was his date was now unmistakably with someone else.

"We're heading over to Nine Muses. You guys want to come?" They looked at us, waiting.

"I don't know. Do we?" Adonis asked as a vacant cab pulled up.

All around me the bars and restaurants were full, the music was blaring, people were laughing, and with no makeup and still reeking of suntan lotion I wasn't dressed for any of it. But when I looked at Adonis—taking in his tanned skin, green eyes, dark hair, perfect lips, and strong Greco/Roman nose—I thought, *Oh, what the hell. Sometimes you just have to say yes. Besides, he's already been fully vetted by Yanni and Kat, so how bad can it be?*

"I need to call Kat," I said, smiling and stepping out of line.

"How do you think I found you?" he said, grabbing my hand as we joined his friends.

29

"Are you going out with Adonis again?" Kat asked as she loaded up the dishwasher, pausing long enough to give me a look that said I couldn't just brush this off.

"Yup." I closed the fridge and leaned against the door.

We'd just finished a leisurely dinner on the patio, and it was one of the first nights Adonis hadn't joined us. Though he'd be arriving any minute to pick me up for another late night on the town. And the truth was, I couldn't wait to see him. I'd been in Mykonos for a full five days now, which was one day longer than I'd originally planned, and I just couldn't bear the thought of leaving.

I mean, with long afternoons on the beach, delicious lunches, lazy siestas, cocktail hour, and dinner parties that turned into late nights in town, the idea of going back to Manhattan where all I had to look forward to was a stack of rejection letters and a furlough notice was something I didn't want to dwell on.

And as long as I stayed put, I wouldn't have to. Because Mykonos was like the ultimate safe haven, offering nothing but sunny days, zero crime, and a laid-back, life-affirming attitude I'd quickly gotten used to. And as long as I carefully avoided CNN and *USA Today,* I'd never have to think outside the bubble.

Besides, I had it all worked out. I only had two more trips to work near the end of the month. So I figured I'd just call Clay, have him post them on the trip drop/swap board, and keep feeding the kitties until I returned.

Though I knew I couldn't keep staying with Yanni and Kat; they'd put up with me long enough. And I already had a lead on a cheap room in town.

"So, is this getting serious?" she asked, closing the dishwasher and wiping her hands on a towel.

I tried to shrug casually, but I could feel my face turn every shade of red. Adonis was great. He was sweet, smart, fun to be with . . .

"Have you met his family?"

I looked at her. "We've known each other less than a week! He hasn't even tried to kiss me yet!" I said, shaking my head.

"Well, then he is serious." She smiled. "So meeting his family would be the logical next step. Relationships tend to move a little quicker here, Hailey."

I just shrugged and poured myself a glass of water. I had no idea if Adonis was serious, or if I even wanted him to be. I was only looking for fun, and a nice little escape from reality. But dinner with his parents? Not so much. "To be honest, I don't really want to meet them," I said. "His mom sounds kind of scary."

Kat laughed. "All Greek mothers are scary. Especially when it comes to their sons."

"Did you have problems with Yanni's mother?" I asked, taking a sip of water and looking at her, wondering if she'd been holding out on me, as she'd never mentioned it before.

But she just shook her head and laughed. "Yanni is sixty-three; his mother passed away years ago. And from what I've seen, that's the best kind of Greek mother-in-law to have."

. . . .

We were having a drink at the Caprice Bar, which had become our favorite hangout even after sunset, as it was one of the few places in the nightlife-intensive town where you could actually have a conversation. Usually we were joined by several of Adonis' friends, but tonight I was glad it was just us, as I was hoping to get to know him a little better.

I had all the basics covered. Like I knew he'd grown up in Athens, had gone to the London School of Economics, where he'd gotten his master's in business, and that he was preparing to take over his father's company, as his dad, in poor health and spending most of his time on the mainland, could no longer manage his properties in Athens, Thessaloniki, and Mykonos. I knew Adonis spent his summers on the island and his winters in Athens—except for the one coming up, where he planned to stick around as they broke ground on their latest hotel.

But even knowing all that, I still had a lot of unanswered questions. Like why he was still single at thirty-one when he lived in a place where most people married before their twenty-first birthday. And even more important, why hadn't he tried to kiss me?

"So," he said, taking a sip of his wine and gazing at me. "I was wondering if you'd like to have dinner tomorrow?"

"Sure." I shrugged, wondering why he was acting so formal. I mean, we'd had dinner together every night, except tonight.

"I meant, at my home. With my family. My mother will cook."

Oh, great, I thought, remembering my conversation with Kat and wondering what the heck I was getting myself into. Then I looked at Adonis, nervously awaiting my response. And he was so sweet and kind, and if he wanted to bring me home so his mother could cook for me, then how could I possibly say no?

"Sounds good," I said, smiling faintly and hoping my voice didn't betray how I really felt.

And then he closed his eyes, leaned in, and kissed me.

"What took you so long?" I whispered, breaking away.

"I wanted you to want it as much as I did," he said, leaning in to kiss me again.

"You've got to tell me everything you know about her," I said to Kat as I dabbed on some shiny peach lip gloss.

"We've never met." She shrugged, helping me fasten my necklace.

"But what've you heard? What's she like? What am I up against?" I begged. Adonis would arrive any second, and I was desperate for all the heads-up I could get.

"Well, they're quite wealthy, as you know. And even though we've never formally met, I've seen her from a distance, and she seems very . . . well . . . traditional."

"You mean she dresses in black and rides a donkey?"

"No. More like she is the true head of the family, the matriarch, and they all do as she says."

I collapsed onto the bed and looked at her. "That does not sound good."

But Kat just shrugged. "Hailey, I'm no expert on Greek culture, and my situation is a far cry from yours. I'm fifty-six years old! No one's going to mess with me. But I doubt anyone will mess with you either. Adonis is wonderful. And if he wants to bring you home to dinner, then they'll just have to trust his judgment. Besides, you look beautiful." She smiled.

I looked in the mirror, and not that I thought she was right about the "beautiful" part, but I had to admit I didn't look half bad. The long afternoons on the beach had turned my skin a nice golden brown, while the hot, arid climate worked wonders in keeping my frizzy hair tamed and under control. I may have even lost a few pounds, which seemed pretty unbelievable with all the big meals we indulged in.

Then I looked at Kat standing beside me. And even though she was smiling, I knew she was worried about me.

"Kat, I've decided to drop my trips and stay till the end of the month. But I've imposed on you and Yanni long enough, so I'm moving to a room in town."

"Nonsense. I won't hear of it," she said, shaking her head in dismissal.

"But I insist. You guys have been more than generous, and this friend of mine, Chloe, that I met through Adonis, she found a room that's available, starting tomorrow."

"Yanni will never allow it," Kat said, shaking her head. "We have plenty of room, and you're not an imposition. And just in case you haven't noticed, hospitality is like a religion here; it's taken very seriously."

"But you and Yanni are leaving soon, and—"

"I'm afraid I can't consent," she said, her voice sounding final.

And just as I'd started to craft a defense, Adonis pulled into the driveway. "Have fun," Kat said, smiling as she placed her hand on my shoulder. "And don't worry. Everything's going to be fine."

Adonis drove along narrow, winding roads to a part of the island I'd never seen before. But with the absence of streetlights, and the moon still in its crescent stage, it's not like I was seeing it right then either.

He made a sharp turn onto a long, unmarked drive, and we headed toward a huge, sprawling house at the end. And the way the headlights shone, lighting it from below, it loomed large in a way that seemed almost eerie.

"This is your house?" I asked, trying not to sound amazed. But jeez, it was even bigger than Yanni's.

"I know, it's huge," he said, parking the Jeep and killing the engine. "But it's actually three houses. My sister, her husband, and their twin boys live in one; my grandmother is in the other; and the rest of the family stay in the main house."

"And what about your house? You don't get your own?" I joked.

"Afraid not." He shook his head. "I'm not married, so I live with my parents."

I stared at him, cringing. *Oh my God! He lives with his parents?* I mean, I couldn't imagine going out with someone like that back home.

"I know it's a weird concept," he said, noticing my reaction. "It's just how we do things. But don't worry. I keep my own apartment in Athens, so it's not like I'm a complete mama's boy. Besides, nobody lives here year-round; they usually only come for the occasional summer weekend. So most of the time I have the place to myself."

I nodded weakly, feeling embarrassed for judging him.

"And by the way," he said, opening the door, "there are going to be a few extra people joining us tonight."

"Oh?" I glanced at the big scary house that was getting more intimidating by the second. "Who's all coming?"

"About twenty of my closest relatives." He laughed. "But don't worry, it'll be fine."

"If you say so," I mumbled, opening the door and preparing for the worst.

"And one more thing."

Oh God, what now? I thought. *I mean, why did I even come here?*

"I have something for you."

I turned to see a small gray box resting in the palm of his hand. "What's this?" I asked, not entirely sure I should accept it.

"Just open it," he urged.

I glanced at him and then down at the box, hoping things couldn't possibly move *that fast* here. And when I lifted the small, hinged lid, I found the most beautiful pair of gold earrings—far nicer than the ones I'd tried in the store that day.

"Oh, they're beautiful," I said, tracing the intricate design with the tip of my finger. "But I can't accept them." I snapped the case shut and handed it back.

"But you have to! In our culture it is very rude to return a gift," he said, pushing the box toward me.

"That's not true." I laughed.

"Okay, tell you what. You put them on, and if they're hideous I'll take them back, and we'll never mention it again."

"And if they're not?"

"Then you have to wear them to dinner." He smiled.

I removed the earrings I was already wearing and replaced them with the ones in the box. And when I looked in the rearview mirror, there was no denying they were completely stunning.

"So you're keeping them?" he asked.

"Well, they're not exactly hideous." I shrugged.

And then he leaned in and kissed me. And as I kissed him back, I was thinking maybe we could forget about this whole scary dinner thing and just head downtown.

But then he pulled away, looked into my eyes, and said, "Ready to meet my family?"

Upon entering your hotel
room check under the bed,
behind the curtains, and inside
the closet. And don't forget
the peephole.

30

Adonis' mother was named Irene, which oddly enough meant "peace." Because even though she was gracious, and pleasant, and welcomed me into her home, shaking my hand warmly while giving me the triple cheek-kiss, I knew immediately that Kat was right—she ruled that house with an iron fist, and her eyes didn't miss a thing.

And unfortunately, for most of the time, her eyes were focused on me.

We were sitting at the large, food-laden table with Adonis on my left, and a cousin who was named either Christos, Georgos, or Tassos on my right when someone asked me to pass the *kotopoulo*. *Kotopoulo. Kotopoulo.* I gazed at the three platters nearest my plate, wondering which one contained the *kotopoulo*. Was it that lamb dish on the blue-and-white platter? Or the baked fish with his head still attached, cloudy eyes gazing up at the ceiling? Or maybe it was the one that looked like chicken?

Knowing I had only a one-in-three shot of getting this right, and feeling Irene's eyes blazing into me even though she was talking to her sister-in-law, I blindly reached out and grabbed the plate directly in front of me.

Gripping the heavy ceramic platter by its edge, I was struggling to lift it without dumping the contents when Adonis leaned over and quietly whispered, "He means the *other kotopoulo*." And then he picked up the chicken dish and passed it to one of his two hundred cousins whose name I couldn't remember.

Oh jeez, of course! KotoPOULO. Like pollo. *Like* el Pollo Loco. *And I was about to give him the lamb, which is called "arni." Duh!*

I looked down at my plate and cut into my own *kotopoulo* as Adonis gave me a brief squeeze on the knee. "Um, this *kotopoulo* is really good, er, Mrs. Vrissi," I said, still not comfortable with calling her by her first name.

"*Efharisto,*" she said, giving me a crisp little nod. "Do you enjoy cooking, Hailey?"

"Well." I took a sip of my wine. "Not really." I looked up to see her staring at me, her face frozen, expressionless, and I knew I had about thirty seconds to find a way out of this, or at least offer some plausible explanation for my lack of domesticity. "I mean, I'm on the road a lot, you know, for work, so most of my meals come from airports and vending machines," I said, unintentionally tacking a nervous laugh onto the end of that.

"I see." She pressed her lips together in a thin line that bore no resemblance to a smile. "And this 'on the road' bit. Adonis tells me you are an air hostess?" She peered at me from the head of the table.

"Um, I'm a flight attendant, yes," I said, noticing that everyone was now staring at me, which made me so nervous my hands started to sweat.

"Well, I can imagine how that must be very amusing for a year or two while you are still quite young," she said, lifting her wine and looking at me. "And how long have you been flying?"

"Six years," I said, knowing immediately after it was out that I'd just blown the interview.

"Well, I can't imagine you'll be doing it too much longer if you want to start a family."

And to *that* I said nothing. Which was the best move I'd made the entire evening. Obviously we were experiencing a bit of a culture clash, as I'd always thought flying was a great job for moms, since it allowed generous amounts of time off, along with the opportunity for occasional escape. But really, it was a moot point. I mean, I wasn't so sure I was ever going to have a family. And if I did stop flying, well, most likely it wouldn't be by choice.

And even though Adonis had his hand on my knee, squeezing it in a private proclamation of solidarity, I couldn't help reaching up and fondling my new earrings, reminding myself how at least one person at this table liked me.

"Those are beautiful earrings," Adonis' sister Anna said. "Did you get them here?"

She was smiling at me, and I knew she was just trying to smooth the tension by saying something nice. But I also knew it'd be a lot better if I didn't mention that they were a gift from her mother's most cherished son. "I got them . . . a few days ago," I said, cringing at how suspicious that sounded.

"Oh really, where?" asked the ever-alert Irene, slipping on the glasses that dangled from a gold chain around her neck and peering at me from across the table.

"Oh, well, um, I don't exactly remember the name," I stammered. "But it was one of those little shops? You know? In town?" I was sinking, drowning, failing miserably.

"She bought them at Lalaounis," Adonis said suddenly, squeezing my knee even harder. "We ran into each other on her way out."

He bought these at Lalaounis? Jeez, even I've heard of them. They're like the Cartier of Greece!

I looked at Adonis and smiled, feeling myself relax as I sliced a dolma in half. "That's it," I said. "Lalaounis, that's where I got them."

By the time Irene was leaning in for the triple cheek-kiss good-bye, I actually thought she might bite me.

"Your mother hates me," I said the second we were in the Jeep and heading down the driveway.

"No, she doesn't." Adonis shook his head and turned onto the road.

"Uh, sorry but you're wrong. She despises me." I gazed at his profile, wondering how he could have missed all the signs. I mean, if I was sure of only one thing in this world, it was that Irene Vrissi not only hated me, but was casting an evil spell on me at that very moment.

"Hailey, trust me. I know my mother. And believe it or not, that actually went quite well."

Okay, if that went well, I can't even imagine how a bad night might go. That woman had taken issue with my lack of culinary skills (and lack of interest in learning any); my profession and lifestyle, which were completely bound together; and during the dessert course had actually balked at my family tree, narrowing her eyes when I explained that as far as I knew in my convoluted, mostly European, mixed-up mongrel lineage there wasn't a trace of Greek DNA to be found—anywhere.

I shook my head and gazed out the window, wondering how many girls before me had suffered that fate. Maybe that's why Adonis was still single. Irene had scared them off, or turned them into ogres.

"Should we go downtown?" he asked, turning to look at me.

But feeling tired and deflated, I shook my head no. "I think I should just head back to Kat's," I told him, watching in surprise as he pulled over and parked beside a low stone wall.

"Hailey, look at me," he said, reaching for my chin and turning my face toward his. "I didn't bring you home to upset you. I brought you home because it's important to me that you meet my family. And I know in some ways she may seem like a typical pain-in-the-ass Greek mother, but the truth is, she only wants what is best for me. And believe me, that didn't go nearly as bad as you think. You were nice and polite, and yet you stood up for yourself when you had to. Trust me, she will respect you for that."

"I don't know," I said, gazing into his eyes, wanting more than anything for that to be true.

"Listen." He trailed his finger down my temple, over my cheekbone, and around my ear to the beautiful earrings he'd given me. "*I* like you. And if you like me too, then nothing else matters, right?"

And the truth was, I did like him. And like he said, it's not like she lived there. She only showed up for the occasional weekend. So avoiding her in the future should be a total breeze.

31

On my fifth day of calling in sick, Kat cornered me. "What's going on?" she asked, sitting on the edge of my bed.

"What do you mean?" I inserted the earrings Adonis had given me, and avoided her eyes in the mirror.

"Hailey, don't get me wrong, I love the company, and don't want you to leave, but you can't keep calling in sick."

"I know." I looked at her and sighed. "I tried to drop my trips, but nobody wanted them. And it seemed stupid to fly all the way to New York for only five days when I could just call in sick." I shook my head and sat next to her. "I just really love it here."

"And Adonis? Do you love him too?" she asked.

I gazed down at my hands, which I'd been unconsciously clenching. "Well, I really, really like him. I know that much. But love? I guess I've never really been in love. I mean, certainly not with Michael, and he holds the distance record in my sorry relationship history." I shrugged.

Kat looked at me, her face full of concern. "Listen Hailey, you're welcome to stay, for as long as you like," she said, getting up from the bed. "But just remember, it's a lot better to be furloughed than fired." I watched her walk out the door, knowing she was right.

Just a few more days, I thought. *Then I'll say good-bye.*

And then, hearing Adonis' Jeep in the driveway, I looked in the mirror, combed my hands through my hair, and ran out the door to join him.

"I have something to ask you," Adonis said as we strolled through town, holding hands and peeking in shop windows.

I smiled at him, but my mind was elsewhere, still echoing Kat's words and the glaring fact that soon, I'd have to leave. But just because you know something in your head, doesn't mean your heart is in on it.

"Well, you know that I'm staying for the winter, to supervise the construction of our new hotel?"

I nodded, waiting for him to continue.

"Well, I was wondering if you'd like to stay with me?" He stopped, and pulled me against a whitewashed wall, holding both my hands in his and gazing into my eyes. "Well?" he asked, looking scared and nervous while he waited for my response.

"Oh, I—" I glanced at the crowds of tourists, trying to imagine what it would be like when the weather turned cold, the shop doors closed, all the people went home, and we were left with only each other. Would I still think it was magical? Or would I be bored to tears?

"You don't have to answer right now," he said. "Just promise you'll think about it. Okay?"

I searched his face, wishing I could say yes, but knowing it was impossible. "Adonis, that's a really nice offer, but I have a job back home and—" I stopped. I had a job and what? I didn't have an apartment. I didn't have a book deal. All that was waiting for me in Manhattan was the possibility of a pink slip and a rather large outstanding balance on my Atlas Visa card. Oh yeah, and Jonathan Franzen. Though I was willing to bet he hadn't noticed my absence.

"I will take care of you." He smiled, pulling me into his arms and kissing me.

Was he asking me to marry him? Or just shack up for a while? And why was I so tempted? Why was this so damn appealing? I mean, what kind of independent, modern woman was I?

I moved away from his lips and nuzzled his neck, closing my eyes and breathing in his scent, a mixture of sun, sea salt, and Davidoff Cool Water—which I was learning to tolerate.

And as I felt his lips brush softly against my ear, he whispered, "I love you."

I just stood there, pressed against his body, staring at the wall before me. *Did he really just say that? And am I supposed to say it too? I mean, do I love him?*

He pulled away and gazed into my eyes. "*S'agapo,*" he said, leaning in to kiss me.

"Um, *s'agapo,*" I whispered, thinking how much easier it was to say "I love you" in Greek, since it really didn't feel like it was all that serious.

"*Kalispera,*" I said, taking a seat next to Chloe, an American girl who'd lived with Adonis' friend Stavros for the last four years.

"I heard you met the mother," she whispered, looking at me while sipping her drink.

"Yup," I said, glancing at Adonis at the far end of the table, and taking the glass of wine that Panos poured.

"And?" She looked at me expectantly.

But I just shrugged and sipped.

"Come on. She's a bitch, right? Made you feel second-class? Like her son was slumming just by talking to you?"

"It wasn't that bad," I lied, wondering how she could possibly know all that.

"Please." She rolled her eyes, not buying it for a second. "It's all the same. Did you know that Stavros' mother refuses to call me by my name? She just makes this *tsk* sound whenever she wants my attention," she said, her short blond hair swaying as she shook her head. "Listen, there's a lot of us expats living here, and we all put up with it in one form or another. Most of these moms have had nice Greek girls picked out for their sons practically since birth, so when their boys don't play along they take it out on us. Adonis was supposed to marry Stavroula. Have you met her?"

What? Is she serious? I just stared at her, my mind racing back to that dinner at Kat's, and the woman named Stavroula who'd given me the creeps. "What do you mean by 'supposed to marry'? Like, an *arranged* marriage?" I asked. Surely she was joking.

"Kind of." She shrugged. "But not exactly. Some of the more traditional parents like to play an active role in hooking up their kids. You know, like, 'Your son has the hotel, my daughter will inherit the bakery.' That kind of thing."

"Sounds more like a business merger," I said, my head spinning with all this. *I mean, how could it possibly be worth it?* "So why do you stay?" I asked, watching as she slid her blue-and-white evil-eye pendant back and forth across its thin gold chain.

"Well, just look at this place." She shrugged. "It's paradise."

I gazed across the table then, watching as Adonis laughed at something Dimitri said, and when I caught his eye he smiled at me. And as I smiled back, it felt as though nobody else was there, like we were all alone on our beautiful little island. But then Christos spoke, and Adonis looked away, and I was back inside the crowded bar, feeling foreign and confused, with no idea what to do.

•   •   •

"Oh my God, I thought you'd disappeared, got lost in the maze, never to be seen again," Clay said from thousands of miles away as I sat on the patio, gazing at the ocean, with the phone clutched tight to my ear.

"So how are the cats, and Jonathan?" I asked.

"Fine, everything's fine. You have a huge stack of mail, though. And a message crammed under the door from some Dane guy. Isn't he the hottie from Starbucks?"

"What kind of mail?" I asked, not wanting to talk about Dane. I mean, I barely ever thought of him. "Anything other than bills? Or Current Single Occupant? Any pink slips or book deals in that stack?" I asked.

"Nothing from Atlas. But there are three plain envelopes with no return address."

"Open them." I said, closing my eyes and hoping to hear the right words—the life-changing kind.

"You sure? You don't want to wait till you get back?"

I may not be coming back, I thought. "No, just rip into them. But you don't have to read the whole thing. Just skim it and give me the gist," I said, trying for patience, though it felt like forever.

"Well, the first one just basically says—"

"Rejection?" I asked, pressing my forehead against my knees.

"Sorry."

"There's still two to go, right?" I laughed, feeling so desperate I'd actually crossed my fingers.

"Um, yeah, but they pretty much say the same thing."

"Well, there's still two more out there that haven't refused me," I said, talking around the huge lump in my throat.

"Actually, there's one. I just found a postcard that says, well, basically they're not interested."

"Oh, okay," I said, wiping my eyes with the back of my hand, determined not to dwell on the fact that my life's dream had just been canceled, leaving me stranded, without a backup. "Any news about the layoffs?"

"Not a word," he said. "But everyone's on edge, and morale is in the hole, so Atlas has instituted yet another one-day mandatory seminar. This time it's called "Aware," and they promise to pay us fifty American dollars in exchange for one of our days off, when we'll fly to one of five bases to partake in six fun-filled hours of skits, inspirational videos, motivational lectures, heartfelt speeches, and a candid and informative Q and A, in yet another misguided, ill-informed, desperate attempt to boost our spirits and put the bounce back in our step before they file Chapter Eleven and pass out the pink slips. Business attire is required, and those not adhering will be immediately dismissed so that they can conference with their supervisor, and attend at a later date." He laughed.

I laughed too, because that's what we always did when we ragged on Atlas and their stupid evangelical corporate seminars. But sitting here, on the long wood bench, with the sea all wide and glistening before me, all that nonsense felt like it was worlds away. Like it had nothing to do with me. And I had to admit, I really liked that.

"So when are you coming back?" he asked. "Everyone misses you, but no one as much as me."

"I miss you too. And I'll be home soon," I said, hanging up and wondering if that was true.

SOME EXAMPLES
OF UNACCEPTABLE
PASSENGERS

Intoxicated

Under the influence of drugs

Traveling in an incubator

Displaying unruly, obnoxious,
   or disorderly behavior

In a malodorous condition

Naked above the waist

32

On Saturday night I cooked dinner for Adonis. And having never cooked anything other than limp Ramen noodles, burnt rice and beans from a box, and the occasional soggy omelet, I borrowed Chloe's English-language Greek cookbook, figuring as long as I followed the recipes, it couldn't be all that difficult.

I'd been in Mykonos just over three weeks now, writing in my journal, e-mailing Clay, and saying *"s'agapo"* so often I'd almost come to believe it. And it was starting to feel so comfortable and so natural that I'd decided to take Adonis up on his offer.

I had it all worked out. I figured I could keep my job at Atlas by either dropping all my trips, taking thirty-day leaves (I was eligible for six a year), or if that didn't work, then I'd just commute to New York, fly my trip, and return to Mykonos the second it was over. And even though I knew that probably seemed crazy to a regular person, in the world of flight attendants it was just another lifestyle option.

Besides, after six years of city living I'd failed to make a life for myself, so why not try to build one here? And even though the only writing I'd done was just a list of silly observations in my travel journal, I was sure that once I got settled I'd get back to it. Though I was through with trying to get published. Apparently I just didn't have what it takes. Or in the case of Martina at Chance Publishing, I refused to do what it takes, since there was no way I would rewrite my story just to fit her narrow, censored vision. And now that I was no longer writing with the hope of a book deal, I was free to write whatever I chose.

But I hadn't told Adonis yet, as I wanted it to be special. So I figured I could do it over a nice home-cooked meal.

With Irene safely ensconced on the mainland and Adonis off to work, I hopped on his Vespa and headed for Mykonos Market, filling my basket with the necessary ingredients while imagining myself in a crisp white apron, with hair neatly pulled back and skin glowing from the warmth of the oven, as I lovingly prepared some of Adonis' favorite foods. I mean how hard could it be to throw together a dinner of *tzatziki* and pita bread, a finely shredded mixed green salad, cheese-and-onion pie, roasted leg of lamb with potatoes, and baklava for dessert?

But later, as I stood gazing at my self-induced Martha Stewart nightmare, my apron resembling a drunken Jackson Pollock canvas, my hair a barely contained mess, and my face glowing beet red and glistening with sweat, I realized I might have been just the teensiest bit overambitious.

I mean, when I'd first pored over that cookbook, creating a menu and making a list, it had all seemed so easy. But now, confronted with a petrified roast, runny *tzatziki,* a cheese-and-onion pie reduced to a thin layer of crud on the bottom of the baking dish, and a salad dressed in blood as I had accidentally "finely shredded" my index finger instead of the lettuce, the only thing remotely edible was the pita bread and baklava. And that was because they came from a bakery.

And hearing the sound of Adonis' Jeep in the driveway, I started dumping it all in the trash, knowing there was nothing I could do to save it.

"*Ya sou agape mou!*" he called, strolling into the kitchen with a steaming hot pizza box.

"I'm afraid dinner didn't quite work out," I told him, tossing the crusty roasting pan into the sink and shrugging pathetically.

"No problem, I brought provisions," he said, placing the box on the counter and handing me a piece.

"You had that little faith?" I asked, using my fingers to separate a thread of cheese suspended between my teeth and the crust.

"I thought it might be a little ambitious for a virgin." He smiled.

"But I had it all planned out," I said, shaking my head. "You'd praise the meal and fill your plate with seconds as I smiled shyly and told you I'd decided to stay." I glanced at him nervously, wondering how he'd respond.

"Oh, Hailey," he said, looking at me and smiling. Then he dropped his pizza, leaned in, and kissed me.

At first it started as one of those brief, chaste kisses that couples who've been together a while use to replace the deeper kisses that initially kicked off their relationship. But as I turned my head and reached for my wineglass, his lips once again found mine. And within a matter of seconds, we were engaged in a full-blown make-out session.

Staggering against each other, we kissed furiously while our hands worked at ridding each other of the shirts and pants that were only getting in the way. He untied my drawstring as I undid his belt, and then releasing all five buttons on the fly of his jeans, I was sliding down to the food-splattered floor, bringing his pants along with me, when the front door slammed hard against the wall and someone shouted "*Putana!*" at the top of their lungs.

And when I looked up, I saw Irene Vrissi standing in the doorway, eyes blazing.

"*Metehra!*" Adonis yelled, yanking up his pants and jumping in front of me, trying to hide me from her view as I cowered behind him and watched as a very angry Irene Vrissi charged us like one of Hemingway's bulls, letting forth a stream of rapid-fire Greek so completely incomprehensible the only word I understood was the one she used the most—*putana!*

Which basically translated to Adonis' mother calling me a slut.

I grabbed the drawstrings on my pants, racing to get them retied, and by the time I looked up she was standing before us, all four feet eleven of her, hands clenched on hips, lips pressed tight, and cold brown eyes narrowed into angry slits.

"What is this?" She stepped forward, now just inches away, as I hid behind her son, whom I was all too happy to use as a human shield. "You seduce my son? *In my house!* And what have you done to my kitchen? Look at this mess!"

I glanced at the sink overflowing with dirty dishes, the stove covered in crusted crud, the counters slathered with onion skin, meat juices, and cheese crumbles, and cringed.

"Mother, please," Adonis pleaded. "You cannot talk to her like that."

"I am not speaking to you, Adonis. I am talking to her, this, this—"

She pointed at me, shaking with rage, and I knew if she dared call me a *putana* just one more time, I would reach around Adonis and punch her.

"Mother, this is ridiculous. I am a grown man, and if I want to marry Hailey, I will do so."

Um, excuse me? Marry? Uh, who said anything about getting married?

I looked at Adonis, my eyes wide and mouth hanging open in shock as he pulled me close, placing his arm firmly around my shoulders.

"Is this true?" she asked, her eyes blazing into mine.

But I just shrugged and stared at the floor, wishing it contained a trapdoor, or some other easy form of escape.

"I haven't asked her yet, but if she agrees, then yes. We will be married," he said, gripping me even tighter. "I can't believe you tricked me, Mother. That's an all-new low. Even for *you*." He shook his head angrily and started to move past her. And I watched as Irene Vrissi glanced from me to him, then clutched at her heart and staggered backward, as though she would fall onto the cold marble floor.

But I knew a fake heart attack when I saw one, so I just stood there, shaking my head and rolling my eyes as Adonis shouted *"Metehra!"* and rushed to her aid, managing to catch her just seconds before her knees pretended to buckle. "Mother, are you okay? Please God!" he yelled frantically, struggling to hold her upright.

And while Adonis' eyes were squeezed shut, as he begged the gods to spare his mother's life, Irene's remained open, narrowed, and fixed on mine.

And then, gazing up at her son, she whispered, "Why don't you say good night to the girl, Adonis? I'm so weak, and I'm not feeling well."

And I stood there watching in complete disbelief as he lifted her into his arms and carried her up the stairs.

I shook my head, rolled my eyes, and headed for the sink, rinsing all the dirty pots and pans before stacking them in the dishwasher. I mean, obviously Irene was acting out in some kind of frantic, last-ditch attempt to get her son's attention away from me and back on her. So clearly it was only a matter of time before he calmed down and clued in. And while I waited, I figured the least I could do was get the place cleaned up; then maybe we could head out to town and grab a drink at one of the two bars that stayed open during the off-season.

I shut the dishwasher, grabbed a damp sponge, and had just started wiping the counter when Adonis appeared. "Hey," I said, going over to hug him. "Is everything okay?" I searched his face while keeping mine straight. I mean, even though I thought the whole thing was pretty hysterical, I knew better than to be the first to laugh.

But Adonis didn't hug back. He just stood there stiffly. And then taking a deep breath, he looked at me and said, "I think it's better if you stay at Kat's for the next few days. I'm afraid your being here will only aggravate my mother's condition."

I just looked at him, my face breaking into a smile. "Oh, okay," I said, already starting to laugh.

"It is for the best," he said, turning his back on me in a way so final I just stood there, staring at the back of his head, as the truth slowly began to sink in.

Adonis was dumping me for his mother!

"Just take the Vespa," he said from over his shoulder.

"But Adonis—" I started.

"Hailey, you don't understand. She depends on me. My father is ill, and I'm all that she has."

And when he finally turned to face me, I saw that his jaw was clenched tight and his eyes were all red and watery. And knowing that anything I said would be pointless, I just nodded, grabbed my stuff, and left.

I buttoned my coat and flipped my collar up around my ears, to guard against the cold night air. Then I hopped on the scooter, kick-started the engine, and had just flipped on the lights when I noticed a small white car parked at the end of the drive. Assuming it was Irene's, I drove right past it and turned onto the street, my eyes watching the road while my brain tried to make sense of what had just happened.

Obviously I'd been ambushed, sneak attacked, and sucker punched. Hoodwinked in the Greek mama equivalent of shock and awe. But how Irene had found out was beyond me, as Adonis had sworn time and again that she never set foot on the island during winter.

Noticing someone following closely behind, I moved to the side of the road, allowing them plenty of room to pass. And as I watched the little white car go by, with two smiling faces hanging out the windows, I knew.

And I just sat there, feeling breathless and shaken as I watched Stavroula and Eleni speed away. Leaving me with the sound of their laughter filling up the sky and echoing back at me in the crisp, still night.

Then after a while I gripped both handles and headed to Kat's. Feeling thankful she'd had enough foresight to leave me a key.

33

"I'm going to miss you," Kat said, leaning in to hug me.

"Me too." I gazed around the Athens International Airport, thinking how even though I'd miss her and my long afternoons of doing and thinking about nothing, it was time to get back in the game and stop procrastinating. Because while that life might be great for Kat, I was way too young to retire.

Besides, Kat had no mother-in-law to contend with, and who's to say where I'd be if there'd been no Irene Vrissi. Because the truth was, saying *"s'agapo"* just wasn't the same as saying "I love you." So I guess in a weird way, I had her to thank. I mean, Irene Vrissi had saved me from myself.

"Yanni and I will be in New York in the next month or so. I miss my kids." Kat smiled. "But don't worry. I want you to stay put. My home is plenty big enough for all of us."

I looked at Kat, and I knew it was time to stop taking advantage of her abundant generosity. "I think it's time I find a place of my own," I told her. "But I promise to keep feeding the cats."

She just nodded, and as I turned to leave she called, "Hey, it'll be a New York crew! Say hello if you see anyone I know!"

I smiled and waved, then headed for the boarding area, wondering if Kat missed flying. Probably not Atlas, I decided, handing over my ID, but definitely the people.

As I settled into my Business Select aisle seat, I wondered if this would be the last time I'd get to do this. Because even if by some small miracle Atlas didn't give me the boot, I knew it'd be a while before I'd get this kind of time off again.

Shoving my carry-on under the seat in front of me, I inserted my iPod earpiece and retrieved my yellow legal pad and pen. I'd decided to heed Martina's advice, and rewrite my story the way she suggested.

I mean, ever since I'd finished my first Judy Blume book, I knew I wanted to be an author, a *published* author. And now that I was being given the chance, I knew I had to take it. And even though I still thought Martina was a nut bag, and totally disagreed with her inane ideas, it all came down to one thing—my desire to be published overrode just about everything else. And pretending as though journaling and writing for myself was enough was completely delusional. Besides, everything else I'd tried had failed. So it's not like I had much of a choice.

I was tapping the end of my pen against my pad of paper when someone tapped me on the shoulder. And when I looked up I saw Lisette.

"Oh, hey," I said, removing my earpiece. "What are you doing on an Athens flight?"

"I wanted to fly something different." She shrugged.

"So how's it going?" I asked, thinking this was the most we'd talked since the day I took the apartment.

"Okay." She glanced briefly at the woman sitting next to me, then whispered, "Sorry about the way things turned out."

But I just shrugged. Because while it really wasn't okay, the truth was, I'd gotten over it a while ago.

"Did you find a new place? Because I'm looking for a room-mate." She smiled awkwardly.

"What happened to Dan?" I asked, wondering which one had tired of the red-hot ass spankings first. But she just rolled her eyes and shook her head. And while I did need a place to crash, it certainly wouldn't be with her. Because now that I was starting fresh, I was determined that all of my mistakes be new ones. "Well, I'm actually set right now," I told her. "But I'll let you know if I hear of anyone."

And as she started to walk away, she said, "Oh hey, do you want this? I was gonna throw it out, since it's from two days ago, but you probably haven't seen it."

She handed me the *New York Post,* and I shoved it in my carry-on. Then I focused on my legal pad and got back to work.

It wasn't until I was on the subway heading back into the city and fighting to stay awake that I remembered the paper Lisette had given me. I retrieved it from my bag, and glancing briefly at the cover, I decided to continue my news strike for just one more day. I headed straight for Page Six (which in this particular edition was actually on page eleven), searching for the "Just Asking" section, which was like a Jumble for velvet ropers.

"Which seemingly straight Slavic supermodel slinks out after
   sunset to swap saliva with her same-sex sweetie?"
"Which handsome hotelier is hooking up with a hot hot hot
   Helsinki hellion?"
"Which massive married movie mogul is making moves on his
   male manicurist and masseur?"

And even though I didn't know the answers to any of these clues, that didn't stop me from guessing. Then, after reading about the latest on Britney Spears' marriage woes and Madonna's latest children's book, I glanced at the bottom, where in the lower right-hand corner was a picture of Cadence.

Novelists were not the usual Page Six fodder, unless they were involved in a major real estate transaction, had engaged in something sexy or scandalous (or both), had a drug and/or drinking problem, had written a tell-all about the fashion industry, or in what was probably Cadence's case had so much freakin' beauty and talent that people just wanted to take their picture. So in an act of complete and total masochism, I held the paper close to my face and stared at the photo, soaking in every last detail.

Cadence was wearing a slinky white dress, and gold stilettos that made her legs look even longer than they already were. Her long shiny hair was held in a sleek, low ponytail, and her tan, sinewy arm was wrapped snugly around the waist of a familiar short-haired blonde dressed in low-cut jeans, a tiny white tank, and silver stilettos. And they were both looking directly into the camera, smiling radiantly.

I stared at the two of them, guessing at what they could possibly be engaged in.

Just another night of fun and frolic, and celebrating their fabulousness?

On their way to a Beautiful Members of Mensa photo shoot?

Or had Cadence simply run out to buy the fixin's for her dinner with Dane when she ran into an old friend?

Shaking my head at my pathetic envy, which apparently knew no bounds, I decided to just read the caption and get it over with.

LITERARY SENSATION CADENCE TAVARES AND HER LONGTIME
GAL PAL, EVIE KEYS, ARRIVING AT THE OPENING OF—

Wait—gal pal? I stared at the picture again, my heart beating faster as I studied the photo with newly informed eyes. Okay, this was the *New York Post,* not the *Podunk Periodical,* and the only

time you ever read the word "gal" in this rag was when it was followed by the word "pal." And since everyone knows that "gal pal" is
code for "sapphic sister," "same-sex sweetie," or the more blatant
"lesbian lover," there was no mistaking what this meant.

Oh. My. God. She's gay!

It wasn't until the guy sitting next to me peered over my shoulder, looked at my paper, and said, "Who's gay?" that I realized I'd
said it out loud.

"Um, no one," I said, quickly folding it up and shoving it back
in my bag.

34

"Hailey? Are you better now?"

Oh great. I was in the JFK flight attendant lounge, with just moments to spare before I had to go brief, when Lawrence decided to pay me a visit. I didn't need to look up to know it was him; I'd recognize that smarmy voice anywhere. I glanced up from my keyboard and concentrated on keeping my face calm, still, and expressionless while waiting for him to continue.

"I've yet to receive your doctor's note," he said, one hand placed firmly on his hip while the other fondled his Drakkar Noir–drenched neck.

"That's because I don't have a doctor's note," I told him, focusing back on my computer screen, looking for a good trip to pick up.

"I need a doctor's note," he insisted.

"Larry," I said, knowing how much he hated to be called that. "Cut me some slack, will ya? That was my first sick call in over a year."

"And if you read your memos you'd know that we've recently remodeled the sick-leave policy. You must now provide a doctor's

note for every sick call, making sure it includes the three Ds—
doctor's name, diagnosis, and dates of illness. Yours is way over-
due, and I need it on my desk by the end of the week."

"Fine," I mumbled, refusing to look at him, though his perva-
sive cologne assured me he was still there.

"And make sure you sign up for 'Aware,' as bids are due by the
end of the week. And if you have any questions, please, don't hes-
itate to ask." This last part he said in a loud, upbeat, "we're all just
friends here," singsongy voice that told me the base manager was
somewhere in the vicinity.

"Hey, I have a question for you," I said, turning to face him.
"Why are we spending all this money flying all these employees to
all these bases—springing for food, hotel rooms, and instructors—
when you're furloughing flight attendants, cutting the pilots' pay,
no longer reimbursing us for that measly dollar we tip the hotel
van drivers, *and* according to both the *The Wall Street Journal* and
your daily memos, we're supposedly on the verge of bankruptcy?"

I watched his jaw clench and his face turn red as he glanced
briefly at Shannon, our base manager, and then back at me. "Well,
Hailey, as you know, customer service is the primary, cornerstone
component of this industry," he said in his "Academy Award winner acceptance speech" voice.

I crossed my legs and nodded.

"And with the impending companywide operational transformation Atlas has implemented due to the current climate of
unprecedented industry struggle, we feel it imperative to immediately address the alarming decline in morale and overall lack of
commitment that is currently being displayed amongst the flight
attendant group." He paused, sneaking another peek at Shannon,
who as far as I could tell hadn't heard a single word of this. "So in
response to *your* feedback, we've formed an advisory committee,
who paired with a review board, who then met with an outside
consultant, who instituted a program that we believe will effi-

ciently provide for a positive impact on employee production, resulting in a renewed dedication to the return of profitability of Atlas Airlines." He smiled triumphantly.

I waited for a moment, to see if he had anything to add to that,
but apparently that was all he'd memorized. "Okay," I said, nodding and getting back to my computer.

I mean, I knew I'd have to attend "Aware"; I really didn't have a
choice, as Atlas loved nothing more than their annual flight attendant roundup, where we'd sacrifice an off day to attend a seminar
that would explain the "new direction" the company was taking,
and what we must do to "prepare."

During the last six years, I'd already survived "Backstage Pass,"
where fashion-challenged supervisors tried to convince us that Atlas
Airlines was the hottest, most exclusive ticket in town, while sub-
liminal techno music pulsed in the background; "The Encounter,"
where we lounged in crazy round chairs that required assistance to
get in and out of, drank company Kool-Aid out of a plastic volcano
cup, and watched a film on corporate branding that left us with an
identity crisis so severe we were no longer sure if we worked for
Atlas, Target, Nike, or Starbucks; "Verbal Judo," where we learned
how to be sympathetic but firm oral warriors; "SASSY," where we
discovered that the new Atlas message was Safe Affordable Styl-
ish Savvy and all about You (but that's You the customer, not You
the flight attendant); and "Atlaspalooza," which is still too embarrassing to talk about.

Atlas had tried to reinvent itself so many times, I felt like I was
working for Madonna.

So later that evening, when I returned to the penthouse, I
picked up the phone, called Kat, and asked her to get one of
Yanni's doctor friends to write me a note, including a detailed explanation of my inability to work due to illness, and making sure
every single word was in Greek. I mean, it's not like Lawrence ever
specified what language it had to be in.

Ever since my return from Mykonos, I'd been so busy with flying and writing that nearly two weeks had passed before I actually found time to see Clay.

"Hey," I said, rushing up the stairs in front of the Metropolitan Museum of Art. "Am I late?"

"Not at all." He leaned in to hug me. "I got here early. It's such a beautiful day I just wanted to be outside. Wanna take a walk?" He smiled hopefully.

"No, let's go inside while we can still get in free," I said, fearing the loss of yet another Atlas perk—free membership to the Met.

He looked at me, eyebrows merged together, and I knew he was thinking of the best way to negotiate this. "Okay, one exhibit, a quick spin around the gift shop, and then Belvedere Castle," he offered.

"Two exhibits, ixnay on the gift shop, and then you buy me a pretzel in the park," I said, waiting as he weighed his options.

"Deal," he said finally, trailing me up the steps and into the building.

Attaching our little metal "M"s to our collars, we headed for the Modern Art gallery, both of us talking quickly and listening patiently while we caught up on the events of the last several months that couldn't be properly conveyed in an e-mail or phone call. I mean, some stories required dramatic hand gestures and facial expressions to really get the point across. And as I watched Clay dramatize a showdown with a customer in a T-shirt that read "Fuck You, You Fucking Fuck," which ultimately involved a planeload of outraged passengers, six flight attendants, a gate agent, two OOs (one, a conflict-resolution specialist who taught Verbal Judo), and finally the captain, who resolved the whole mess by handing over his jacket and extorting her promise to keep it zipped until reaching her final destination, I realized it was the first time I'd ever gone that long without seeing him, and just how much I depended on his friendship, advice, and overall presence in my life.

"So have you called him yet?" Clay asked, changing the subject as he stopped in front of a Lichtenstein.

"No." I shrugged, knowing exactly who he was talking about, as Clay truly believed that Dane and I belonged together.

"What are you waiting for?" he asked, gazing at me instead of the painting.

"Listen," I said, turning to look at him. "I know you think he's cute, and now that he's apparently single and not dating Cadence like I thought—"

"All good reasons to pick up the phone," he said, steering me quickly to the other side of the room.

"Yeah, well, I just feel that ever since I broke up with Michael, I've had a few false starts. I mean first there was Max in Paris, and then there was Adonis in Mykonos." I shook my head. "And it's like, even though they were nothing alike, with totally different backgrounds, from totally different cultures, in both those situations I was all too eager to just pack it up and move, to say *adiós* to my life so that I could go live theirs. And it wasn't until I was confronted with some huge, glaring flaw that I woke up."

"But Hailey—" Clay started, then abruptly stopped, probably because he knew I was right.

"And the fact is, I have to build my own life, from my own dreams, before I can go merging with someone else. And if I keep allowing myself to get sidetracked, that will never happen. I mean, how many men do you know who let some woman distract them from their goals?"

"But you can build your life *and* call Dane. It's not like he lives in Europe; he's just a few floors down!" He looked at me, and I knew he thought I was crazy, but I was serious about what I'd said, and this time I was planning to act on it.

"Look at them," I said, pointing to Botero's *Dancing in Colombia*. "They're having a great time."

"Don't change the subject."

"Clay, forget it, I'm done. Besides, I can barely stand the guy. And if you were ever forced to hang around him for more than a few seconds you'd know exactly what I mean. He's arrogant and annoying, and he acts like he's this major player in publishing, when the reality is he's just a creepy . . . sapphic sycophant."

"A what?" Clay looked at me, eyebrows raised.

"I just made that up. You know, like the male version of fag hag?"

"That'll never catch on." He laughed.

But I just shrugged. "Look, I'm not calling him, and that's final. I'm revising my book, saving my money, and I'm through with dating. So tell me, what's going on with you?"

"I'll tell ya," he said. "But only if we go to the park."

We made our way outside and headed straight to Central Park, where we stopped at a cart and bought some warm, salty pretzels and a couple bottles of water. And just as we were strolling down the path toward the castle, Clay sighed and said, "Peter and I are moving."

I stopped in my tracks and stared. "But, when? And where? And what about Atlas? And what about *me*?" I cried.

"Okay," he said, nervously twisting the cap on his water bottle. "When? Soon. Where? California. Atlas? I'm either taking a leave, getting furloughed, or quitting so I can go back to school. And you? Well, that's the hardest part."

I stood there looking at Clay. If he was happy, then I was determined to be happy for him. But that didn't mean I wasn't devastated for me. "How did this happen?" I asked.

"Peter got a promotion that required a transfer to Los Angeles. And you know how I've always loved California, and you know how I'm so over these winters. So when he asked me to join him, I said yes. I'm hoping to get into UCLA, so I can get my master's in psychology."

"And how soon is soon?" I asked, blinking hard and trying not to cry. He was my best friend in the whole world, and he'd been such a major part of my life for the last six years I had no idea how I'd fill the big empty space he'd leave behind.

"Well, we're headed there this weekend to look for a place to live, and then we'll probably be moving shortly after that. But Peter's so attached to New York he's determined to keep the apartment. So we were wondering if you'd want to sublet?"

"Are you serious?" I asked, tearing off a piece of my pretzel and searching his face. I'd been to the apartment only once before, but I remembered it as being full of light, with a surprising amount of storage space.

"We'll leave most of the furniture, so you won't have to worry about that, and I know he'll keep the rent reasonable, since he'd rather have someone in there that he can trust. So, are you interested?" He looked at me.

I did need a place to live, and so far everything I'd seen was either out of my league or completely unlivable. But I wasn't sure I was up to staying in his old place, using his old furniture. I mean, it would seem weird without him. "I have to think about it," I said, slipping on my sunglasses so he wouldn't see me cry.

Then I leaned into him, and he put his arm around me, and we headed toward the castle.

I had just left the service elevator and was rushing through the lobby on my way to meet Clay and Peter for dinner when I ran smack into Dane and Jake. And having no choice but to acknowledge them, I reached down to pet Jake while carefully avoiding eye contact with his owner, as he'd recently crammed another message under my door that I hadn't bothered to answer.

"How've you been?" he asked.

"Great! Really, really busy though, flying, writing . . ." I met his eyes reluctantly, knowing I wasn't at all convincing.

But he just nodded. "Where you headed?"

"Mark's. My best friend and his partner are moving to L.A., so we're meeting for a last supper."

"We're headed that way too. Mind if we tag along?"

I glanced down at Jake, who was gazing up at me with those irresistible big brown eyes, and then I looked at Dane and shrugged.

And as we headed across the street, weaving our way through traffic, we pretended not to notice when our hands awkwardly bumped together. "So how was Greece?" he asked as I sank my hands deep into my pockets, keeping them safe from any further accidental contact.

"I stayed a little longer than planned," I admitted.

"I hear Atlas is going to furlough. Will that affect you?" He looked at me with concern.

"Well, they sent me a warning letter. But it really depends on how many people take the leaves they're offering."

"Are you taking one?"

"I wish," I said, shaking my head. "My friend Clay, the one who's moving, he's taking one. But unfortunately, I don't have anything else lined up yet. I guess I'll just stick around and see what happens."

"And the book?" he asked, gazing at me.

"Five rejections, and one pending." I shrugged, not wanting to tell him I'd decided to revise my work as per the suggestions of a reality-challenged editor. "Well this is me," I said, peering in the restaurant window, searching for Clay and Peter and hoping they wouldn't see me talking to Dane, since I'd never hear the end of it.

"Well, good seeing you." He smiled.

"Yeah, you too," I said, bending down to pet Jake.

"Call me if you want to hang out sometime," Dane called as I went inside.

But I just smiled and waved, knowing I'd be moving to a new neighborhood soon. Then I'd never have to run into him again.

35

After accepting Clay and Peter's offer, I coaxed Jonathan Franzen into a plastic bag, packed my belongings, and headed for Chelsea. And even though Jonathan would no longer get to enjoy a room of his own, I made sure to position his tank near a window so he could appreciate the view of the fire escape, and the dirty brick building next door.

With the deadline for the Atlas leave program long gone, and still no word from the sixth publisher, my dreams of following Clay and receiving low-priority stand-by travel for the next five years were sadly not to be. So all I could do was just sit back and wait while Atlas tabulated the takers, so they'd know just how many heads to chop.

The second I finished the rewrite for Chance Publishing, I dropped it in an envelope and sent it to Martina, adding "Requested Material" in big, bold letters along the front, so that whoever handled the package would know that someone actually wanted to see it, and that it wasn't just another wannabe destined for the circular file. And now that it was out there, making its way through the system, I tried to stay focused on how awesome it would feel to finally be a published author, while ignoring the voice in my head that was calling me a sellout and accusing me of writing a book I'd never want to read.

I still spoke to Clay nearly every day, and I could hardly wait till he and Peter were settled so I could go visit. I'd even considered swapping my Atlanta "Aware" seminar for the one in L.A. so I could see his face when I mocked the supervisors, reenacted the skits, and relayed just how stupid it all really was.

And even though I spent nearly all of my time either flying or working on my second book, in the moments when I found myself alone with nothing to do, I couldn't help but feel incredibly lonely.

I'd just returned from a Brussels layover and had swung by the flight attendant lounge to check my mailbox before catching the bus, when Jennifer, whom I hadn't seen since Puerto Rico, rushed toward me and said, "The numbers are out."

I stared at her, taking in her red and watery eyes.

"The cutoff was just below you. You're safe."

"And you?" I asked, already guessing the answer.

"I'm junior to you. So it looks like I'm outta here," she said, sniffing and looking away.

"I'm sorry." I felt awful for her, and more than a little guilty that I'd been spared. "What're you gonna do?"

"I guess I'm going home." She shrugged.

"To *Alabama*?" I asked, unable to hide my surprise. I mean Alabama might have been home, but Jennifer was East Village through and through. During the last six years she'd even managed to lose her accent, and I just couldn't imagine her living anywhere else.

"Both my roommates got axed, so they're leaving too. I have nowhere else to go." She tried to smile, but it was too much of a stretch.

"You can stay with me," I offered. "I have plenty of room."

"Thanks, but I already called my parents. Besides, I want to buy a house someday, with a real yard instead of a fire escape. And I'll never be able to do that here." She shrugged.

I just nodded, knowing it was true.

"Well, good luck," she said, leaning in to hug me. "Call me if you get a Mobile layover."

I watched as she grabbed her bags and left; then I sat at a vacant computer, logged into my e-mail, and clicked on the one regarding "Atlas Transformation Furlough Notice," scanning the document and feeling a twinge when I saw the cutoff was just two below me.

Which meant I was now the third most junior person in the entire Atlas system.

I just sat there staring at the screen, not quite sure how I felt about that. Because even though I'd managed to keep my job, the job as I once knew it was over.

In my new life as number three from the bottom, I'd no longer choose when and where I flew, as now the good people in scheduling would be deciding that for me. I'd be required to keep my cell phone turned on, fully charged, and by my side at all times during my "on-call" periods, which could last as long as a week and encompass an entire twenty-four-hour period. I'd be forbidden to consume any alcohol, or stray too far from home, and my bags must always be packed, and my uniform pressed and ready, in the event I was needed to fly anywhere in the world, at any given time, on a moment's notice.

In briefing, I'd be the last to sign up for duties, which meant I'd be assigned to all of the tasks no one else wanted. And the crews would treat me as though I was new, even though I had six solid years stashed firmly under my apron.

With the drop of a snowflake, or a hint of rain in the southeast, my cherished and few "off" days would transform into "on" days. And I could definitely plan on spending Christmas, New Year's, and all other holidays anywhere within the Atlas system—except home.

I would be a Ready Reserve. Which in the Atlas caste system made me an untouchable.

And since I'd barely survived this dreadful existence during my first year and a half of flying, I had no illusions about what I was in for.

So once again, my life was regressing. But this time, with the way things were going at Atlas, it held little promise of moving forward.

I logged off, grabbed my bags, and headed for the bus stop, knowing I should be grateful for keeping my job, even though I was pretty sure I no longer wanted it.

The first time I was charged with a Failure to Be Accessible I'd just returned from a seventeen-hour duty day, and was so exhausted I forgot to call scheduling and ask permission to go home. And for my punishment, I was banned from flying until I'd contacted Lawrence, apologized profusely, and followed up with a signed letter detailing exactly why and how the unfortunate event had occurred, including a point-by-point outline of how I'd ensure that I never, ever "jeopardized the integrity of the Atlas operation" again.

The second time took place when I failed to notice I had limited cell phone reception on the third floor in Bloomingdale's.

"Hailey Lane, please."

I shifted my two Medium Brown shopping bags to my other arm and squeezed my phone between my ear and shoulder. "Speaking," I said, wondering who I could possibly know with such an insincere, affected voice.

"This is Lawrence Peters."

But of course, I thought, pushing through the revolving glass door and making my way to the corner of Sixtieth and Lex.

"Hailey? Is this you?" he asked, sounding a little irritated.

I considered snapping it shut and pretending we got cut off, but I knew he'd only hunt me down eventually. "Yeah, it's me," I sighed, pausing to gawk at a table full of knockoffs.

"I need you to come to my office immediately."

I rolled my eyes and picked up a faux JP Tod's purse. "I'm busy," I said, running my hands over the smooth, slick vinyl.

"Yes, I can see that. Apparently you've been too busy to answer your phone. Because for your information you've just received your second Failure to Be Accessible, *which, I might add,* requires a face-to-face meeting with *me.*"

"I don't know what you're talking about," I said, shaking my head and moving on to the fake Burberry scarves section. "I only have one FTA, *which, I might add,* I've already apologized for." I dropped the scarf and smiled at the dead-on voice impersonation I'd just delivered.

"Scheduling tried to reach you approximately two hours and ten minutes ago. You were to fly a Cincinnati turn. But even though you're on call, you failed to answer your phone."

"That's totally ridiculous. I've had my phone with me the entire day, and it hasn't once—" I held the phone away from my ear and looked at it. *Oh crap!* There was an envelope on the display, and the red light was flashing! Had scheduling really tried to call me? And how had I missed hearing it ring? "Um, I'm not sure how this happened," I said, breaking into a cold, clammy sweat, and attempting a verbal backtrack. "I've had it on this whole time, I swear. I mean, is it too late? Because I can still get to JFK—"

"You've already been replaced," he said, back to his usual, smug self. "I expect to see you in my office tomorrow afternoon, one o'clock sharp."

"But that's my only day off! Can't we do this before my next trip?" I pleaded. The last thing I wanted was to go to the airport and see him.

"If you care about saving your job you'll be in my office tomorrow at one, where I'll move you from Verbal Warning to Written Warning.

I stood on the corner of Lex and Sixty-first, fuming. *"If I care about saving my job?" Who the hell is he to threaten me like that? And what if I've just now decided that I don't actually care about my job? What then? I mean, obviously I'm just days away from getting the call from Martina that will change my entire life. So why am I still putting up with this crap?*

"So what comes after Written Warning?" I asked, adding a little chuckle to the end of that, so he'd know just how seriously I *wasn't* taking his threats.

"The next step is *Final Warning,* followed by *Termination.* And trust me Hailey, you don't want to go there."

"Hmmm," I mumbled, crossing the street against the light. I was living dangerously now.

"I'll see you tomorrow, in my office, one o'clock. Or I'm afraid I'll be forced to take drastic measures," he said, with barely concealed rage.

"I'll pencil you in," I said, rolling my eyes and snapping my phone shut.

BELLY LANDING

When the landing gear is
inoperative, the aircraft will
slide across the runway until
coming to an eventual stop.
You should then evacuate
using any available exit.

36

Dressed in the brand-new sweater and jeans that had gotten me into this mess in the first place, I headed out the door and over to Fifth Avenue, so that I could feed the kitties, collect the mail, and straighten up a little before Kat and Yanni's visit next weekend.

I found the cats in the library, sleeping side by side on the velvet settee, and I settled alongside them, petting their soft, white fur while I sorted through a pile of mail that seemed to be mostly junk, until somewhere in the middle I came across a plain white envelope with the words Chance Publishing embossed on the front.

I just sat there, holding it in my hands and thinking how light and insignificant it felt considering how the contents were about to change my entire life. Then, hooking my finger under the flap, I tore it gently along the top, knowing I'd want to keep this for many years to come.

Then I took a deep breath, unfolded the single sheet of paper, smoothed it across my lap, and read:

Dear Ms. Lane:

While I appreciate the opportunity to read your revised manuscript, I'm afraid that the plot, with its lack of conflict and struggle, makes for an insubstantial read and just doesn't work for us.

Though I wish you the best of luck in finding it a good publishing home.

Sincerely,
Martina Rasmussen

I just sat there, reading the letter over and over, until the words became a fuzzy blur on the stark white page, wondering if there was something I'd missed. I mean, I'd done everything she'd asked: revised the parents so that they were supportive and emotionally available; altered the best friend, making her less self-serving and more loyal; heck, I'd even given the protagonist a complete emotional makeover so that she was lighthearted and less burdened. I'd given Martina *exactly* what she'd asked for, turned my novel into something I couldn't even relate to, and she was *rejecting me?* Because there was no conflict? She was the one who hated all the conflict! She was the one who had ordered a conflict-free story!

And as I sat there, breath shallow and hands shaking, the truth slowly sank in, as I realized I'd now have to:

A.   Meet with Lawrence, where I'd be forced to grovel, suck up, and do whatever necessary to compensate for my attitude yesterday when I was still under the delusion that I was a writer.

B.   Learn to love my low-seniority status, and transform myself into the best Ready Reserve Atlas Airlines had ever seen, if I was going to have a chance in hell of keeping my job.

C.   Surrender my dreams of creative fulfillment, go back to school, and enroll in some solid courses like business or computers, so that maybe someday I could retire my wings.

So I guess in a way Martina really had changed my life. By making it even worse than it was.

I crumpled the letter into a tiny, hateful ball and then checked my watch, seeing I had barely enough time to make my meeting at JFK. And now that I could no longer afford to make the leap from "Written" to "Final" warning, I knew I'd better get off the couch and onto the bus, like, pronto.

Since I didn't have time to mess with that stupid service elevator, I was waiting for the normal one, praying I wouldn't run into Dane, when my cell rang.

"Hello?" I said, cringing at how abrupt I sounded, but really, I was in no mood to chat.

"Hailey? Is this a bad time? You sound irritated."

I rolled my eyes and punched the elevator call button three more times. Irritated wasn't the half of it. Especially compared to the river of self-pity, self-doubt, low self-esteem, and self-loathing I was wading in. But even though my mom and I were getting along much better these days, it's not like I was gonna share any of that with her.

"Hey, Mom," I said, attempting a lighter tone. "Listen, I'm stepping into an elevator, and then a subway and bus. Can this wait?"

"Well, I just wanted to give you the news," she said, ignoring all the obstacles I'd just placed in her conversational path.

"What news?" I asked, watching the numbers descend with each floor, wondering when we'd be cut off.

"Alan stopped by the other night with a dozen roses and an apology."

"And?" I said, trying to move this along, since left to her own timing, it could go on forever.

"He says he's made a huge mistake, and begged for a second chance."

I rolled my eyes and made my way through the lobby and onto the street. "At this point wouldn't that actually be more like a four-teenth or even fifteenth chance?" *I mean jeez, maybe I'm not to blame for my pathetic love life. Just check out my gene pool!*

"You should have seen him, Hailey," she said, ignoring my sar-casm. "He looked so upset."

"Mom, can you please cut to the chase? I'm about to enter the subway, and then we'll definitely be cut off. So just say it. He looked sad, you turned to Jell-O, and now you're back together, right?" I stood on the corner, rolling my eyes and shaking my head.

"Actually, no," she said quietly.

"Oh," I mumbled, feeling terrible about the way I'd just spoken to her.

"I told him I was leaving the country. Then I wished him well and sent him away."

"Where you going?" I asked, giving my watch a worried glance, but knowing there was no way I could hang up. "I mean, are you serious?"

"I've sold the house and I'm moving to China."

I leaned against the wall, dazed.

"I'll be teaching English for a while, and after that, I'm going to travel the world, volunteering along the way. Who knows where I'll end up?"

"Wow," I said, not knowing what else to say.

"And it's all because of you, Hailey. You inspired me. With the way you live your life, embracing change, seeking adventure—you're just so fearless!"

Okay, that doesn't sound at all like me. I mean, obviously she's confused me with someone else. "Uh, Mom, although it may look like that on the surface, I've actually made some really bad deci-sions over the last few years. I mean, I'm not fearless, and I shouldn't be anyone's inspiration, especially yours," I told her.

But she just sighed. "Hailey, it doesn't matter how things worked out in the end, it's the fact that you tried them in the first

place! Look at me. I've been in the same town, doing the same
thing my entire life. Just going along and never messing with the
status quo. Then one day I was on the escalator in Nordstrom and
I realized I could stay here, donating all my time and money to
South Coast Plaza, or I could sell the house, pack my bags, get on
a plane, and do something that matters."

I just stood there, letting her words sink in. "I'm proud of you,"
I said finally, my eyes swelling with tears. Partly because she was
breaking out of her box and getting a life, and partly because it
highlighted just how stagnant and small my own world had become. It was like everyone around me was moving on, *literally*,
while I was still stuck in a six-year ground delay. "Can I see you before you leave?" I asked.

"I'm flying in later this week. Does that work?"

"Sounds good," I said, knowing I was on call but hoping I could
work something out. Then, wiping my face with the back of my
hand, I headed down the subway stairs, knowing if I lingered any
longer I'd definitely miss my bus.

"Oh, and Hailey, did you read that bit about Jude Law and—"

Oops, lost her. I closed my phone and got on the subway, and
by the time I'd made it to midtown, I had a message. But knowing it was just my mom wanting to engage in a deep analysis of
celebrity sex lives, I decided to ignore it. I mean, I was glad at least
some part of her was still recognizable, but that didn't mean I
wanted to indulge it.

I made my way onto the New York Airport bus and smiled at a
group of flight attendants from another airline as I headed for the
very last row. Then I grabbed a seat and stared out the window,
wavering between fear for my own bleak future, and resentment at
being forced to waste my only day off like this. So by the time I got
to JFK, I was a complete and total wreck.

And as I stood outside Lawrence's office, nervously adjusting
my sweater and jeans, I checked my watch, confirmed the time,
then took a deep breath and knocked.

But as time passed with no sign of response, I was just about to knock again when he opened the door, looked me over, and said, "I'm very busy right now. Please return in fifteen minutes."

I narrowed my eyes, peering around his puny frame, taking in every square inch of his cramped little office. His desk was cleared, his phone lights were blank, but his computer screen didn't lie, displaying his current participation in a down-and-dirty eBay bidding war.

And even though I knew he was enjoying a sick, passive-aggressive game of watching me sweat while messing with my off day, I also knew there was nothing I could do about it.

"Okay," I said, forcing my lips into a smile. "I'll see you at one fifteen." Then I marched down the hall, pushed into the bathroom, and headed for the row of sinks, where I stood with my eyes closed taking deep, Zen-seeking breaths.

Relax. He's trying to get you all riled up so he can fire you. Do not take the bait! You need this job.

Turning on the taps, I ran my hands under the cold, wet spray, filling them with soap and watching as the rinse water ran gray with the disgusting accumulation of city smudge and public-transportation grime. Then I dried them on a towel and headed back into the lounge, bought myself a cup of weak but very hot vending-machine coffee, and sat there alternately sipping and blowing for the next fifteen minutes.

"Welcome," Lawrence said as I stood in his doorway for the second time. "Have a seat."

I grabbed a chair, crossed my legs primly, and watched as he settled behind his desk, arranging his features into a grim expression.

"I know the adjustment to Ready Reserve is a challenging one, but with two Failures to Be Accessible, coupled with your blatant, insubordinate attitude, I have to level with you, Hailey. I'm very tempted to put you on Final Warning. He leaned back in his chair and gave me a smug, "I'm the boss of you" look.

"But Lawrence—," I started, pausing as his phone rang and watching him raise a stubby, authoritative finger as he lifted the receiver.

"Yes?" he said, eyes fixed on me. "Of course, I'll be right there." Then, getting up from his desk, he nodded at me. "Stay put. We're far from finished."

I watched as he left the office, then rolled my eyes and shook my head, wondering too late if he'd rigged some kind of nanny-cam that had just recorded my insubordinate facial expressions. Insubordination was a major offense at Atlas, considered far worse than failing to be "proactive," or not taking "ownership" of passenger complaints. And since flight attendants were the least supervised of all the employee groups, Atlas management worked overtime at keeping us in a constant state of paranoia, with their toll-free, anonymous hotlines that encouraged us to rat on each other, and the infamous "ghost rider" program that always left me wondering which of my passengers was actually a company spy. I even knew of flight attendants who, convinced that the layover hotel staffs were in cahoots, refused to use the phones and collected all of their garbage into separate bags to be dumped later at a secret, undisclosed location.

But as the minutes ticked past I knew he was just dragging this out to annoy me. So I reached into my purse and retrieved my cell, figuring I'd kill the time by listening to my mom's message.

Pressing the VOICE MAIL button, I waited to hear my mother's list of theories on the most recent celebrity love triangle, but instead got, "This message is for Hailey Lane. My name is Hope Schine, and I'm an editor here at Phoenix Publishing—"

Oh my God! Phoenix Publishing was the sixth rejection letter I hadn't yet received. And now, apparently they'd decided to just ignore my SASE and deliver the bad news in a more up-close and personal way.

"I wanted you to know that we all love your book. You really managed to capture the voice of a teenage girl, and write about her struggles in such an authentic, realistic way. I don't know if you're working on anything else, but we'd like to offer you a two-book deal. So if you could please call me back, I'd be happy to go over the details, and answer any questions you might have. My number is—"

Wait—did she really just offer me a deal? And not just for one book, but two?

I listened to the message again, and then left Lawrence's office, heading outside to the noise and chaos of people getting picked up and dropped off, hugging hello and waving good-bye. Then I leaned against the yellow brick wall and returned Hope's call.

And after accepting her offer, I reapplied my lip gloss, ran my hands through my hair, and headed back inside the airport. Making sure I took my time going through security before I got in line at Starbucks.

Standing in Lawrence's doorway, venti skim latte in hand, I watched as his face contorted with barely checked rage. "I specifically told you to stay put. But what do you do? You go on a coffee run, which is not only disobeying my orders, but also displays a complete disregard for my time." He leaned back in his seat and arranged his hands into a rigid little steeple. "You'd think that someone who came so dangerously close to being furloughed would be a little more grateful to be here," he added, shaking his head and giving me a disdainful look.

"By 'here' do you mean here in your office, or here on Earth?" I asked, lowering myself onto the seat across from him and watching his jaw twitch and his eyes bulge out as he faced his computer and began typing furiously.

"Three weeks ago you were four minutes late to sign in," he said, firing off a list of my most recent Atlas misdeeds. "Two weeks ago you wore your own black cardigan sweater instead of the Atlas-mandated navy blue one. *And* you were recently seen in the Salt Lake City concourse wearing the white blouse without its designated red-and-blue scarf, opaque hose which you know are only allowed with the skort, and a pair of nonregulation clogs with visible staples. Never mind all the other uniform infractions you've incurred over the last six years." He took his eyes off his screen just long enough to give me a sorry shake of his head. "Your latest doctor's note, written in Greek, was *not* amusing; your behavior following an in-flight death was questionable at best; *and,* I happen to know that just the other day, upon returning from London, you deplaned with an Atlas water bottle poking out of your bag. And don't try to deny it, Hailey, because I *saw* you, and I saw the bottle of water. But even though that is considered *stealing,* which by the way is an offense punishable by *termination,* I didn't write it up, because I knew you were in enough trouble already." He turned away from his screen, crossed his arms, and looked at me. "What do you have to say for yourself?"

I sat there sipping my latte with what I hoped mimicked a thoughtful expression, and then I uncrossed my legs, leaned toward him, and, resting my elbows on his desk, said, "Hey Larry. Do you remember when we first started flying to Europe, and how you used to take, well, not just bottles of water, but also mini bottles of liquor, unopened bottles of wine, leftover cheese trays, rolls of crackers, and all those boxes of assorted chocolates that you lifted from first class? And how you'd set it all up real nice in your hotel room and invite everyone to come party with you? Remember that? And then that one time when you were too hungover to work the flight back from New Orleans, so we put you in an empty coach-class seat, gave you a pillow and a blanket, and let you sleep it off while we covered for you? Do you remember any of this, Larry? Or how about the time when you showed up forty minutes late for that midnight flight to Las Vegas, and you called scheduling from your cell phone, assuring them you'd been there the whole time, but just forgot to sign in? And how we all vouched for you? Or that time when you sicked out during your Rome layover because you met some guy you wanted to spend more time with? Do you remember any of this, Larry? Do you remember back when you were one of the *very worst offenders*?" I leaned back in my chair and smiled.

"I could fire you," he whispered, face red, hands shaking, eyes filled with fury.

"Go ahead." I shrugged. "And then maybe I'll take a little stroll over to the base manager's office, have a little chat with Shannon, and see if I can't take you with me."

And seeing the panic on his face made me smile even wider.

"You wouldn't do that," he said, though it sounded more like a question than he probably intended.

But I just sat there sipping my coffee. *Would I do that? Probably. Yet, why should I bother? Why should I waste my time challenging this dweeb to a duel? I mean, I am so over Lawrence, and I am completely over Atlas; so wouldn't it be better just to walk away with my dignity intact, secure in the knowledge that while he may be the big cheese down here in the bowels of JFK, upstairs, where it really counts, he's just another pale peon?*

I lifted my ID from around my neck and dropped it on the desk between us. And when he looked up, his face bore a priceless expression of shock and fear.

And wanting that to be the way I always remembered him, I stood, finished my latte, and then leaving the empty cup on his desk said, "Good luck to you, Larry."

Then I walked out of his office, and away from Atlas.

37

It wasn't until I was sitting in the back of the cab, and crossing the Fifty-ninth Street Bridge, that I felt like I might throw up. What the hell had I just done? I mean, was I insane? Everyone knows that a debut novelist has no business quitting their day job, and now I'd gone and done exactly that. Taking my flight benefits, health insurance, and free Met Museum entry, and kissing it all good-bye in one well-executed yet poorly planned moment.

I shook my head and gazed out the window, wondering if there would be a SWAT team of Atlas supervisors all lined up on the other side of the bridge with guns drawn and ready as they directed me to put my hands in the air and surrender my wings, uniform pieces, and flight manual, nice and easy.

When I got to my apartment, I headed straight for the kitchen, and having run out of wine, champagne, or anything remotely festive (since I wasn't allowed to drink while on Ready Reserve), I poured some Pellegrino into a champagne flute and sat on the couch, where I listened to Hope's message over and over again. Then I looked at Jonathan Franzen swimming laps in his tank, and thought how ironic it was that after working so hard to rebuild my life, I had no one left to share it with.

And after calling my mom, Kat, and Clay, and telling them the good news, I'd just poured my second celebratory glass of water when my cell rang.

"Congratulations!"

"Um, thanks. Who's this?" I asked, recognizing neither the voice nor the number.

"Dane."

"Oh, hey," I said, wondering why he was calling and what he could possibly be praising me for. *I mean, it's not like he'd know about the book deal; it just happened.* "So, congratulations for what?"

"Your two-book deal!"

"Oh," I mumbled, wondering if Clay had somehow contacted him, since he was always trying to get us together.

"You don't sound all that excited," he said.

"I am, really. I'm just wondering how you know, that's all."

"I saw it on Publishers Marketplace."

And since I had no idea what that was, or why he'd be reading it, I didn't say anything.

"So who's handling the deal for you?" he asked.

"Um, I am," I said, while thinking *Here we go again.* I mean, he always made me feel like I had no idea what I was doing. I mean, maybe I didn't. But, still.

"Do you have anyone to read over the contract?"

"No," I said, rolling my eyes. Jeez, this guy was a total buzz kill. Couldn't I just concentrate on being happy, and leave all the small print for later?

"Well, it's something you should consider. Those contracts can be pretty confusing if you don't know what to look for. I'd be happy to help," he offered.

"We'll see," I said, shaking my head and sipping my sparkling water.

"So, any plans to celebrate?" he asked.

"Well, my friends are flying in from Greece this week, so we'll probably go to dinner or something," I told him, suddenly feeling like a total loser, despite my recent success. "And my mom's coming into town as well." *Lame, Hailey. Sad, pathetic, and lame.*

"Well, what about tonight? Flying off to any exotic locales?"

"Does the corner of Twenty-third and Eighth count?"

He was silent for a moment, and then he said, "How about dinner? With me. Tonight. I'll take you anywhere that'll accept a last-minute reservation."

I sipped my sparkling water and gazed at Jonathan Franzen. *Well, at least someone wants to celebrate with me. And even though Dane totally gets on my nerves, it still beats takeout. Besides, it's just one meal, so how bad could it be?*

"I know just the place," I told him.

38

I could smell the rich aroma even before Dane opened the door. *"Entrez,"* he said, motioning me into his apartment. "Welcome to Chez Dane." And when he smiled I noticed he was cuter than I'd allowed myself to remember.

"Nice dress," I said, eyeing the stained and wrinkled white apron he wore over his faded jeans and striped cotton shirt.

"You remember Jake?" he said as the friendly chocolate lab hurried over to greet me.

I leaned down to pet Jake, patting him on the head and scratching under his chin, thinking how nice it would be to have a dog like this to come home to every day.

"So, I hope you like champagne?" he asked, popping the cork and filling two flutes, stopping just before the bubbles ran over the top and down the sides. Then, handing me my glass, he lifted his. "To Hailey Lane, New York City's newest literary sensation!" He smiled, tapping his glass against mine.

"Uh, let's not get carried away here." I laughed.

"Don't downplay it. It's a huge accomplishment. Do you have any idea how hard it is to get a book deal?"

I thought about the months of struggle, isolation, and self-doubt. And how at one point I'd been so desperate I ignored my better instincts and completely sold out. "Yeah, I think I know."

"Most people are never offered a deal. And those who are work for years before they get it," he said.

I remembered how I'd been given similar statistics when I became a flight attendant. *Only two out of every thousand applicants makes it this far,* they'd told us at orientation. *Now look around you and know that several more won't make it through training.* "Well, I guess I got lucky." I shrugged, thinking how funny that sounded. "Though it does feel pretty incredible. I mean this entire day has just been so surreal. First I got a rejection letter that made me feel two levels below rock bottom; then I got the call from Hope that sent me soaring so high I marched into my supervisor's office and quit my job." *And now I'm having dinner with you,* I thought, taking a sip of champagne.

"You quit Atlas?" he asked, his mouth hanging open in shock.

"Um, yeah." I shrugged. "I guess I had no business quitting my day job, but, well, it's a long story."

He looked at me and smiled, but I could tell he was worried. "Hailey, I'd really like to help you navigate your way through all of this if you'll let me."

I finished the rest of my champagne, set my glass on the counter, and looked at him, knowing it was now or never. "Look, no offense, but what makes you think you know your way around any better than me? I mean, you're not actually a writer, are you?"

But he just looked at me and smiled.

"I mean, I'll probably just look it over, and if I have any questions, then I know where to find you," I said, feeling bad about the tone, but sheesh, if this guy really wanted to be my friend then he was gonna have to stop butting in all the time.

"Sounds good." He nodded, heading over to check on the stove. "We have standard boilerplates for all the major publishers, including Phoenix, so just let me know if you need anything."

I watched as he checked under lids and stirred something in a pot as my stomach filled with dread. "Wait," I said, moving around the counter till I was standing next to him. "Why would *you* have a boilerplate for Phoenix?"

"Because I'm general counsel for McKenzie and Thurston," he said.

I just stood there looking at him. I had no idea what that meant.

"You've never heard of us?"

I shook my head. Once again, he was making me feel completely uninformed. But apparently I had a lot to learn.

"We're a literary agency. You've been to my office, so I just assumed you knew." He shrugged. "Anyway, I handled Cadence's contract, and most of Harrison Mann's—"

"And now you're offering to handle mine," I said, feeling so embarrassed for all those months of brushing him off and thinking he was arrogant and pompous, when actually, he was only trying to help.

"It's up to you," he said, reaching for the knob and turning down the heat.

"Well, if you're good enough for Harrison Mann . . ." I laughed, feeling my face warm and redden. "But I should apologize," I said, shaking my head and looking at him. "For blowing you off all this time. I guess I've just wanted this for so long, but I wanted to do it myself, without any help. And now that it's finally happened I feel like I've just been invited to join some exclusive private club, only I don't know any of the rules."

"That's where I come in," he said, smiling and holding my gaze, making me so nervous I quickly looked away.

"So, do you need any help?" I asked, motioning toward the simmering pots.

FLY ME TO THE MOON

"It's under control." He smiled. "But you can put on some music, if you'd like."

I browsed through his CD collection, surprised to see we had such similar tastes. And after choosing the *Garden State* soundtrack, I wandered over to some shelves where a group of colorful ceramic Mexican folk-art pieces were displayed.

"Where'd you get these?" I asked, lightly running my finger along the edge of a brightly painted animal that looked like a coyote, but I couldn't be sure.

"I traveled through Mexico for three months the summer between grad school and law school," he said, grabbing his wineglass and coming over to join me.

"What'd you study in grad school?"

"International affairs. Here, this one's my favorite," he said, lifting a ceramic piece depicting a classroom scene where the students all had horns and the teacher was sticking her tongue out at them.

"Oh my God, that so reminds me of high school." I laughed as he looked at me and smiled. "Um, so where in Mexico did you go?" I asked nervously.

"All over. Oaxaca, Chiapas, Michoacan—"

"Sounds awesome." I said, moving on to another interesting piece.

"Have you been?"

I shrugged. "A few short layovers in Mexico City, some day trips to Tijuana, a couple long weekends in Cabo—you know, all the usual haunts when you grow up north of the border."

"You're from California?" he asked.

"Born and raised in the OC." I nodded.

"I grew up in Studio City."

We stood there for a moment, gazing at each other, and I wondered if he was going to kiss me. But just as he moved toward me, my cell started ringing. And even though I was more than willing to ignore it, Dane smiled and said, "You should probably get that."

I raced toward my purse, grabbed my cell, and flipped it open, though I was sure it was too late.

"This is Shannon Atkins from Atlas In-flight Service, I'd like to speak with Hailey Lane, please."

Oh my God! Is this for real? Does she really think she can still harass me even after I've quit? I mean, what is with these people?

But I didn't say any of that. Instead I just rolled my eyes and said, "Speaking."

"Oh good, I'm so glad I caught you! You probably haven't even realized it yet, but it seems you've lost your ID."

"Excuse me?" I said, wondering what the heck she was talking about.

"It's sitting right here on my desk. It looks like the lanyard broke, so it must have just fallen right off your neck without you even noticing. Lawrence found it on the ground right outside his office, and he brought it to my immediate attention. So when do you think you can come by and get it?"

"Well, I'm not exactly sure," I said, gripping the phone and trying to digest this most recent turn of events. Was she really unaware of the fact that I'd quit? And had I really scared Lawrence straight? So to speak.

"I'll just keep it locked in my desk. But don't forget to call before you come in, since you know you can't enter the lounge without it. Enjoy your weekend, Hailey!"

"Um, you too," I said, closing my phone and wondering if Atlas had become like a bad boyfriend that I'd never be able to shake.

"Is everything okay?" Dane asked, already sitting at the table.

I looked at him and smiled. "You're not gonna believe this," I said, heading over to join him.

The cabin is secure when all baggage is finally stowed.

39

"I swear, Chez Dane is by far my favorite restaurant." I smiled, leaning back in my seat feeling happy, lazy, and full. "I don't know anyone who can throw together braised short ribs and pumpkin orzo on a moment's notice. What'd you do? Attend Cordon Bleu between all of your other accomplishments?"

"Nope, just a hobby," he said, refilling our wineglasses.

"And I bet Jake loves the leftovers," I said, glancing over at the chocolate lab lying on the living room rug and noticing how his head perked up at just the mention of his name.

"So when do I get to read this book of yours?" Dane asked, leaning back in his chair and smiling.

"Uh, when it's revised, edited, copyedited, bound, and sitting on the shelf in Barnes and Noble?"

"You're gonna make me wait?"

"Well, you didn't seem all that interested before it sold," I teased.

"I didn't even realize I had it until I called you."

"Fair enough." I shrugged.

"So," he said, pushing his chair away from the table. "Should we head out on the town? Or stay in and watch a movie?"

I looked at him standing across from me and realized I'd been having such a surprisingly nice time just hanging with him and Jake that I really didn't feel like going out into the cold and crowded night. "What movies do you have?"

"I've got a pretty good selection in the den. Why don't you choose one while I put this stuff away." He smiled.

"Need any help?" I asked.

But he just shook his head. "The movies are in the cupboard, under the flat screen. I'll meet you in the den in ten," he said, smiling and heading for the sink.

I made my way down the hall, and the second I reached the den I looked at the couch and thought, *Oh crap, Cadence's book is still under there!* And I knew that no matter what it took, I needed to get it back on the shelf while I had the chance.

But I also had to pick a movie.

And knowing I only had ten minutes or less to accomplish both of these tasks, I wasn't sure which to conquer first. I mean, if I went straight for the book and then Dane came in and I hadn't picked a movie, he'd wonder what the hell I'd been doing all that time. But if I took too long picking a movie, then I ran the risk of getting caught with my hand under the couch.

Okay, I decided, *I'm just gonna pick a movie, any movie, and then I'll go find that stupid book.*

But when I opened the cupboard I found four shelves chock-full of DVDs. *Great,* I thought, quickly scanning the titles, *this is gonna take forever.* Apparently he owned all of my favorite movies, and I had no idea how I'd choose just one.

I ran my fingers over the cases: *American Beauty, Chinatown, The Pianist, Eternal Sunshine of the Spotless Mind, Se7en, Pulp Fiction, High Fidelity, Annie Hall, Requiem for a Dream, Ghost World, The Shawshank Redemption, Harold and Maude . . .*

Knowing I didn't have time to waste I reached for *The Gradu-*

ate, which I hadn't seen in years but which always made me laugh, followed by *Silence of the Lambs,* which I'd recently seen on TNT but wouldn't mind seeing again; then I tossed them onto the table, slammed the cupboard door, and made a beeline for the couch.

Slinking around the back of the sofa, I quickly scanned the room, making sure that other than me, the den was completely empty. Then, giving myself the all-clear, I dropped to my knees, bent forward, and slid my arm under as far as it would go.

I was down on all fours, feeling around as best I could, hoping I could locate the book before coming across anything disgusting, when I realized that with my arm bent the way it was, and with the couch being kinda long, it was quite possible I would crawl like this forever and still not maximize my full potential.

So straining my neck and peering over the top, I checked to make sure I was still alone. Then I flattened myself on the ground, turned my head so that my cheek was resting on the smooth hardwood floor, and pressed my nose firmly against the brown damask upholstery. And keeping one eye closed, I scoped with the other, trying to make out the shape of a bestselling book in the sliver of shallow, dark space before me.

Unable to see anything but black, I inched my body forward like a Navy Seal on a highly sensitive, top-secret mission, sweeping the sliver of space with my left arm, which, stretched to its full extent, was beginning to ache from all the strain.

Where the heck was it? I mean, the couch was long, but it's not like it was all that wide. So where the heck could it have gone?

And by the time I'd made it to the end, I'd barely collected so much as a dust ball. But knowing it was under there somewhere (since I'm the one who'd put it there) and sensing the minutes slipping away, I decided to head back where I came from, arm sweeping, and double-checking the entire way.

I was inching backward, keeping flush to the floor and using the toes of my black leather boots for leverage, when I felt the very tips of my fingers graze something that felt like it might possibly be made of paper. And crushing my body as hard as I could against the back of the couch, I extended my arm so far I thought it would pop from its socket, as my fingers frantically reached for what I now knew was Cadence's book.

And just as I grasped it, I felt someone breathe softly in my ear.

"Shit!" I jumped, pulling away from the couch, and turning to see it was only Jake. "Jeez! You scared the heck out of me," I whispered as he sniffed at my face and licked my cheek. "Go on now." I pushed him with my free hand, the one that wasn't throbbing and still partially wedged under the couch. "Go find your master. I'll be through in a minute," I told him, anxious to get back to work before Dane came in and found me like that.

And just as I slid back to the ground, pressing myself against the couch and getting into position, I heard footsteps.

Followed by the sound of Dane's voice saying, "Looking for this?"

And then I closed my eyes and froze.

And then I reviewed my options.

I could either:

A. Stay put for as long as it took, refusing to budge, breathe, or speak.
B. Pretend I'd lost an earring, and was just looking for it.
C. Get up and own up.

I chose A.

"Hailey?" Dane said, his voice filled with worry. "Are you okay?"

I lay there for a while, trying not to think about how much worse this probably looked from his angle; then I took a deep breath, retrieved my cramped and throbbing arm, and got up from the floor, awkwardly unfolding my body until I was finally standing before him.

"Oh, hey," I said, having decided to take the nonchalant approach, and casually ridding myself of tiny pieces of lint. "I, um, I thought I dropped something." I shrugged, avoiding his eyes and suppressing a nervous laugh.

"Was it this?" he asked, holding up Cadence's book.

My arm was aching, my knees were bruised, my hands were sweaty, and my face was on fire. I'd been caught flat on the floor, minesweeping under his couch, and the whole time he knew exactly what I was up to, which made me wonder just how long he and Jake had been watching me before they'd let their presence be known.

Though it's not like I was about to ask. I was far too humiliated to do anything now but go home, lick my wounds, and pack up my belongings so I could move to another state.

"Um, I should probably go," I said, heading for the door as he quickly stepped in front of me, blocking my path.

"Hailey," he said, reaching for my good arm.

I stood there staring at his feet, wondering how on Earth I was going to get out of this. And when I finally found the courage to look up and face him, I was even more humiliated to see him looking so amused. I mean, even though it might have been funny for him to watch, believe me, it wasn't such a riot having to live it. So I shook my head and stared at the ground again, thinking that if I could have any of the superpowers, I would definitely choose invisibility.

"I should explain," I said finally.

"You don't have to explain anything," he said.

"Yeah, well, I think I do," I told him, wanting nothing more now than to just get it over with. "Look, the last time I was here, I was checking out your books, and I came across the one by Cadence, and I know it was none of my business, but I—"

"Hailey, I'm not dating Cadence," he said, rubbing my arm, trying to get me to look at him, but no way was that happening.

"Okay, fine," I said, wishing he'd just let me finish so we could all go live our separate lives. "But still, I pulled it off the shelf and—"

"And you read the dedication, misinterpreted the whole thing, assumed I was dating Cadence, tossed it under the couch, thought I was a slimeball for asking you out, avoided me like the plague, started taking the service elevator, fled to Greece, moved out of the building, only to show up here tonight just so you could retrieve it and put everything right."

"Yes," I said, shaking my head sadly while my face burned with shame. "Except *no!* Not the last part. I mean, I didn't come here just for the couch." I finally looked at him, and once my eyes met his, I couldn't look away.

"Then why'd you come?" he asked, dropping the book and moving toward me.

"Um, because I know you like to cook . . . and because you offered to celebrate with me . . . and—" I stopped. He was standing very close now, holding both my hands in his and gazing into my eyes. I swallowed hard.

"And?" he said, his lips warming into a smile.

"And, I guess, basically, because you were number three on my list of people I wanted to celebrate with," I whispered, closing my eyes as he leaned in and kissed me on the side of the neck.

"Oh yeah? And who were the other two?" he asked, nibbling on my ear now.

"Um, a fifty-six-year-old woman and a gay guy. Oh yeah, and my mom. So you're actually number four," I said, laughing nervously.

And while I was laughing, he kissed me. Brushing my hair off my face and pushing his mouth first gently, then urgently against mine. And everything about this kiss felt so good, and so right, and so natural, and so safe that I felt like I was finally home.

And as he moved in even closer, wrapping his arms around me and holding me tight, I happened to glance down just as the toe of his shoe collided with Cadence's book, tapping it on the corner and sending it all the way back under the couch.

But I didn't say anything. We just kept on kissing.